THE GRAVEYARD BELL

ANDREW JAMES GREIG

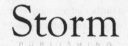

Storm
PUBLISHING

Ebook ISBN: 978-1-80508-482-2
Paperback ISBN: 978-1-80508-484-6

Cover design: Blacksheep
Cover images: Shutterstock

Published by Storm Publishing.
For further information, visit:
www.stormpublishing.co

ALSO BY ANDREW JAMES GREIG

The Girl in the Loch
Silent Ritual

A Song of Winter
The Bone Clock
The Devil's Cut

No man is an island,
Entire of itself.
Each is a piece of the continent,
A part of the main.
If a clod be washed away by the sea,
Europe is the less.
As well as if a promontory were.
As well as if a manor of thine own
Or of thine friend's were.
Each man's death diminishes me,
For I am involved in mankind.
Therefore, send not to know
For whom the bell tolls,
It tolls for thee.
John Donne 1572–1631

ONE
PUFFLING

Robert Jameson lay stomach down on the clifftop, brown hair blowing in sympathy with couch grass, his camera catching each aerial encounter. He briefly regretted having left his tele-photo in the boat, but he needed to catch the first puffins making landfall from up close. He had no need for hides or camouflage – the small birds had never learned to fear humans. Here, exhausted and at the end of their journey, they only had one thought – to find their burrow and partner after eight long months at sea.

One puffin veered towards him, making for the burrows close to where he lay. Short, stubby wings fought an updraft as Atlantic winds met the island's towering cliffs. Basalt columns guarded Staffa's sea cave entrance – nature's Gothic cathedral, born in fire and christened in the restless sea.

Robert checked the image, then smiled with satisfaction now that he had the shot he wanted. With the pressure off, he was able to relax and be more leisurely in his framing. With a sellable picture in the bag, everything else was a bonus.

Puffins were his favourite birds. Though they were often described as comical clowns, he had the deepest respect for these long-lived adventurers. Spending eight months of each year touring the wild Atlantic Ocean, they returned in a short breeding season to find the same life partner and hopefully produce a single puffling.

The last thought gave Robert some disquiet. Lucy was his lifelong partner, but the prospect of having their own children remained an elusive dream. They were booked in for fertility treatment on the mainland, a final and desperate attempt to give meaning to their lives and fill the void that was eating them both from within.

That concern mirrored the other worry Robert kept hidden – his loyalty to Lucy. He imagined more fertile soil and guilt swept over him in waves.

Out at sea, a fishing boat made slow progress towards the island. Robert shifted position to try and frame it more artistically but gave up after a single shot. Without the telephoto, it would just be a dot in the frame. He returned to the puffins, tumbling out of the sky and beginning to fall like April rain. Their numbers were increasing now that the vanguard had made landfall, and he was soon so busy with his camera that even the sly thought of forbidden fruit slipped from his mind.

He was alerted by a change in the seabirds' calls. Skuas and gulls had become used to his prone figure lying in the grass, but something had attracted their attention. Robert began to stand, stretching arms that had become unresponsive, his back complaining at being exposed to the chill sea wind. A figure approached, climbing up the steep grassy slope and making for the top of Fingal's Cave. The visitor stopped when he noticed Robert, then headed urgently towards him.

Robert waited until the man was closer, the face obscured by the hood of his waterproofs, then raised a hand in greeting when he recognised a fellow islander. His hand lowered when he saw the anger revealed in his visitor's face.

'What are you doing here?' Robert asked cautiously.

'You have to leave Siobhan alone. Do you understand? Don't go near her ever again.' The words spat forcibly in his face.

Robert stepped backwards in surprise. 'What are you talking about?' The guilt returned, accompanied by the first shiver of fear. If she'd told him what he'd done, what he intended to do...

'You know. Give me the camera – I want those photos you took of her deleted.'

Robert clutched his camera closer as a hand extended to grab it from him.

'I'm not giving you my camera. What's got into you? Have you gone completely mad?'

The fist caught him entirely by surprise, smashing into his jaw and spinning his head around. Robert tasted the metallic tang of blood in his mouth, then his tongue ran over the sharp edge of a broken tooth. He staggered back under the force of the blow, fighting to stay upright until one foot encountered nothing but air and he felt himself tipping backwards.

Time moved in slow motion. Robert's arms windmilled in empty space, fighting against gravity. When the fist turned into a hand, grasping at the camera, his backward fall was momentarily arrested, so he stood suspended above a sickening drop – and then the strap broke.

Robert's scream became another wild bird call until basalt columns far below fractured his cry with a harsh impact of bone against rock.

Underpinning the soundscape, the sea surged restlessly into the cave and back out again. A rhythm that mirrored the Earth's breath. In the agitated waters, a body stained the sea red. Caught in currents, it seemed to debate whether to stay in the cave or head out to the open sea, moving first one way, then the other. The uncertain dance attracted inquisitive seals, warily deciding whether this was a predator or food.

They kept a safe distance, large dark eyes drinking in the threat.

It was the beginning of April, and the first puffins were returning from the Atlantic – feather-gowned circus monks under a voluntary vow of silence. They paid no attention to the tragedy – focussed on awkward landings, they found last year's burrows and called for their mates. Some would wait for days, some for weeks before their life partner returned from a winter spent exploring the wild Atlantic. For a few, like the body in the cave, there would never be a homecoming again.

TWO

GRAVEYARD BELL

This was the worst part of the job – advising next of kin. Sergeant Suzie Crammond checked her appearance in the patrol car rear-view mirror, patting down her errant brown hair before placing her regulation cap squarely on her head.

'Let's do this.' Suzie kept her tone brief and to the point, taking refuge in procedure.

In the passenger seat, a WPC exchanged a look of sympathy as if she'd read the sergeant's mind. She took a deep breath and followed the sergeant to the door of a terraced house. At a nod from her boss, she pressed the doorbell and a chime sounded from deep in the hallway.

They waited with faces set, listening for the reluctant sound of approaching footsteps. Suzie had glimpsed a pale face watching from an upstairs window, had seen the head duck back when their eyes met. It was always worse when you knew the family, and here in Tobermory everyone knew each other – apart from holidaymakers who descended as predictably as summer rain and no longer registered unless they caused trouble.

For some reason, the distant door chime made Suzie recall

the graveyard bell – that mechanism of last resort for those inadvertently buried in Victorian times. It was an inappropriate image; this body wasn't coming back from the dead.

She'd been to the scene. Taken to Staffa by the same tourist boat operator whose customers had reported a body in the cave. He'd set the wee ferry boat headfirst into the waves, anxious to get this trip over with and return to business as normal. Her hands had been sore from hanging onto the boat to avoid being thrown around. PC William Aitkin accompanying her had had no such qualms, face split into a grin at the madness of it all – only returning to sobriety whenever he caught her eye.

The mooring had been wet and slippery. Stones slick with green slime and treacherous underfoot. The constable had offered her a hand which she had reluctantly accepted, not trusting her sensible black shoes with insufficient grip for this expedition. William had let go once they reached safer ground, embarrassed at the small intimacy with his superior. She'd turned to see if the ferryman was accompanying them, but he had insisted he had to stay with the boat and talked vaguely of tides and weather. He preferred not to meet her eye, checking on overhead clouds like a seasoned mariner.

She had understood. Death can have a fascination for some, is something best avoided for others. They'd known each other – the ferryman and the corpse. Spent a childhood at the same school, played in the same rugby club, drank in the same bar. He'd pointed silently to the well-worn path towards the cave, and she'd tilted her head in acknowledgement of all the things he hadn't said.

The man's skull was leaking brain soup into the water, and he'd attracted a shoal of tiny fish to the feast. An arm had caught in the crevice between two basalt columns, wedging him firmly enough to have defeated the first attempt of the tide to remove him. She'd looked up, imagining the fall from above. Had he fallen on purpose? She had sent the constable back to the boat to fetch rope and insist the ferryman return with him.

Between them, they had managed to anchor the body more securely. Blue nylon was wrapped around his torso and tied off to a metal railing. Of course, her radio didn't work – not this far out and blocked by the mass of the island itself. She'd had to use the boat radio, confirming a body had been found and requesting Oban to send out a team to recover and investigate. They'd been given instructions to keep the site secure until a RIB could make it, carrying a detective and single forensics officer.

Suzie had received the official confirmation earlier today. Robert Jameson had been positively identified by the ferryman. Cause of death – misadventure, likely accidental fall from the cliffs above the vast sea cave.

Lucy Jameson opened the door, her face bleached with prescience and holding onto the frame for support.

'Can we come in?' Suzie had taken off her cap without realising, standing on the threshold like a mourner.

Lucy stared at the floor and pulled the door open. They entered directly into a living space, wood burner patiently waiting to be lit. The house felt unnaturally cold as if the seawater from Fingal's Cave had only recently ebbed out of the place – as if death lived here.

'Please, sit down.' Lucy gestured towards the seats, face muscles failing to force the smile she tried for. 'Can I get you anything?'

'No. We're all right, thanks.' Suzie saw her swaying on her feet. Had she even eaten anything since her husband had been reported missing just twenty-four hours ago?

'Please, sit down, Lucy.'

She behaved like an automaton, knees folding and hands clasped together on her lap. Tears dripped silently onto the worn carpet.

'Clare, can you make us a cup of tea or coffee?' Suzie directed the comment to the constable. 'Is that all right, Lucy? What can we get you?'

The constable stood, awkwardly looking around her before deciding where the kitchen might be.

'I'm fine, thanks,' Lucy replied, without looking up.

Suzie didn't try to contradict such an obvious untruth. She squatted down in front of Lucy, held her hands.

'I'm so sorry. That's Robert's body they found. Is there someone we can call – a friend or neighbour?'

Lucy engaged with her at last, her cheeks wet with salt water. 'I can't...' The words choked off as her body spasmed, breaths gulped in between despairing cries for her love.

Suzie wrapped her arms around her, held the quivering body close.

'I'm so sorry.' She realised she was repeating herself, sought for other words of comfort and failed. She caught the constable's eyes, mouthed 'tea' above the sobs and held Lucy tight until the shaking lessened.

'How?' Lucy had recovered sufficiently to utter the one syllable. She raised her head up from her chest to plead for an answer – anything that would help her world make sense again.

The constable clattered around in the kitchen, her unseen progress marked by the sound of a kettle being filled, cups gathered, cupboard doors opening and closing. Suzie felt her thigh muscles complaining at her awkward stance, felt Lucy drawing away. She straightened up from her crouch, sat on an uncomfortable hardback chair and attempted to explain the inexplicable.

'We think he must have lost his footing on the cliff edge. He's a keen photographer, isn't he?'

Wildlife photographs adorned the walls: stags rutting in early autumn mist, their breath clearly visible in golden light; iconic white-tailed eagle with a salmon in its claws; otters companionably holding paws as they floated on their backs. Suzie imagined otters making a feast of Lucy's husband's spilt brains in the cave. She banished the unwelcome image from her mind as quickly as it had arrived.

Lucy managed a nod, wiped her eyes to clear her vision.

'There was a thorough investigation of the scene.' Suzie brushed over the fact that the Oban detective had climbed to the top of the island for a cursory look, evidence of puke still adhering to his jacket and a face set like thunder. He'd been accompanied by a young forensics guy, white scene-of-crime suit attracting the unwelcome attention of skuas. They must have spent all of ten minutes up there before being intimidated by the birds, returning with the firm opinion that the skuas had most likely made Robert slip over the cliff edge.

'It looks like he just lost his footing and fell.' *Or deliberately chose that final option for whatever reason.* Suzie kept her thoughts to herself.

'He takes care; he's always wary of the cliffs.'

The present tense. She'd not let him go – not yet.

'Accidents happen, Lucy. Even to the most careful.'

The constable brought in three steaming mugs, offered one to their host who took it and held it in two shaking hands.

'Thanks, Clare.' She motioned the constable towards a small table. 'Can you bring that over for Lucy?'

She waited until the mug made a safe landing on the occasional table before continuing.

'I know this is a dreadful shock. If there's anything we can do to help? Anyone we can ask to be with you...?'

Lucy's expression was devoid of emotion. She looked lost, isolated.

'I only have Rob.'

Suzie took a sip from her own mug, tasted coffee where she had expected tea. Drank it anyway.

'We found his boat. It's now moored down at Tobermory

pontoon – it can stay there as long as you like. They're not expecting you to pay anything.'

Lucy didn't respond, returning her attention to the same patch of carpet as if it held the secrets of the universe. A reason for why her husband had never returned home.

'Do you know what he was doing? On the island?' Suzie pulled her notebook out of her uniform, pen held in readiness.

'Puffins. He wanted to photograph the first puffins. Had a magazine article ready to be sent off. He said he'd be back in time for tea.' These last words more accusatory.

Suzie had seen it before. Loss turning to grief turning to anger. Railing against the universe or God or whatever was responsible for ruining a life.

The words were condensed and entered into her notebook. *Photo puffins for magazine.* At the same time, she recalled the items recovered with the body: house keys; wallet; clothing; sensible walking boots.

'What camera did he have? We didn't find it.' Suzie saw confusion sweep across Lucy's features.

'I don't know. Canon, I think. He carried it in an aluminium case, along with his binos.' She caught the interrogative stare before Suzie had time to articulate. 'Swarovski – green, cost a fortune.'

Again, the turn to anger in her voice.

'Thanks. We'll have another look. Maybe they're still in the cave – underwater.' *Canon camera, Swavorki (sp) binos* joined the other comments in her notebook. She exchanged a helpless glance with the constable, sipped from her mug.

'Who are your neighbours?' Suzie asked conversationally, as if they weren't there to tell Lucy her husband was dead – his skull crushed against basalt and lungs full of salt water, brains mostly eaten by opportunistic fish. Her imagination was running a reel inside her mind with a variety of aquatic creatures enjoying the unexpected snack.

Lucy looked up in surprise. 'Airbnb on the right. Zieliński on the left.'

'Do you know the Zielińskis at all? Are they friends?' Suzie tried to keep the desperation out of her voice. They couldn't stay with her indefinitely – they couldn't leave her like this on her own.

'Yes. We sometimes have each other round for meals. Maria's lived here for ten years or so, works part-time at the Co-op.'

'I'm going to ask her to pop in, if she's at home. Is that all right?' Another purposeful look towards Clare, followed by an imperative jerk of her head as the message didn't get through. The constable made for the front door, leaving them both alone. Lucy hadn't responded, lost within her own thoughts.

'We'll bring any of his belongings back to you, if we find them.' *And see if there's any clues on the camera, assuming it survived the drop and immersion in salt water.* She'd have to call in a diving team, keep the cave off-limits until they'd finish. That would be a week at least before they'd be able to fit in a search. She wasn't going to be popular with the tourist industry.

'Thank you.' Lucy sounded like a little girl.

'If there's anything we can do.' Suzie realised she was repeating herself again.

The constable returned, leading a concerned thirty-something woman into the room.

'Oh Lucy, this is awful.' Her voice betrayed her Polish roots. She immediately pulled Lucy into her body and stroked her hair repeatedly.

'I'll look after her.' She directed this at Suzie with a no-nonsense tone in her voice.

The sergeant mouthed a 'thank you', stood and returned her notepad to her uniform.

'I'm so sorry, Lucy. We all are.'

Suzie meant it. Any death somehow matters more on an

island, more so than on the mainland. Their community was more fragile, more susceptible to being damaged – but she could only offer words, and words were inadequate to fill the void Lucy had fallen into.

'We'll keep in touch.'

They left Lucy to the care of her Polish neighbour, Suzie replacing her cap for the short walk back to the car.

'Call around the ferry boat operators. Tell them the island is off limits for the next few days – or until we've had a police dive team look for his missing gear.'

'You think someone's robbed him? Someone killed him for his camera stuff?' The constable asked in disbelief.

She started the short drive back to the station, unsure of what to think.

'No, I'm sure it was an accident. Just a terrible accident.' Suzie realised she was only trying to convince herself and the young constable.

THREE
SKÚMUR

Teàrlach Paterson thought he recognised the woman's voice coming from reception and swivelled his neck to see who Chloe was speaking to. Lucy Jameson had been a few years below him at the high school in Tobermory. They'd gone to the same parties, knew the same group of friends and at one time he'd hoped she might find him interesting enough to go out with. She hadn't. He wasn't surprised – she had been vivacious, a naturally gifted academic whilst he'd always been taciturn and, as an incomer, had never really fitted in.

'Wait here, I'll see if he's available.' Chloe peered around the door to his office, allowing him full view of the woman.

'It's all right, Chloe. We go way back.' He beckoned Lucy in, saw the vivaciousness had evaporated and understood why.

He'd seen the news item a week ago – well-respected wildlife photographer dies from tragic fall. Should he have sent a card, some words expressing regret? It was too late now. They'd not crossed paths since the last day at school – him running around idiotically with all the other final-year schoolkids. Reverting to childhood and a last chance to play in the safety of the playground before adult life tied them all in straitjackets. She'd signed his white school shirt, left the faint imprint of lip gloss on his cheek. He remembered being inordinately pleased as if he'd been bestowed a great gift. That was twenty years ago, another world entirely. The image of his aunt and the white-painted stone cottage that had been his childhood home appeared so vividly in his imagination that he could smell the sea.

'Come in, Lucy. Please, take a seat.' He stood and they awkwardly shook hands across his desk as if they were playing at being the grown-ups they'd become. She settled into the chair opposite, hands clasped primly together on her lap.

'I'm so sorry to hear what happened to Robert.' Teàrlach found he was tongue-tied, unsure what to add.

'Thank you,' Lucy responded. 'It all seems so unreal... I've not really come to terms with it yet.'

Teàrlach called out to Chloe, knowing she'd be listening intently to everything being said. 'Can you make us a coffee, Chloe?' He lowered his voice to a more conversational pitch. 'Can I offer you anything: tea, coffee, water?'

A smile appeared and Lucy fleetingly returned to the young woman he remembered. 'Water, please. That would be nice.'

'Tap water?' Chloe enquired through the open door.

'Yes, thanks.' Lucy breathed heavily, her shoulders collapsing into her body. She lifted her chin and spoke as if she'd rehearsed a speech.

'I didn't know where else to go. There aren't any private investigators on Mull, and I knew you'd set up here in Glasgow.' She paused, looking around his office as if surprised to find herself there. 'I need someone to help me.'

Teàrlach waited for more. She sat opposite him, frowning. He could tell her hands must be flexing in her lap by the muscles twitching in her arms. In reception, the coffee machine started spluttering and the hiss of escaping steam made it sound like a train was approaching.

'I'll help in any way I can, of course.'

She sent him a look of gratitude, the smile making a reappearance. Chloe brought in the drinks, raised her eyebrows at Teàrlach and closed the intervening door behind her to give them some privacy.

'I don't know where to begin.' Lucy frowned again. A hand swept long blond hair away from her face so it cascaded behind her back.

He remembered the hair. Lucy owed her genetic makeup to some long-lost Scandinavian adventurer, leaving his trace in the blueness of her eyes and her blond genes.

'The police say that Robert fell accidentally. Lost his footing above Fingal's Cave whilst trying for a photograph. Or maybe he was startled by a bonxie which dive-bombed him and made him lose his balance.'

Teàrlach had read the local news report days after the event. The newspaper journalist had taken it upon himself to warn of the dangers of walking too close to cliff edges, reminding walkers to carry sticks and wear hats to fend off attacks by great skuas. He'd had personal experience himself of being targeted by those aggressive birds. Amusing to see other hapless walkers fending them off, but not so funny when you're the subject of their attention. Half the time he thought the birds did it for fun, or pure maliciousness.

'Do you think something else happened to him?' Teàrlach tried a leading question. She was here for some reason – he just didn't know what.

'Did you know the word skua comes from the Old Norse?' She changed the subject, interrogating him through her own blue Nordic eyes.

'No. Figures.' He wondered where this was going.

'Skúmur in Old Norse means "dark or ominous person". That's who I think murdered him.'

Teàrlach felt his eyebrows raising in surprise.

'Murdered? What makes you think Robert was murdered? The police investigated, didn't find any evidence to the contrary as far as I know.' He waited for her to explain herself.

'No, they didn't find any evidence.' Lucy sighed again, drank from the glass of water.

Teàrlach took the time to mirror her, sipping his coffee and watching her keenly. This was a woman who'd recently lost her husband, someone she loved more than anyone else. It was natural for grief to take strange diversions. Maybe this was her way of dealing with his death, trying to make sense of it all by imagining some rationale other than a simple slip on a cliff edge. He wondered how he would be able to reassure her and tell her to save her money. There was nothing they could do to bring Robert back or to explain his death any other way than a tragic accident.

'Robert's camera gear and binoculars were never found. The police called in a dive team to search the cave – nothing.' Lucy's glass hit his desktop in emphasis.

'Maybe he left them up top somewhere? Puffins may have dragged them into their burrows – or a tourist might have kept them for themselves instead of handing them in?' Teàrlach searched for simple explanations. 'He was on Staffa alone, wasn't he? The news said his was the only boat there when the ferry arrived.'

'That's the line the police held to as well,' she responded.

Teàrlach opened his hands, palm outwards in supplication. 'I don't see how you think there was anyone else involved?'

She nodded as if expecting the response he'd given her, reached down to the bag she'd brought and pulled out a magazine. Lucy skimmed through the pages with a look of concentration. Teàrlach read the cover – *Scottish Birdwatcher*. A full colour photograph adorned the front page, two swans flying over the iconic Eilean Donan Castle, backlit with the ghostly green glow of an aurora.

'Here!' She placed the magazine down in front of him, pointed to a page full of puffins – comical clown faces peering out at him.

'I don't see what this has to do with your husband's death,' Teàrlach eventually responded after looking more closely at each shot.

'Because these were taken on Staffa by Robert the day he died. That's his style, I'd recognise his photographs anywhere.' Lucy challenged him to disagree.

'You may be right, but it's quite possible these were taken by someone else – or maybe they're stock photographs Robert provided?' Teàrlach searched the small print for a photographer's name with difficulty, squinting his eyes to bring the minute letters into focus.

'They claim to be taken by a David Webster,' Lucy helpfully added.

'OK.' He was struggling to find a way to close this down. She was clutching at straws, creating a narrative where anyone but her husband or sheer bad luck was to blame for his death.

'You think I'm crazy, don't you?' Lucy said quietly.

Teàrlach wondered if he was really that easy to read. 'No, of course not. I think you've had a terrible shock, that's—'

'Just look into it for me,' she interrupted. 'I know Robert's photographs. I'd recognise them anywhere.'

Her finger rested on the magazine where a puffin's head poked out of its burrow, framed by moving grass. It was a great shot, the puffin commanding the focus away from the blurred background.

He studied the picture. It looked no different to all the other pictures of birds he'd seen. 'The police are better placed to look into this, Lucy.'

'The police can't be bothered. They say there's no reason to investigate and there's no evidence that these are his photographs. The magazine refused to pass on David Webster's details claiming data protection, but he's the only person who knows what happened. I need you to find him and ask him what he's doing with Robert's camera.'

FOUR

CAMERAWORK

'Wildlife photography is all about waiting for the wildlife to come to you.'

Sam stood in a damp huddle with the other three members of the expedition, sheltering in the lee of the minibus. Even so the wind managed to cut through three layers of clothing as if they weren't there, leeching warmth from his bones. The other three members of the group stared at the guide as hungry as messianic cult followers searching for wisdom in the wilderness. They were in the wilderness right enough – the sea at their backs and tree-covered hills in front being erased in lowering grey mist. They'd left Tobermory just an hour ago in spring, but here on the west coast the weather had turned to winter.

He had joined the tour ostensibly to improve his photography skills, take instruction from a professional and bag shots of sea eagles. The guide was confident this was the one spot on the island where they could be all but guaranteed to spot them. Sam took note of the 'all but guaranteed'. If he was brutally honest with himself, which he rarely was, he'd accept he was running away from a failing relationship and this new hobby was just another diversion.

He allowed a moment of self-pity to intrude. Everyone else seemed to manage careers, relationships, life. Why was it so difficult for him? Sam didn't even know why he'd chosen Mull as a holiday destination. He'd never been here before, had no connection with the place. When he'd seen the tour advertised online, it had all looked so idyllic. Rugged outdoor types with all the gear, driving around in 4x4s, boat trips to far-flung islands. The website displayed photographers positively tripping over puffins, soaked by the spray from diving whales, enjoying companionable drinks in pubs. And the sun – always shining, sparkling off an aquamarine sea, outlining eagle feathers in laser-sharp definition. He lifted his head to look morosely in the direction the guide was indicating, his stare failing to penetrate rain so fine it existed in an indeterminate state between liquid and air, and all the wetter for that.

He had left his partner behind on the mainland, continuing the tour of Scotland in their small campervan without him. He'd hoped that taking the two weeks at Easter would give them space to rekindle a flame that had dimmed to faint embers. A break from his teaching job where adolescents circled him like spotty sociopathic piranhas. Steve was always wrapped up in his graphic design business, taking it home most nights so the two of them coexisted more than cohabited. Instead of the holiday bringing them back together as he'd anticipated, the claustrophobic campervan interior only served to reinforce their level of disconnect. It seemed to Sam that the closer they were forced together, the greater the need to escape had become; two magnets sharing the same poles.

'Spread yourselves out, find a good location and try to remain as still as possible. We don't want to disturb the wildlife. All the best shots come from patience and keen observation. Have your finger on the shutter release at all times, you never know what's going to appear right in front of your lens!'

Sam followed the group, searching for somewhere sheltered

where he could wait out the next few hours without risking hypothermia. They were on a spit of open ground which doubled as an unofficial lay-by, overlooking a mile-wide channel separating Mull from its smaller satellite island of Ulva offshore. The wind and rain had total and unfettered access which it used to good effect, coating his new camera and lenses with a corrosive mix of salt water before he'd even taken his first shot. Around him tripods were being extended, cameras positioned, and hoods pulled around heads as the team hunkered down to get 'that shot'. He couldn't see a single bloody thing moving, even the tough highland cattle had gone to ground rather than remain grazing in this weather.

He struggled with the tripod, slipped the camera into the socket at the top as he'd practised earlier, then realised the camera was pointing out to sea in entirely the wrong direction.

'May be otters,' he explained in response to querying looks from his fellow enthusiasts. As one they pulled out binoculars and scanned the coastline, eventually giving up and focussing back on the hill with a few pitying glances sent his way. There must have been a simple way of swivelling the mount around, but his fingers had become unresponsively numb and the prevailing wind was at his back, so this is where he would stay. Even in a group this small, he still managed to be the odd man out. The sea blended almost seamlessly into the overcast sky, a washed-out grey panorama that would require all the software magic available on his laptop to produce anything worth printing.

The narrow sea channel, sheltered as it was, still managed to be whipped into white horses by the strength of wind funnelling between the two land masses. A pair of oyster-catchers patrolled the stony beach just a few hundred metres away, looking as wet and dejected as he felt. He focussed his telephoto lens on them anyway, their long red bills and orange legs the only splash of colour in a monochrome world. They probed the shoreline with as much success as he had with life, moving on between failed attempts to find anything worthwhile before trying somewhere new and repeating the same, fruitless exercise. Further out at sea a small fishing boat made brave progress against the wind, see-sawing forward in a way that made him feel sick just looking at it. Sam shifted his viewpoint from the sad oystercatchers and increased the magnification until the boat filled his screen.

Now he had to work out how the tripod pan mount worked as the boat slipped out of his field of view. Cursing under his breath, he tried loosening one of the adjusting arms until the camera moved freely, overshooting his target and causing him to track back until it filled the screen once more. He tried a few shots, then a few more as two fishermen appeared on the deck. They were struggling to throw nets overboard and added much needed action and interest to an otherwise boring snap. When the sun made a temporary appearance, sending a golden shaft of light between two banks of cloud, it caught the boat and the image popped out of the screen. Sam pressed the remote shutter control, holding the button down in his sudden excitement that he'd somehow managed to catch a perfect shot. The camera whirred, shot after shot taken within milliseconds of each other as it entered burst mode. The other photographers turned around at the sound, following the line of his telephoto as the sunbeam disappeared. All they could see was an uninspiring small boat on a grey sea. Exchanging looks that spelt out Sam was a sad case, they returned to scanning the skies for the outline of a large bird of prey.

Sam was oblivious to their disdain, playing back the shots on his screen until he found the one where the sun illuminated the boat and fisherman under a golden spotlight. A red roof caught the light like a drop of fresh blood. Zooming in to check the focus, he frowned, then zoomed in some more. That bundle of netting looked more like a body than fishing gear. The thought was instantly dismissed – what was he thinking? This was a wildlife tour on a Hebridean island, not a television crime series where improbable murders occur amongst photogenic scenery. Not that today was proving particularly photogenic. Behind his back one of the photographers let out a yell, shouting he could see a golden eagle. The tour guide instantly hushed him, reminding them all to keep quiet unless they wanted to scare the bird away. He was roundly ignored as cameras swung upwards, the unmistakable barn door wings of an eagle seeming to scrape the distant treetops. Sam awkwardly manoeuvred his camera to join them, fishing boat forgotten until the air was thick with multiple shutter releases and excited exultations from photographers announcing they'd caught it. The eagle ignored them all, eyes seeing further than any land-trapped animal. An object floated on the sea surface, defying the pull of the sea. The eagle watched for movement, saw only the random tug of waves, and leisurely tipped a wing to ride the wind out to sea. Uncaring of the huddle of excited photographers below, the bird soared overhead and out over the water.

As the day ended, the weather started to clear. The minibus disgorged the group of photographers at a viewpoint high above Dervaig, just in time for them to catch the first proper glimpse of the sun that day. It sank towards the horizon, red fire doused in the sea and painting the departing clouds in varying hues of crimson. The opportunity was too good for the tour guide, who fetched his own camera from the vehicle, taking shot after shot of a stunning sunset, then stepping back from the group to include the minibus and photographers outlined against the dying day. Satisfied he had the perfect publicity shot for his website, and with his small group of photographers expressing delight with their expedition, they returned to Tobermory with the promise of a meal and a few pints at the pub foremost in their minds.

Sam spent the journey bent over in his bus seat, viewing the day's shots with difficulty as he was thrown from side to side. The one of the boat, caught in a solitary shaft of sunlight, held his attention. Whatever the fishermen had thrown overboard, it was too large to be a creel and more substantial than a net. Try as he might, Sam couldn't shake the chilling thought that he'd inadvertently photographed them disposing of a body.

FIVE

PUFFINS

Teàrlach's hands automatically went to the back of his head after Lucy had gone, tilting back in his chair until the twinge in his side warned him to stop. She was insistent the photos in the magazine were Robert's, had pleaded with him to investigate and he'd eventually given in. What exactly was she hoping he'd be able to accomplish?

Dee interrupted his chain of thought, arriving in the outside office and exchanging banter with Chloe. At least the two of them were firm friends now – there was a time after Dee first joined when he thought one or the other would leave. Their last case had forged them into a close-knit team and left a seven-centimetre scar in his abdomen – large enough to accommodate a knife and then the surgeon's tools. Now each one of them shared a close relationship with death, which left them closer than ever.

'Here's your wrap!' Dee's voice broke his reverie.

He caught the paper bag mid-flight before it could disgorge its contents over his desk.

'Thanks, Dee. Wait!'

She turned on her heel, poised in the open doorway with

her head tilted quizzically to one side and eyebrows raised in enquiry. She blinked as her hand unconsciously swept waves of red hair away from her face, revealing green eyes bright with humour.

'Chloe! Can you join us?' Teàrlach pushed his wrap to one side of the desk, leaving space to open *Scottish Birdwatcher* to the page Lucy had shown him. He could feel the two women exchanging a look without having to raise his head.

'Has someone lost a parrot?' Dee joked.

'Someone's lost a husband,' he replied drily. 'The woman who was here earlier, Lucy Jameson. I knew her from when I was at school on Mull.'

The two women remained silent, although their interest quickened at the possibility of hearing salacious snippets about his past.

'Not like that,' he quickly added. 'Did you see the news item about a photographer who fell off sea cliffs a week ago?'

'Saw something,' Chloe acknowledged. 'That was her guy?'

Teàrlach nodded in confirmation, aware that she'd undoubtedly heard everything that had been said in his office.

'Why are we getting involved?' Dee came straight to the point.

'She's convinced the photos in this magazine were taken by her man, Robert Jameson. His body was recovered from inside Fingal's Cave on Staffa, near the Isle of Mull – police divers and a ground search found no trace of his camera or binoculars.'

'Probably taken by a tourist.' Dee spoke as if light-fingered thieves were a regular occurrence.

Teàrlach couldn't disagree. 'Point is, everyone is convinced that he was the only one on the island. He'd taken his own boat which was still tied up by the pier and his body was discovered by tourists making one of the first trips of the season.'

'Could be another person made their own way there and

left before the ferry arrived.' Chloe suggested. 'Is it far? Could you take a canoe or something?'

'You can kayak there, long as the wind isn't against you.' Teàrlach studied the puffins in the hope they'd be able to offer some advice. 'Point is, this cave is deep – sixty or eighty metres, perhaps. Police divers aren't going to go that far down. His gear's more than likely on the sea floor.'

Dee was shaking her head. 'I don't see what we're meant to be doing for her. He lost his footing or whatever, bashed his head on rocks and drowned. Where do we come in?'

They both stood patiently at his desk, Dee tearing into her wrap and chewing noisily, Chloe adopting her confused expression.

'She's convinced something happened on the island that the police couldn't discover. Something that caused Robert to lose his life. I don't know how we can possibly give her any answers as to why he died, but we can investigate this photographer and confirm he hasn't taken Robert's camera.'

'We're looking for lost property now?' Dee managed with a mouth full of food.

'She's an old friend, I said we'd look into it.' His reply sounded inadequate even to his own ears. It must be almost twenty years since he'd last seen her. His memory provided a snippet from a beach party, a fire lit, bottles emptied and an unknowable future lying in wait for all of them. Lucy's hair had shone in the flames as she danced around the fire. He remembered thinking he was in love but feeling powerless to do anything about it.

'Dee, see if you can access the original photographs from the magazine. Chances are they were emailed. If they won't play nicely, then you can do whatever you need to do. There should be metadata, right?'

She nodded vigorously in return, red hair flying around her face as she fought to swallow her food.

'Absolutely. If it hasn't been removed, then it will have the camera details, date, time – even location it was taken at. Should be enough to prove the photographs came from the place he was on the day he died at least.'

'That's what I thought.' He shut the magazine, handed it to Chloe. 'See if you can find this photographer, David Webster, so I can have a chat. It's probably all above board, but at least we can try to put her mind at rest.'

They left him to enjoy his late lunch. Lucy's unexpected arrival in his office had brought the past back with a vengeance. Years growing up on the Inner Hebridean island that became home. The cottage he shared with his aunt was his now, in desperate need of attention since she died. He really ought to do something with it, but like everything in his past, he filed it away under forget.

Outside his window, the sun was fighting a battle with April showers, and the showers were winning. The Clyde kept being erased by returning sheets of rain, smearing the glass and turning Glasgow into an impressionist painting. Teàrlach imagined plummeting off the cliffs above the sea cave, hitting the unforgiving rocks and drowning without anyone there to watch him die. Staffa always struck him as an otherworldly place – lava flows frozen as columnar basalt met the sea. Legends had the cave as home to the Irish warrior Finn MacCumhaill, a base from which to fight off marauding Vikings. Others said hell was underneath.

Teàrlach wasn't convinced about that – hell was all around them. He glanced at the filing cabinet, pulled open the top drawer and retrieved the letter that had lain there unopened since his abusive father had died. Lucy had brought the past back into his life – he took it as a sign to deal with something he hadn't wanted to face and prepared to open this last missive from beyond the grave.

'I'll work from home.' Dee's interruption stopped him

before he'd begun. 'Don't feel comfortable hacking from the office – too easy to be tracked.'

'Aye, sure. Whatever works best.' He transferred the letter to his jacket pocket, deciding to deal with it later.

Dee's smile remained in his memory like a Cheshire cat's long after the sound of her motorbike had faded into the busy Glasgow traffic. He couldn't change the past, but he could attempt to bring Lucy Jameson some comfort in the present.

SIX

YOU'RE LOST

Dee Fairlie roused herself from a disturbed sleep, looked out on blue skies being steadily erased by a bank of grey clouds coming in from the west. The bedside clock digits swam into focus showing 9:30 and she leapt out of bed in a panic. Dee washed in haste, threw on yesterday's clothes and regarded herself in the bathroom mirror. Green eyes stared back at her, tousled red hair threatened to remain unmanageable for the day. A pimple had erupted on her chin during the night, no doubt encouraged by the greasy pizza she'd wolfed down last thing before hitting the sack. A tube of concealer hid the worst of the blemish by the time she'd finished with it.

She leaned over the metal balcony of her modern apartment overlooking the Clyde, sipping a morning coffee and watching the river making slow progress out to sea. If she had a boat, she could sail on that languid watercourse and make her way across the Atlantic Ocean to America. A familiar ache started some- where in the centre of her chest. It had taken her the best part of a year to realise that this orphan had finally found a family. Maybe something more than family.

Teàrlach had discharged himself from hospital after his

stabbing last August. Six months for his stab wound to heal and she knew it still gave him occasional pain.

'Unhealthy places, hospitals,' he'd said at the time. 'No one here gets out alive.'

He'd said it with gallows humour, and she'd searched the internet afterwards, finally finding the quoted source as the singer Jim Morrison. It figured – he also had poetry running in his veins, riding high on youth and rebellion before drug-fuelled entropy had its inevitable way. Entropy had affected Teàrlach too – or something akin to that. Maybe it was the enforced rest, laid up on a hospital bed with tubes carrying liquids in, tubes carrying liquids out. He never allowed himself time to think, and in those bedridden days, he'd changed somehow – grown even more introverted. The death of his father had occurred at the same time, a final severing of an umbilical Teàrlach had wanted to cut for most of his life.

Following last summer's close encounter with death, he'd deliberately kept her at arm's length after risking his own life to save hers. Now they both set boundaries: he for 'professional reasons' or so he claimed – she for self-preservation. They would have made a great couple if they were only brave enough.

Dee sighed, letting that thought join the Clyde. Life moves on, and so must she. Her office was in the second bedroom, repurposed to house the tools of her trade. Computer screens waited for Dee to give them a meaningful task, the soft whirr of electric fans the only sound. She selected a track on her mobile, sent it to the TV soundbar with a flick of her finger and The Doors started playing 'You're Lost Little Girl', Jim Morrison's velvet tones filling the room. A touch of the mouse and three screens burst into life. An email remained unopened from last night. The subject was simply titled, 'Enquiry Reference Fairlie, Dee – 739365. The sender was Scotlandspeople.gov.uk. Dee took a deep breath and prepared to view the results of a search she'd put off ever since turning sixteen. For all her life she'd been adamant that she'd never search for her birth parents. They'd abandoned her to a life in care, had never once attempted to contact her. Why this sudden need to try and find them – and why now?

Her phone vibrated in her pocket, and she muted the music before turning the screen towards her with trembling hands. It was Teàrlach.

'Hi, Teàrlach.' She hoped the nerves she felt weren't too obvious in her voice.

'Hi, Dee, how did you get on with the birding magazine and those photographs?'

Dee clicked on a file on her desktop, opened a photo gallery of bird pictures.

'They didn't want to send me the photos, claimed copyright protection but offered to sell me prints at a rip-off price.'

'No joy, then?'

'Didn't say that. I'm looking at the originals now – and the metadata is still on them. The date stamps show they were taken during the time Robert Jameson was on Staffa, and the camera was the same Canon EOS 90D that his wife said he used.'

'Interesting. Chloe's tried to find the photographer credited for the shots but has drawn a blank. He doesn't show up in any other magazines or social media. Can you see if you can find him?'

'Sure. I'll make a start now – what was his name again?'

'David Webster.'

She typed the name into an open notes app. 'If he has Robert Jameson's camera, he may know something about his death.'

'Precisely! Although I'm still working on the assumption that this is an accident we're looking at.'

She could hear Teàrlach pause.

'How are you doing? You all right – unlike you to lie in?' He had dropped his voice.

She glanced at the screens, the unopened email from the Scottish agency.

'Fine,' she lied. 'Doing away. Are you going over to the island?'

'I need to have a look around myself – and I thought I'd check on my aunt's cottage, see if the place is still weathertight. I may have to spend some time doing some DIY.'

Dee attempted to imagine Teàrlach fixing up a house. Failed.

'Best to stick with what you're good at. Why don't you leave building to the professionals?' *And give your side a chance to recover*. The advice remained unvoiced.

'You should come over as well. You could use a break,' he said lightly.

Dee read too much into the invitation.

'Maybe. When were you thinking?'

'We could go tomorrow – the Oban ferry should have space.'

'Aye. All right,' she answered as casually as she could manage. 'Be good to give the bike a run. I'll get back to you about this David Webster.'

'OK. Let me know if you find anything. I'll let you know which ferry I'm on – catch you soon. Bye, Dee.'

'Bye, Teàrlach.' The sound of his voice died. She replaced her mobile on the desk and stared at the central computer screen. The message waited on her to do something.

Her fingers reluctantly reached for the keyboard.

SEVEN
BAIT

John Stevenson stood at the extent of the shoreline, breaking spray covering his face in a fine mist. These rocks were only visible at low tide, and the bladder wrack and laminaria with their large flat fronds were treacherous and slippery underfoot. John threw the cable holding his hydrophone as if he were casting a lure, watching as it dipped beneath the sea surface to capture the quieter sounds underwater. A plastic bottle served as a makeshift float, holding the microphone at two metres depth and bobbing with each wave crest.

He pressed record, and the small digital recorder strapped to his waist glowed a single red eye in response. A quick check that recording levels were correct, then he eased headphones over his ears and was immersed in an underwater world of muffled surf and breaking bubbles. John listened for the sounds he sought: the whistles and clicks of dolphins; the pig-like sounds of the minke whales. What he heard was the sound of a woman's voice, so clear that he spun around to search for whoever had snuck up on him. He was alone. John slipped the headphones off but heard nothing but breaking surf and the wind blowing across his newly exposed ears.

He eased the headphones back into place, unsure whether he wanted to hear the sound again but couldn't resist the urge to do so. There it was. A woman singing – underwater. His imagination furnished the disembodied voice with a body, then a mermaid's tail and long, golden tresses catching the ebb and flow. It was preposterous – yet at the same time it was undeniably real, the level meters on his recorder confirmed the sounds were there. This wasn't the first time he'd heard her, but never as clearly as this. On other occasions he'd been able to rationalise that the sound had been playing on a boat and his sensitive equipment had picked up music transmitted from inside the hull – but there were no boats out today.

John stayed immobile for minutes, listening to the voice rising above the breaking surf until the first wave broke over his feet. The tide was turning, and these rocks would soon be underwater. Hastily, he reeled in the small underwater microphone, wrapping the cable around the makeshift bottle float and stepped carefully back to the safety of a stony beach. There was no one else around, not on such a grey April day. His attention switched from the cold sea and back to the track leading to his van, debating whether to risk a quick dive in search of the sound.

The rational part of his mind encouraged caution, but he needed to know where this voice was coming from. John considered his options – the tide was coming in; he took that as a positive. The sea wasn't too rough, and relatively shallow on this part of the coast. He'd dived here before. On the negative side, it was unwise to even try a shallow dive without someone there with him.

Caution lost the argument. He quickly returned to his van, pulled on his wetsuit before he could change his mind and waded out in the direction from where the sound appeared to originate. John took a deep breath, then plunged under the water. He could still hear her, and now that her voice came directly to his ears, he could pinpoint the direction. John surfaced and began swimming out, away from the rocks and the surf that threatened to throw him bodily back to land. He took one last deep breath, then curled his head down, aiming his body like an arrow pointed downwards.

Visibility was better than he anticipated without goggles, a blurry representation of the seabed coming to meet him. There was nothing he could see that was out of the ordinary, certainly no mythological mermaid swimming to greet him. Here the kelp grew in profusion, crabs waved claws in protest at this alien intruder. Small fish darted away to avoid being eaten, shoals performing underwater murmurations as they repeatedly changed direction. John's gaze was fixed towards an abandoned creel, anchored to the seabed with ropes caught on rock. The sound came from there and from whatever package had been left inside.

He tugged at the ropes, attempting to dislodge the creel, but it was held so tightly he couldn't shift it. John only had so much time he could hold his breath, and his arm stretched inside the creel opening to withdraw the source of the woman's voice. He gripped the package, began withdrawing his arm and the creel entrance pulled tight, gripping his arm like a vice.

John's initial feeling was of exasperation – caught like a lobster. He pushed his arm back into the creel and the grip on his arm lessened. This time, he tried pulling out slowly, but the mechanism at the entrance gripped him just as hard as before. He attempted to see how the creel was gripping him, but his vision wasn't sharp enough to render sufficient detail. More angry than anything, John released the package. He needed to take another mouthful of air, the urge to breathe was beginning to hurt his chest.

He pulled out of the creel, only for his arm to be gripped once again. Frustrated, he tried a quick jerk before the mechanism could respond. It was no good, he was caught fast.

Now the panic started. His chest had begun to contract in an attempt to pull air into his lungs and he fought against that urge whilst trying to escape the abandoned creel. No matter how hard he pushed, pulled, twisted or turned, the entrance held him fast. Trails of blood had begun weeping from cuts in his trapped arm, spiralling out into the cold water. He could feel the sting of salt in his wounds and redoubled his efforts to escape. His spare hand tried to force the jaws of the creel apart and he felt sharp metal. What was going on? This wasn't a normal creel – no fisherman he knew had ever loaded the entrance with the equivalent of a steel gin trap.

Bubbles of air escaped his mouth as he fought, rolling up towards the surface just two metres above his head. He couldn't stand, the trap was holding tight and the ropes were too well secured to the seabed for him to break free. Beneath the rising tide of panic, John knew he was going to die. He could only hold on for a few more moments until the urge to breathe would fill his lungs with water. His violent struggles only briefly lifted the creel off the seabed, raising clouds of silt until he could no longer see the device that held him down.

When he gulped the first, choking mouthful of seawater, it took a long, painful eternity until he could no longer see anything; there was only the sound of his last air escaping as bubbles. When that, too, was silenced, his thrashing body quietened into stillness.

EIGHT
LOBSTER

Sergeant Suzie Crammond stood beside the abandoned van and scratched her head where her cap had rested moments before. The call had come in over breakfast, two wild swimmers in a panic over a swimmer who never surfaced and his discarded pile of equipment on the beach. She'd had to eat on the move, a skill they hadn't included in police training but an important one to learn. Constable William Aitkin was taking the two women's details, his pen scratching so loudly on his notebook she could hear it above the wind.

She tried the van door – it had been left unlocked. The interior was relatively clean, just an untidy pile of clothes on the passenger seat. There was a Greenpeace sticker on the window, Safeguarding Our Oceans pamphlets in the dash. Nothing there to suggest the occupant had decided to take his own life. She checked the trouser pockets – empty.

'Thank you, ladies. We'll be in touch if we need anything else and thank you for bringing this to our attention. You'll have to find somewhere else for your swim, I'm afraid – until we've checked the scene.' PC William Aitkin's Somerset accent was clear as Suzie withdrew her head from inside the van to view the two wild swimmers.

They exchanged worried looks with each other, then with Suzie as if she might associate them with a potential drowning.

'We tried looking for him,' one of the women pleaded. 'It's just so deep and without a mask...'

'You did everything you could. Best to leave this to professional police divers with the experience and equipment.'

Suzie's tight smile gave her little comfort. The two police officers watched them until they'd driven out of sight.

'Did you find any ID on the beach?'

The PC's blank expression told her all she wanted to know.

'Let's go back down. There's no note or anything in his van.'

They walked the ten-minute hike back through cattle pasture, Suzie placing her feet with care. Highland cattle followed their progress, dark eyes scarcely visible from underneath long fringes. A forlorn pile of recording equipment remained in a heap on the pebble beach, the wind playing with a coat that had been carelessly left covering it.

Sergeant Suzie Crammond looked down at her shoes plastered with mud. Normally, the soiling of her regulation black footwear with an amalgam of ruminant droppings and honest Mull earth would have caused her some concern, but her attention was focussed on the shoreline below. Oystercatchers caught sight of her, veering away with alarm calls ringing in the chill morning air, searching for less haunted feeding grounds. She watched the birds fly until they rounded a headland, their burbling call fading into the distance.

'Forensics won't find anything – the tide's coming in,' Suzie muttered to herself but made towards the shoreline anyway, just in case there was something of interest left by the same waves that the missing man had presumably entered. A small crab scuttled sideways, brown kelp clung to the seafloor, waves made a half-hearted effort to make some impact on the black rocks which shrugged off their feeble attempts at erosion. 'Check the coat pockets,' she called over her shoulder, irritated by the constable's inactivity. 'Put your gloves on!'

He straightened, searched his own pockets before pulling on a pair of black nitrile gloves and bent back to the task.

She sighed, looked out to sea. 'Where did you go?' The words were whispered, lost in the soft sounds of the incoming tide. Suzie scanned the area the two women had stated they'd seen him dive, calculated currents to work out in which direction a body might be taken. It didn't matter, the Oban police would have to be involved. Two bodies in as many weeks and all she had were the two constables – Clare and William.

'Found this!' The PC was waving a brown wallet in the air; water droplets described arcs with each semaphore move. He looked like a crab himself, ludicrously semaphoring from a crouched position.

Suzie picked her way across the uneven rocks, feeling her soles slip and slide each time they made hesitant contact with the ground. He'd stopped waving it by the time she'd returned, latex-covered fingers riffling through the contents and producing a wad of paper.

'Driving licence!' A pink plastic card emerged. 'Mr John Stevenson, an address in Fort William. Could be him,' the PC added with his usual dubiety.

She felt an initial sense of relief that they hadn't found another islander, immediately followed by guilt for having had that thought. Whoever he was, there'd be family, friends – maybe children missing a dad. Suzie had seen enough.

'We'd better take all this back to the car, we can't leave it on the beach. I'll radio through to Tobermory coastguard but it looks like he never surfaced from his dive.' The first spatters of rain impacted her face, and she turned to watch a bank of dark clouds heading from the west with a telltale mist fast approaching across the sea.

'The witnesses said he wasn't wearing any sub-aqua gear, just a wetsuit.' The PC spoke with an air of finality – the diver's death an inevitability.

The heavens opened before they made it to the patrol car, and they sat dripping onto their seats with heavy rain drumming on the roof. Suzie tried the radio without much hope of there being any reception – the signal was weak on this part of the island and the rain would only make it worse.

'Sorry, William. That gate needs to be taped to stop people using the beach until the dive team have been.' She handed the constable a roll of police tape.

'Are we not waiting for the coastguard to do a search first, ma'am?'

Suzy sighed in response.

'If the coastguard find a body, I'll call it off. But those women said they saw him dive and never re-surface. My guess is he managed to get himself trapped somehow – old fishing gear, seaweed, foot caught between rocks. The dive team will likely take days before reaching us out here off the mainland. It's a body recovery at this stage.'

The PC retrieved a waterproof from the back seat, pulled it over his wet uniform with difficulty and left the shelter of the patrol car. The prospect of having the Oban police trampling over the island was bad enough, but what really concerned her was the possibility of a second unexplained death this month. She told herself they were unconnected, just accidents. Two completely unrelated incidents coincidentally occurring so close together. The troubling thought remained with her all the way back to the police station and the call through to the Oban branch.

When she'd given the details to the Oban detective, she breathed a sigh of relief. John Stevenson was their problem now, and the Fort William police would have the job of notifying the next of kin. The light outside brightened, sunshine catching the roof of the patrol car visible from the small office window and patches of blue showing in the grey sky. She hoped taping off the beach would be enough to keep the scene secure until forensics and a dive team could make it over. Now that the sun was shining, she felt her concerns lessening. The two deaths, happening so close to one another, had shaken the whole team. But they had to be just a terrible coincidence. The island would return to normal: petty crime; drink-driving; the usual suspects taking most of her time. She checked her watch, felt her stomach rumble. There'd be fresh pies in the baker's on the high street, and it did no harm to remind everyone the police were keeping an eye on things.

NINE
TOBERMORY

Teàrlach didn't see Dee on the ferry crossing over to Mull. He thought they'd meet up on the boat, then found her phone wasn't receiving calls when he tried to contact her. She was probably running late and would make the next one. Motorbikes always found space on board, unlike cars which were best booked in advance.

The last time he'd made this journey it was to bury his aunt. More mother than aunt – the pain of her loss still squeezed his heart like a fist. If only he'd known she was ill... She'd not told anyone. Determined not to be a burden, to protect him from the cruel fact of her cancer.

Teàrlach stared absent-mindedly over the sea as the ferry made stately progress towards the only home he'd ever known. His early years were lost – unreliable memories of a string of different houses and flats; arguments and shouting; his dad terrorising them all whenever he'd been on the drink – until the day his aunt had taken him away and saved his life. It was a debt he could never now repay, and the guilt of that omission would be a burden he'd carry to his grave.

A change in the engines alerted him to the boat's imminent

arrival. At the same time a woman's pre-recorded voice advised drivers in Gaelic to return to their vehicles. He joined the queue for the lower decks and the memories he'd suppressed played in his mind like a newsreel.

He headed straight for Tobermory, stopping off at the arts centre café which was far enough away from the main tourist street to be sure of a seat. Teàrlach ordered a double espresso, sat at a table and gratefully sipped at the strong coffee. The letter he carried weighed heavily in his jacket inside pocket, the only item the nursing home had forwarded after his father's death. He'd carried that burden ever since, unwilling to read the contents and on many occasions, only taken out to be binned then reluctantly returned to his pocket.

There was music playing over the café speakers: two girls' voices weaving plaintive harmonies around and over one other. There were elements of Hebridean Psalm singing in the arrangement, and he listened to music his grandfather would have recognised until he felt strong enough to face reading his father's last words. His fingers shook, pulling apart the envelope and withdrawing a letter written in his father's hand. The writing was spidery, crawling across the page with random leaps and scrawls as if the effort of creating each word had almost been too much for him. It was dated August last year, the month he died.

Teàrlach, son, I can understand you not wanting to see me ever again, but I need you to know that I'll soon be dead and gone, and though that may be a good thing for the both of us, there are things I need to tell you. I never meant to kill them. There's no one more sorry that they've gone than me, and I'll take that pain to the grave with me and maybe the afterlife as well.

I loved your mum more than life itself, and you boys were the best thing I ever did. She wanted to leave me. Because of my drinking. I wasn't good to her or you boys when I was drinking, I know. I tried to stop, God knows I did. I went to AA meetings and everything, but when I needed a drink, I could never stop.

The fire was just to scare her, make her come out. She wouldn't open the door, so I got some petrol so she'd come out and I could make it all better and right again. I never thought she'd stay inside with Jamie. I thought you were there as well. I thought I'd lost you all.

Listen, son, I'm no fucking use to you, I know that. You're right to hate me for what I did, and I don't blame you for not coming to see me now I'm dying. I just wanted you to know that I love you. I loved all of you and I killed everything I ever loved. If you bury me, put that on my tombstone.

I'm sorry, son.

Your da,
John Paterson

He'd not signed off with love. Teàrlach doubted that his father was even capable of love. The letter read like a narcissistic plea for forgiveness. A final self-delusion that none of this was his fault. Blaming the drink instead of his own weakness of character. And yet Teàrlach could remember happy times. His mum and dad laughing together, holding each other, kissing, playing with him and his brother. Both sets of memories were as true as the other. Teàrlach was now at the age his father was when the unforgivable happened. Was he so different to his father? There was no simple answer. He'd expected hate to be his response and found he was in mourning.

Teàrlach stared into some middle distance, the artwork and posters on the walls blurring out of focus and the girls' unearthly harmonies echoing inside his head. His father had not asked for forgiveness – he knew that was a gift Teàrlach would have been unable to offer. He'd expressed regret, a degree of self-pity, but at least he'd spoken his truth. His words from beyond the grave remained when a lifetime's utterances had been forgotten. '*I killed everything I ever loved*' – it was a fitting enough epitaph.

The café was slowly starting to fill – mostly women collecting children from school, their excited clamour drowning out the music and shattering Teàrlach's reflective mood. He stood, wincing as a sudden pain stabbed him in the side, waiting until the phantom knife dissolved. The surgeon had warned him that he could expect to feel occasional discomfort until the wound had completely healed. He hadn't mentioned it would feel like an action replay of the stabbing that had put him in hospital.

There was a poster on the wall of two young women, artfully draped over a clarsach and cello. They were on stage, lurid colours picking them out in primary shades; effects pedals at their feet; electronic drums, bass and keyboard player standing beyond the photographer's focus in a blue wash. Two white spotlights made a saltire cross on the back of the stage. The band's name was Deò and they were in concert here tonight. On a whim he bought a ticket, placing it next to his father's opened letter like a talisman to ward off evil. He recognised the word Deo – meaning God in Latin. Somehow the music he'd heard suggested this was no praise group, and the accent over the letter O made this more likely a Gaelic word. Once back in his car, Teàrlach made a quick search of the language that had been commonly spoken in all the Western Isles until the coming of the Second World War. Deò – sounding like Joe-o and meaning air, breath of air, breath, vital spark. He smiled to himself. Going to a music concert was out of his comfort zone, especially on his own, but if anyone was in need of a breath of air or a vital spark, it was him.

His phone rang whilst he was still browsing the web, Chloe's name displayed on the screen.

'Hi, Chloe, what's the problem?' Teàrlach had asked his PA not to contact him whilst he was on Mull unless it was important.

'Not a problem as such. Do you want to take on any other work while you're on a few days' holiday?'

'I'm not on holiday.'

If Chloe felt the reprimand, she didn't show it. 'Well, whatever you call it – it's just I've had someone local to you ask if we could look for their son.'

Teàrlach stared at his phone screen in disbelief. 'On Mull?'

'Hang on,' Chloe said. 'Ah, here we are. Fraser Donald. His son Calum has been missing for over a week and he's asked for our help.'

'How old is Calum?' Teàrlach fetched a notepad from his jacket, held a pen in readiness.

'Twenty-two.'

He paused writing. 'Twenty-two?'

'Aye. Missing for ten days or so. He's a fisherman but went missing on dry land.'

'You explained we mostly look for missing kids?' Teàrlach sought clarification.

'Aye, but he was very insistent. Specifically wanted us to be involved in the search.'

Teàrlach sighed. He could at least meet the guy.

'What's Fraser Donald's address and contact details?'

'He lives on the Isle of Tiree—'

'You said local,' Teàrlach interrupted.

'Aye. He lives on Tiree, but he's staying in Tobermory. Sending you his details now.'

His phone chirped a notification. Teàrlach scanned the

message. Fraser Donald's hotel was only a few minutes back up the hill.

'OK. Let him know I'm on my way. Is this everything he gave you?'

'That's it. Are we taking it on?'

'I don't know. I'll see what it's all about and whether I can do anything for him. I'll be in touch.'

He ended the call and read the brief notes attached to Chloe's message. There was a potted history of his son's work as a fisherman, details about the day he went missing and a photograph of a handsome young guy staring straight into the camera lens with eyes the colour of cornflowers.

TEN

BRAIN CANCER

Teàrlach drove up the steep hill towards a nineteenth-century tribute to Victorian optimism, the four-storey hotel clinging on for dear life to the side of a precipitous hill. It faced out over the harbour towards tracts of remote mainland, encircling the island like a grasping hand. The hotel reception was dominated by a log fire, stacked up so high Teàrlach could feel the warmth even at the front desk.

'Good afternoon. I've an appointment to see one of your guests – Fraser Donald?' Teàrlach handed the desk clerk a business card which was given a glance and then handed back with an apologetic smile. Teàrlach had the strong impression that the receptionist felt sorry for him.

'Sure, Mr Paterson. I'll let Mr Donald know you're in reception.' He indicated two spare seats near the fire. 'Can I get you something?'

'No, I'm fine, thanks.'

Teàrlach ignored the seats, crossing over to look out over the iconic harbour setting through full-length windows. On a good day he'd have had a great view over the Sound of Mull towards the distant Morvern mountains. This wasn't a good day, however he tried to spin it. A bank of low, dark clouds pressed down on the island; rain mixed with hail spattered the large casement windows like gunshot pellets. Teàrlach stared out over the harbour, impressed with the view despite the rain. The marina was almost full – not surprising given the forecast for a storm later. Out in the bay he could make out a larger yacht, one too big for the marina. Some millionaire would be riding out the waves and waiting for the weather to pass. It gave him a small feeling of satisfaction that money couldn't buy the weather – it bought just about everything else.

'Teàrlach Paterson?'

He turned to face the enquirer. A sixty-something man whom he took to be Fraser Donald took tentative steps towards him, hand already outstretched in greeting. He was wiry, temples etched with grey where his naturally dark hair faded and betrayed his age. His cheekbones stood out, giving him a gaunt appearance which only served to accentuate a sharp nose cutting the air like a keel. Teàrlach exchanged a handshake, feeling fragility in the weakness of his grip, looked into eyes that mirrored the lowering clouds and saw pain.

'Fraser Donald,' he confirmed as he shook Teàrlach's hand. 'Shall we sit somewhere more private?'

He relinquished his grip and haltingly led Teàrlach into the guest lounge. At this time of year, the room was deserted. They took seats in a bay window where the sound of hail against glass muffled their conversation, Fraser breathing heavily as he lowered himself with obvious relief into his chair.

'How can I help you, Mr Donald?' He offered a business card which was given a cursory inspection before being slipped into a jacket pocket. Teàrlach's notebook lay in his lap, pen rotating between fingers.

'My son, Calum...' Fraser Donald hesitated, straightened his back so he appeared to grow several centimetres higher. 'He's a fisherman, working out of Tobermory. Mostly creels for lobsters, crabs, prawns. There's precious little out there.' A shaking hand encompassed the view of the sea from the hotel windows. 'It's the marine equivalent of a desert.'

His weak voice struggled to be heard over the noise of the rain against glass. Teàrlach leaned in closer. A fresh squall of rain pattered against the glass in response.

'When did your son, Calum, go missing?' Teàrlach broke the silence.

Fraser dropped his head from a contemplation of the window, pinched the bridge of his nose between forefinger and thumb and surreptitiously wiped the tear forming in one rheumy eye.

'He went out on the *Morning Dew* first light on 6th April. The skipper claimed all hands returned to shore, but Calum's not been seen by anyone since.' His eyes held Teàrlach's. 'Something happened on that boat. I can feel it in my bones. Something the rest of the crew are covering up.'

Teàrlach was close enough to see the broken blood vessels in Fraser's eyes, moisture forming a salty meniscus over his corneas. He wrote in longhand, placed a full stop after '*covering up*'. The coincidence of the date when Robert Jameson fell to his death didn't need a written comment.

'Have you tried phoning him?' It seemed too obvious to ask.

'Of course. He won't pick up. Neither will Siobhan.' He stared into the middle distance. 'We had a... disagreement. I told him that I didn't think being with Siobhan was right for him. Now they've both blocked me.' He gave a tight smile. 'I think that's what it's called?'

Teàrlach gave an affirmative nod. 'Siobhan?' He spoke the name as a question.

'Calum's girlfriend. They've been seeing each other for a few months now.'

'Did Calum have any enemies? What makes you think he never came back with the boat?'

Fraser Donald had the hunted expression of a man who had a secret he didn't want to share.

'Our families have been at war for years,' he eventually blurted out. 'I thought we'd made amends, put all that nonsense behind us.' A look of longing appeared as he reminisced. 'At one point I'd thought we'd be the ones to marry.'

'Who are we talking about, Mr Donald? Are the police involved, have there been threats made against you or your son?' Teàrlach pressed for more information.

Fraser slumped down in his seat as if the effort of sitting straight had exhausted him. 'The police aren't involved. Things like this – they're settled in the old ways.'

Teàrlach had a suspicion what that meant. 'You think someone has taken revenge on your son because of some old rivalry?'

Fraser nodded. 'The gods never wanted our families to be together, and now they never will. Our families have been fighting over land for centuries.' He shook his head in resignation. 'It's madness, of course. Ancient history, but still the enmity remains.'

The pen held position above the notebook. 'Which families are you talking about, Mr Donald? Your own family and who?'

'The MacNeills. Siobhan and Calum were going to announce their engagement. He met her when he made friends with her brothers.'

Teàrlach's pen scribbled rapidly across the page. 'But Siobhan and her brothers are the same MacNeills who you say hate your family?' He struggled to make sense of Fraser's contradictory statement.

Fraser's pained expression answered the question. 'No! She loved him. They both loved each other. That generation have no time for ancient feuds – thank God. No, it was her mother who wanted to break up the relationship before it went too far.

Morag MacNeill had my son killed, Mr Paterson – or she has him prisoner.'

Teàrlach's pen came to a halt. 'That's a serious allegation, Fraser. Have you taken your concerns to the police?'

His head shook in response. 'There's no point. The MacNeills own this island, Mr Paterson, and that includes the police. That's why I want *you* to find out if my son is still alive and to bring him back home to me.'

'Why me, Mr Donald? I understand your concerns regarding the local police, but if you report your son missing, then they'll have to act.'

'Because you used to live here, Mr Paterson, and I've read enough about you to know you're good at your job. Where else am I going to find a PI with those credentials?'

Teàrlach couldn't argue with the old man's logic. It hadn't escaped him that Fraser Donald was talking as if his son was already dead.

'One more thing you should know, Mr Paterson, before you take on this case.'

He engaged with Fraser's haunted expression.

'I've only a few weeks left to live. Brain cancer.' Fraser Donald's finger pointed towards his temple. 'I need to know what happened to my son before I go.'

Teàrlach struggled to find an appropriate response. 'I'm sorry to hear that, Mr Donald.' The words sounded inadequate.

Fraser Donald gave him a sharp nod of acceptance, pushed himself out of his chair and stood swaying as Teàrlach stood to offer his arm in support.

He was too slow to catch Fraser before he collapsed.

ELEVEN
STRAWS

Teàrlach had rushed to lift Fraser off the floor, his unconscious body surprisingly heavy for someone so slight of build. The man's head had struck the table a glancing blow and now fresh blood covered his forehead and Teàrlach's fingers. He drew close enough to feel Fraser's breath on his face just as the receptionist's startled head peered around the door to check on the commotion.

'He collapsed. You'd better call an ambulance.'

Teàrlach had seen the doubt written over the receptionist's face, held up a bloodied hand to gesture him to hurry up and the doubt turned to fear. They'd kept him isolated in the lounge after the ambulance had taken Fraser Donald away – three male members of staff newly appointed as hotel security and standing awkwardly by the exit in case Teàrlach attempted an escape.

Now he sat uncomfortably in the police station, the hard plastic chair digging into his backside and giving him flashbacks to a headteacher's study. The sergeant's office was a glorified cupboard with a strong aroma of damp; lime-green paint covered the walls up to the halfway point as if left by a departing tide, then it switched to an unhealthy cream colour. It must have been quite a few years since a decorator had wielded a brush here. Flaking paint left scars on the walls, dandruff detritus covering the brown carpet tiles. A radiator struggled to overcome the chill of a building mostly left unoccupied, occasional rattles coming from the pipes as the central heating struggled to reach the thermostat's demands. Last year's calendar was sellotaped on the wall behind her back, marker pen outlining what were now historical events in the policing day. She occupied the only comfortable chair, leaning back in her seat with a coffee mug held in both hands to extract the maximum heat as she observed him through narrowed eyes.

'What exactly are you involved with here, Mr Paterson?' She handled his card as if it were infectious, reading the words *Private Investigator* with obvious distaste.

She hadn't believed him when he'd explained that he was only here to check up on Robert Jameson's death for Lucy, and then repeated what Fraser Donald had confided to him before passing out.

What was he involved with? Buggered if he knew. He rephrased his response to avoid alienating the officer sat across from him. He needed to work with the police rather than against them.

'All I know is that Lucy Jameson asked me to look into her husband's death and try and find out anything your lot may have missed.'

Sergeant Suzie Crammond's expression hadn't changed.

'Then I have a message saying Fraser Donald is staying at the hotel and wants me to help him find out where his son is,' Teàrlach continued.

'Calum Donald.' Suzie clarified.

'Yes.'

'Fraser Donald told you he had weeks to live, was suffering

from inoperable brain cancer and you thought it a good idea to subject a man already in a great deal of stress to a load of questions?'

'Yes, but—'

She held a hand up to stop him – a trick she must have learned during her time as a constable on traffic duty.

'It didn't occur to you that he might react badly to such a thing?'

Teàrlach had better things to be doing than to be lectured by the local police.

'He wanted to know what had happened to his son. Fraser Donald came to me, officer. I wasn't looking to take on another investigation whilst I was here.'

Suzie wrote laboriously in longhand, filling her official note-book with neat script.

'Why didn't you bring Fraser Donald here, or at least leave him in the hotel for us to deal with?' she asked, sighing with frustration as if he was adding considerably to her workload.

'I didn't know he was about to collapse, and this was the first I'd heard of his son. I'm a private investigator, not a clairvoyant.' Teàrlach decided to go on the attack. 'What do you know about his son going missing?'

'This is the first I've heard of it too.' Suzie glared at him in an accusatory manner.

'His dad said he never returned from the boat he was crew on,' Teàrlach added. 'The *Morning Dew*.'

She added the detail to her notebook before sparing him another distrustful look.

'What do *you* think is going on?'

Teàrlach saw her eyebrows draw down, and wondered what he'd done to irritate her.

'Look, I've nothing to do with this. I don't have any more idea of what's going on than you do.' He spoke defensively.

Suzie considered him, her enigmatic expression providing no clues even to someone like himself who made his living out of reading people.

'I'll try and question Fraser Donald, once the hospital say he's fit enough to be questioned.' She closed her notebook, a clear signal that he was dismissed, and Teàrlach took his leave.

His thoughts were on the dying father and his missing son. Fraser had made the trip over from Tiree in the slight hope that he'd find someone to take on the search. He could only imagine how difficult that must have been for him – in evident pain and knowing he only had weeks to live. There was no way Teàrlach would be able to not take on the case. He called the Glasgow office.

'Hi, Chloe. I want you to find out all you can about Fraser Donald and his son, Calum. See if there's anything about a fishing boat called the *Morning Dew*, and can you ask Dee to have a look at Mull and Oban police servers to see if anything crops up in relation to any of this?'

'Are we looking for anything in particular?' Chloe's voice sounded distant over the speakerphone.

'See if there's any report of any violence connecting Calum Donald to anyone called MacNeill. Also see what you can find out about the MacNeill family – Fraser basically accused the mother, Morag, of doing away with his son.'

'Sounds like a delightful woman. Has Fraser any idea where his son may be?'

'Not in the short time I was with him. He collapsed when he finished speaking to me, I wasn't fast enough to catch him and now the local police think I decked him.'

'Sounds like you have everything under control. Is Dee with you yet?' Chloe asked.

'She didn't make the ferry. She sent a text saying she'd be coming over tomorrow.'

Teàrlach ended the call, walked back towards the hotel to pick up his car. He'd told the policewoman everything he knew – which wasn't much. Everything but the allegation that Calum might have been murdered or kidnapped.

He was clutching at straws; wasn't that what drowning men were meant to do?

TWELVE
ORPHAN

Dee had made scant progress on the task Teàrlach had set her. David Webster had sent the photographs to *Scottish Birdwatcher* from a free email address. It was the only time that email had ever been used. A search for the name brought up hundreds of potential matches, none of whom looked likely candidates. She tried another tack, searching for the IP address the email had been sent from. Buried in the header was the information she needed, cut and pasted into her favoured analyser tool.

The email had been sent from Dervaig on the Isle of Mull and dated days after Robert's death. Two problems with that: Robert Jameson lived in Tobermory; and he was dead when the photographs were sent.

There wasn't anything to be gained by delaying opening the other email sitting in her inbox any longer. She clicked on it, waited for the software to do its worse.

Dear Ms Fairlie,

Thank you for your enquiry regarding your birth parents. As you

*are aware, there is no record of either parent recorded on your
birth certificate. Despite an extensive search of medical admis-
sions prior to your admission at the Queen Mother's Maternity
Unit in Yorkhill 28th June 1992, we can find no record of antenatal care that may be traced to a mother giving birth at or
around the time you were found in the hospital foyer.*

*I'm sorry that this is not the result you were hoping for. We have
been in touch with Police Scotland and they have confirmed the
search for your mother was shelved some years ago as the case
was considered to have little realistic chance of resolution.*

*In these circumstances we can only advise performing a genetic
search in the hope that you find a close match that may lead to a
family member. I have attached the relevant agency details to
this email.*

*May I extend my heartfelt apologies for not being able to bring
you the closure you seek.*

'Jesus!' Dee sat back in her seat and read it again. She was
hit with a feeling of relief that she wouldn't have to face either
parent. What could she say after a thirty-two-year absence?
Would they even want to make contact? That feeling was
replaced by anger. Anger at whoever left her bundled in news-
papers jammed into a cardboard box in the hospital reception
area one summer evening.

For once her hacking skills were useless. In internet terms
she was born in the Dark Ages, several years before computers
were as common as TVs in every home. No CCTV records to
view, no police reports to read. Whoever her mother was, she'd
managed to have a baby without any medical intervention. Dee
still had a newspaper sheet stained with blood, her only legacy,
the same date as her birthday. Her surname was plucked from

the same paper – an article discussing the first Double Fairlie locomotive built for the Ffestiniog Railway and christened *Little Wonder*.

Dee stopped that train of thought before it started. Self-pity was a luxury orphans learned to live without. She opened a locked drawer in her desk, brought out a yellowed newspaper page and smoothed it flat. Her mother's blood stained the page to the edge – it was all she had.

Dee cut a bloodied section from the border, placed it in a plastic sealed bag and inserted the package into an envelope. She wrote the address of the genetic testing company suggested in the email on the front and put it to one side. There was something too final about this last step for her to deal with right now. She'd already waited a lifetime – she could wait a while longer.

THIRTEEN
ARTS CENTRE

The threatening grey clouds that had hugged Tobermory like a dirty blanket had been swept away on incessant westerlies, leaving blue sky and with the promise of a sunny evening to come. The sea had miraculously changed from sullen grey to sparkling blue – a few yachts had returned now the water was calmer. Teàrlach sat in his car and wondered how he was going to fulfil his promise to a dying man.

His attention was caught by a poster advertising this evening's concert at the arts centre with Deò – they were due on stage in two hours. He wondered if he could ask for a refund for the ticket he'd bought earlier on a whim, then saw the clarsach player was a Siobhan MacNeill. Teàrlach searched through his notebook, confirmed the name as being the same as Calum Donald's girlfriend. If she was the same woman, he could have a word with her after the concert.

In the absence of any response from Chloe and Dee, it was all he had to work with. A couple of schoolkids ambled by, bags slung over their shoulders. They cautiously checked him out as they passed his car, streetwise even here on a small Scottish island. He tried to remember if he'd demonstrated the same qualities for self-preservation at that age, but all he could remember was the crushing boredom of class and the relief when each day ended. That and Lucy.

Her house was a few minutes away. He needed to see her – for professional reasons. His excuse fought a losing battle with the truth.

'Teàrlach! Come in.' Lucy stood back to give him space to pass, a hand distractedly wiping hair from her eyes. 'Sorry, the place is in a bit of a mess.'

She looked tired, the smile she offered forced.

'I can come another time, if this isn't convenient?'

'No. It's fine. Can I get you something? Tea, coffee? You used to like coffee.'

'I'll not stay, Lucy.'

She held the door open, undecided whether to close it or not. Teàrlach saw a half-eaten takeaway left on a chair, mugs collecting on every surface.

'How are you keeping, Lucy?' His question sounded crass to his own ears. He didn't need to be a detective to see signs of neglect, her distracted air.

'Been better.' The smile she gave this time was genuine at least.

He nodded. 'I just wanted to check in, see if you'd heard anything?'

'No. The police said they'd look for his camera gear. Going to call in divers or something.'

There was a growing pile of mail on the shelf beside her. A flyer from a funeral director lay on top.

'I've been to see the local police.' Teàrlach stopped when he saw the hope fill her face. 'They couldn't add anything to what we already know.'

They wanted me to fuck off and get out from under their feet.
Teàrlach kept his thoughts to himself.

'Have you found anything? Do you think he was

murdered?' Lucy's voice was steady, at odds with her demeanour.

'We've not found anything yet, but we're tracing the photographer that tried to pass off Robert's photos as their own.'

'They *were* his, then.' Lucy sought confirmation.

'As far as we can tell, yes. Taken whilst he was on Staffa. The dates and times match up.'

She nodded to herself. 'I knew they were his,' she said quietly.

'We're doing everything we can to get to the bottom of this.'

The room fell silent, waiting for more.

'Is there anything I can get for you, any help I can give you?' He felt unaccountably useless. Surplus to anyone's requirements.

'Just find out what happened to Robert. That's all I need.'

'I'll do the best I can. I promise.'

Teàrlach took his cue and left. Lucy stood like a statue as he drove away, the door still open in invitation.

He checked the car clock – he had enough time to go to the cottage he'd inherited and see if he could sleep there. Teàrlach made his way on the winding island road to the only home he could remember.

He still had quite a few miles to go when he saw police tape covering a track which he remembered led to a small beach. Could this be something to do with the missing fisherman, Calum Donald? Teàrlach decided to take a look and turned off the road, parking on a flat patch of grass which often served as a car park for birdwatchers looking out for sea eagles.

He pulled on his jacket and headed downhill towards the sound of surf impacting rocks. There was a farm track giving access to a rough stony beach, just enough clearance for a small boat to be launched. Teàrlach had a notion to build a small jetty at the cottage and keep a boat there himself, when the day came for him to leave Glasgow for good. He could picture himself putting out into the bay and trying a bit of sea fishing – although Fraser Donald's description of the seas around Mull resembling a desert took the gloss off that romantic idea.

Teàrlach started walking between low and high-water marks. The upper level was identified by seaweed, peppered with polystyrene fragments and the general detritus of flotsam and jetsam that characterises high-water marks all around the world. He could see no obvious reason why the beach had been closed. He was the sole occupant, apart from curious seabirds.

Half an hour later and Teàrlach had reached the end of the small bay. It was bounded by bigger rocks, lumps of black volcanic stone, slippery and treacherous for anyone foolish enough to try clambering over them. He'd found nothing apart from a single pink croc, an assortment of plastic bottles and several strands of green nylon rope. No clue as to why the police had taped off access.

Teàrlach stretched, feeling his muscles protest at being bent double for the last thirty minutes and felt a recurrence of the pain in his side. He massaged the source of discomfort absent-mindedly until the sharpness dulled into a more bearable ache. The doctor had told him there may be some discomfort for a few months, but to make an appointment if the pain remained after six months. It had almost been nine months, but Teàrlach wasn't keen on seeing a doctor; he preferred to let nature take its course. He returned to the car, realised he wouldn't make the cottage and catch the beginning of the concert, and turned back towards Tobermory.

An hour later and he'd taken his seat in the arts centre, facing a stage set for tonight's performance. A clarsach and cello held central stage, keyboards, and drum kit occupied the back. The place was filling up to near capacity with a good cross-section of Mull's residents and smattering of tourists, pre-recorded folk music playing in the background and drowned out by the hubbub of voices and chatter all around him. Then the house lights dimmed and the audience quietened as the lead instruments were picked out in yellow spotlights.

The band walked onstage, quietly self-assured and taking their places behind keyboard and drums. A guitarist carried on his instrument, plugging into an amplifier stage left and fiddled with the tuning even though he must have tuned it already. Then two women took their places at the front, bent over their instruments with electronic tuners for a final check without sparing a glance at the sea of expectant faces caught in the spill from stage lighting. With a quick nod behind them to check everyone was ready, the drummer counted quietly to four and the music began.

Teàrlach had been prepared for what to expect by the recording he'd heard earlier, but the force of their vocals caught him off guard. The first song was lost on him, sung in Gaelic as a call from first the clarsach player with the rest of the band lending support for the response, then with the cello player alternating the lead vocals. The driving rhythm was reinforced by percussion until Teàrlach's diaphragm resonated with the quickening beat. When the song ended, the clarsach player explained it was a waulking song – traditionally used when working tweed or tartan cloth. The band wasted no time, firing into another song with the girls' vocals weaving a tapestry around the bell-like tones of the clarsach and the low bass from the cello.

Teàrlach enjoyed the entire set, although not as much as a group of dancers who'd laid claim to the small space near the stage where they threw each other around like whirling dervishes, linking elbows and attempting to spin each other across the room. When it was time for the final encore, the lights dimmed once more, the dancers stood still and the two girls sang a plaintive melody about a missing lover.

Teàrlach only realised they were singing about Calum Donald when Siobhan sang about a fisherman's love. As the band left the stage to rapturous applause, he headed backstage. He needed to talk to Siobhan MacNeill – the woman Fraser Donald had said his son was romantically involved with and whose family wanted Calum gone.

'Sorry, staff and band only.' The guy was in his early twenties, dressed in a T-shirt emblazoned with the arts centre logo across his chest. An arm blocked the corridor ahead. Teàrlach briefly considered pushing past him but acquiesced.

'I just wanted a quick word with Siobhan MacNeill. I'll only need a minute.' Teàrlach attempted a winning smile.

'What's your name?'

'Teàrlach. Teàrlach Paterson.'

A sheet of A4 was consulted, finger running down a small list of names.

'You're not on here. Can't let you through.' T-shirt gave every indication of enjoying this part of his job.

'Can you just ask her?' Teàrlach produced his business card and received an inquisitive stare after it had been read.

'What's it about?'

Teàrlach held back his impatience. 'I'm working for Calum Donald's dad. He's asked me to find his son, Calum. I just need to speak to Siobhan in case she has any idea where he might be.'

'You'll have to return to the main auditorium. This area is off-limits.'

Teàrlach reconsidered pushing past him but decided against creating a scene. That wouldn't help develop any hope of rapport with the one person who might know anything about the missing fisherman.

'I'll pass on your card – tell Siobhan you're looking for Calum.'

The guy started walking towards him, forcing Teàrlach to retreat down the narrow corridor towards the stage. He raised his hands in surrender.

'OK. I'm here for a few days. If she can call me on that number.'

A door swiftly closed on his face, sealing backstage from the rest of the area. Teàrlach sought for a handle in vain, tried pushing it open without success. He caught sight of an electronic door swipe at the side and gave up. Siobhan would have to wait for another day. An hour's drive lay ahead of him, along twisting single-track roads to what once had been his home. He'd only returned sporadically since joining the army, never knowing when he kissed farewell to the woman who'd become his only family that it would be for the last time. All that lay in wait for him was a cottage that hadn't been lived in for years, memories and ghosts of his past.

FOURTEEN
MORNING DEW

Chloe started the day with a coffee, taking it through to Teàrlach's empty office and his comfortable chair with its view of Glasgow. She spun the seat around to face the window, blowing steam off the surface of her cup, and watched cumulus clouds scudding across an urban sky. This was her favourite part of the day, alone without Dee, Teàrlach or the phone to interrupt her thoughts. From what Teàrlach had said, it was likely he was staying on the island for a few more days – looking into Robert Jameson's death and now searching for this missing fisherman, Calum Donald.

The *Scottish Birdwatcher* magazine was still on his desk, and she idly thumbed through the pages until the puffin photographs filled the page. There was no online trail to the photographer, David Webster, and a search of people living in Dervaig on the Isle of Mull with that name had drawn a blank. She wondered whether Dee had been able to make any progress.

Chloe put the magazine and the identity of the photographer to one side, pulling out the sparse file she'd started on Calum Donald. Teàrlach had asked her to look into the alleged family feud and whatever she could discover regarding Siobhan MacNeill and both families. Calum's photograph stared out of the page, a fishing boat in the background. They say the eyes are the gateway to the soul – she would have dived into the blue of his eyes without any concerns. Calum was a catch!

She frowned in frustration. This sort of investigation shouldn't be run from an office a hundred kilometres away from where the people were – especially when there was no mention of any inter-family feuding in the news or social media channels. Chloe needed to speak to this Siobhan MacNeill, or Teàrlach would have to see her himself. All she'd been able to discover was Siobhan played in some electronic folk group. Even the fishing boat, the *Morning Dew* didn't show up on any registers or Scottish maritime insurance lists. Either Fraser Donald had given them the wrong boat, or he was having problems with his memory. Looking at the text she'd received from Teàrlach, it was more likely the latter. If he was in the last stages of brain cancer, how much could they rely on any of his testimony? Maybe his son wasn't even missing – it had evidently come as a surprise to the local police.

Chloe took the file back through to her own desk and dumped it down. Neither of these jobs gave her any confidence that they were going to provide any results. Robert Jameson's death looked like a tragic accident – a momentary lapse of concentration on a cliff edge. Teàrlach only took the case because he was still sweet on Lucy – she'd picked up on that as soon as he'd set eyes on her. So, what if someone *had* found his camera and passed the shots off as their own? It was hardly anything substantial enough for them to spend any time on. As for Fraser Donald and his missing son – so far nobody else even knew he was missing. Maybe Teàrlach would talk to his girlfriend, this Siobhan MacNeill, and find the whole case was the product of a failing mind.

Chloe pulled up a map of Mull on her laptop and searched

for Teàrlach's cottage. All he'd let slip was that it faced out over to another island somewhere on the northwest coast. There were two likely contenders, the islands of Ulva and Gometra – looking like the one land mass on her map. His aunt's cottage must be somewhere along this coastline. A single road wrapped its way along the coast and as she zoomed in, houses revealed themselves built into the hillsides. She discounted the new ones – Teàrlach had said his aunt had an old stone cottage. Chloe gave up after a while; there were just too many options. Struck with a thought, she called her brother.

'Hi, sis, everything good?'

She caught the note of concern in his voice and regretted not calling him more often.

'Hey, Leo, yeah everything's fine. I wanted to pick your brains if you're OK to talk?'

'Sure. This isn't about ropework again, is it?'

Chloe gave an awkward laugh. The recent events where Teàrlach and Dee had almost lost their lives was too fresh.

'No. We've been asked to look for a guy missing from a fishing boat and wondered if you might have some ideas.'

There was silence from the other end as he processed his sister's question.

'Where are we talking? North Sea?'

'He returned from a fishing boat on the Isle of Mull and hasn't been seen since.'

'So, not lost at sea?' Leo sought clarification.

'No, by all accounts he left the boat along with the rest of the crew but then disappeared. We've been asked to find him.'

'Don't know how I can help, sis.'

'The boat he was on was called the *Morning Dew*, only there's not a fishing boat registered to that name. Is it normal practice to go to sea under an assumed boat name, like false numberplates? To get around fishing quotas and suchlike?'

'I've not heard of it. Not even sure it's something you can do as AIS transponders broadcast the boat's name along with position.'

'Sorry, AIS?' Chloe reached for her pen.

'Automatic Identification System. Any fishing boat larger than fifteen metres has to have one fitted. If it's smaller than that, it still has to be registered and meet build and safety standards. Like an MOT for cars,' Leo helpfully added.

Chloe's pen started to make random patterns on the paper.

'Have you talked to Mum and Dad recently?' Leo's question immediately made her feel guilty.

They'd never been able to reconcile her leaving the church and all it entailed in terms of community and expectations. Leo still paid lip service to religion, made believe for them, but she knew he'd lost the faith. In her case, there was no going back – not from the life she'd led and her attempted suicide.

'No,' she answered simply. 'I'll call them tonight. See how they are. Have you talked to them?'

She could imagine Leo trying to work out what hadn't been said. They'd reverted to speaking in code, cryptic messages that concealed what they really wanted to say. In her case, she had a past that had to be concealed more to protect her parents than herself. Having a drug-fuelled prostitute as a daughter wouldn't play well in the circles they moved in. What was Leo hiding?

'Couple of nights ago. They suggested we both go around for a meal, have a catch-up.'

'Yeah, we should do that.'

'OK. Well, I'm meant to be at work here, so unless there's anything else?'

'No, that's all. Look after yourself, bro.'

'Aye, you too. Bye.'

The phone went silent – the date and time for a family dinner deliberately kicked into the long grass.

'Where the fuck is Dee?' Chloe asked of an empty office.

FIFTEEN

MERMAIDS

Sergeant Suzie Crammond unlocked Tobermory police station on the dot of 9 a.m. The incessant ringing from the front desk phone doubled in volume with the opening of the door, and she reluctantly put down her takeaway coffee to grab the phone.

'Tobermory police, how can I help you?' She stretched to reach her coffee, expertly flicked the lid off with one hand and took the first welcome sip of the day.

'This is DI Corstorphine from Fort William. You discovered John Stevenson's discarded clothes yesterday?'

'Yes, that's right, sir. Sergeant Suzie Crammond here.'

'Good morning, Suzie.'

She could hear papers being shuffled before the DI spoke again.

'Are you any further on finding out what happened to him?'

'No, sir. Coastguard sent a boat out to look for him yesterday. There's been no reports of a body, but Oban are sending out a dive team, should be with us later this morning. They wouldn't come out until the coastguard had completed their search.' She risked another sip from the takeaway cup.

'There wasn't any equipment nearby by any chance?

According to his partner, John Stevenson was involved in some sort of nature survey around the coast. His speciality was recording underwater sounds, so there should be his hydrophone and portable recording gear somewhere.'

'That equipment is in our evidence locker.' Suzie glanced at the pile of cables strewn across the floor of her office. 'Do you want it sent over to you?'

'No, best wait until we know what happened to him. He was swimming off the north-west of the island?'

'That's right, sir.'

'Hmmm. Last contact he had with his partner was on Monday 13th. He was working some ten kilometres further down the coast from the location you're searching – a place called Balmeanach?'

'Is that significant to our search for his body?' She struggled to see why this information was relevant.

'He was working with one of your tour companies, hang on... Here we are, Tauth Wildlife. Could you have a word with them, see if they can shed some light on his movements between Monday 13th and the time he was last seen?'

'Sorry, sir, but that's really Oban's remit. We don't have any detectives on the island.'

'No, of course. I'm sorry, I'll ask Oban to look into it. Do you know anything about this Tauth Wildlife outfit – have you come across them before?'

'No, sir. Not heard of them, to be honest. I'll look into them. I can ask if they know what John was doing?'

'Thanks. It's probably all a tragic accident, but his partner is looking for more information.'

'Understood, sir. I'll get on it today.'

'One other thing...' DI Corstorphine sounded hesitant. 'He was sent threatening messages on social media last week, including a death threat. I'll send you a screenshot.'

'Do you think this might be a murder, sir?'

'I don't think so. The threats originated here in Fort William, not from Mull. Looks more like someone having malicious fun at his family's expense. We'll investigate this end, but if we find anything that points to Mull, I'll let you know.'

There was a momentary pause before the DI continued.

'I've been sent his last set of audio recordings that he emailed through before he went missing.'

Suzie's eyebrows drew down in puzzlement. Where was this going?

'Not sure what to make of them, to be honest. Maybe whale or porpoise. If there's anyone who may have some idea what we're listening to, then it may help clarify what he was doing?'

'I can try, sir. If you send them through to the Tobermory station email, I'll pick them up.'

'Thank you, sergeant. As I say, probably nothing, but if you're able to check those two things out for me, I'd be grateful.'

'Happy to do so, sir.'

'OK. Thanks. Just send any information back to my direct email – I've just sent you the audio. Bye for now.'

'Bye, sir.'

Suzie finished her coffee, walked into her office and fired up the computer. A file with attachments was waiting. She waited until the virus scan declared it safe to open and the sound of distant song came eerily through the small speakers. She wasn't superstitious in any sense – twelve years in the force had been enough to quell any fanciful ideas she might have once had as a young girl. But the unearthly sounds she could hear could never have originated with whales, dolphins or any other aquatic animal she knew.

The sounds she heard were more like the cries of mermaids or sirens.

SIXTEEN

BIRTHDAY

Dee finished packing her bag, adding the laptop, and closed the apartment door. First stop was the office, and Chloe.

'There you are. Thought you'd taken yourself off to the islands with Teàrlach.' Chloe's eyes narrowed when Dee's expected flippant response didn't happen. 'What's up?'

Dee put the motorbike helmet down on her desk, shrugged off her backpack and put it next to her helmet. She debated how much to tell Chloe, but one look in Chloe's eyes was enough to derail any attempt at cooking up a story. Dee wasn't taken in by Chloe's bubbleheaded persona, neither was Teàrlach.

'I need a drink, but a coffee will have to do,' Dee stated simply, making for the gleaming machine Teàrlach had bought in a moment of fiscal madness. She considered how to deal with her dilemma as the machine hissed and gurgled, then took the fresh cup back to the office and sat on what space remained on her desk.

'I've decided to look for my birth parents.' She watched Chloe's eyes widen in disbelief. 'I know,' she added before Chloe could respond. 'I've always said I wouldn't. Not when they just abandoned me as a newborn in a cardboard box.'

Chloe waited on her to continue.

'Thing is, there's no records of any births or antenatal treatment that could be anything to do with my mother, so I'm left with nothing much to go on.'

'What do you plan on doing?' Chloe asked.

'I've a blood sample, from my birth.'

Chloe's expression was so comical Dee had to laugh.

'Don't ask. Call it an heirloom. I was thinking of sending it off to a DNA site to see if there are any matches. I was told not to get my hopes up – it's a long shot at best.'

'What made you change your mind? You always said that you'd never look for your parents.'

Dee sipped her coffee, looking out thoughtfully over Glasgow's mismatched architecture and wondering if her mum or dad were still somewhere out there.

'I don't really know. Something to do with getting older, I suppose. Looking to make sense of life.'

'Good luck with that.' Chloe's dismissive remark brought another smile to Dee's lips.

'Aye. Right enough.'

The two women sat in silence, each preoccupied with their own thoughts.

'You going off to Mull then, with Teàrlach?' Chloe's eyes held more than a trace of enquiry.

Dee processed the unspoken part of Chloe's question. She'd grown closer to Teàrlach in the time they'd been together, to the point where light-hearted flirting now felt uncomfortable. He'd made it clear he wasn't looking for a relationship, at least not with her. She could cope with rejection – it was the one recurring theme in her life – but coping involved too much drinking and casual sex. Neither of which provided the substantial nourishment she desired.

She gave Chloe a wry look. All three of them were damaged goods. Chloe with her history of drugs and prostitution; Teàrlach with his murdered family; her the unwanted orphan.

'What are we like, eh?' It was a question that Chloe didn't need to answer. 'Aye, I'm heading off now. He's not safe to be left on his own for too long.'

They both laughed at the thought of Teàrlach needing protection, but underlying the joke was a fundamental understanding that they all needed one other.

'Why don't you come as well?'

'Me?' Chloe pointed at her chest as if there could be some confusion.

'Aye, you! We've two cases to solve – this photographer and the missing fisherman. You can't do much stuck here in the office. Treat it as a holiday, a couple of days out on the Hebrides. Might even get some sun!'

'I don't know, Teàrlach might not like the office being shut.'

'Chloe, it's Friday. Come for the weekend. It'll be a laugh. Anyway, it's not good for you to be cooped up in here every day. Get some fresh air in your lungs!'

Chloe's face brightened. 'Why not? It's not as if I have a lot on this weekend.'

'You and me both, sister. I can take you on the bike?'

'Not a chance. I have to pack a bag anyway. I'll take the train and meet you over there.'

'Great. I'll see you later.'

She left the office and climbed on the bike. Ahead of her was a four-hour journey and a ferry crossing from Oban. A touch on the electronic starter and the engine roared into life. As Dee steered a course through the morning Glasgow traffic, spring sunshine brought colour to the city's usually grey aspect.

SEVENTEEN
COTTAGE

Teàrlach arrived at his aunt's cottage after 11 p.m., using the car's headlights to tread a path through rough scrub to stand at the front door. He felt in his pockets for the old mortice key, the metal smooth with constant handling, and turned a lock almost seized with neglect and time.

As he pushed open the door, a wave of musty air hit him like a physical force. The inside smelt of neglect, a stale odour clinging to the furnishings. Underlying the air of abandonment, he could still detect his aunt's scent and instantly felt as if something of her remained within these walls.

The light switch toggled ineffectually, and he fumbled for his flashlight, its beam revealing a layer of dust thick enough to write in. He cautiously made his way to his old bedroom, each creak of the floorboards echoing in the silence. Opening the door felt like breaching a tomb.

The sight that greeted him brought him to a halt – a room at once familiar and strange. His books, his model soldiers, even the chest still holding his childhood clothes – all preserved as if in amber.

How could this place remain so utterly untouched by time?

The miracle of its preservation felt almost eerie as if the cottage itself had been waiting for his return.

Teàrlach told himself to get a grip. These were the fears he'd felt as a child. Nights when he'd woken from the same nightmare trying and failing to save his mother and brother from the flames. He felt momentarily embarrassed to be ambushed by these feelings. Now he was old enough to know the past can never be undone and the dead remain forever out of reach.

The cottage reminded him of a time capsule, a frozen tableau from a previous life. He was surprised that no one had taken advantage of an abandoned building – although there was no sign of it from the road so only a local would know it was there, and the locals tended to respect other people's property. Even so, it was nothing short of miraculous that it had remained untouched over the two years since his aunt's death.

One day he'd just left. Taken a commission with the army and said goodbye to the aunt who'd cared for him. He remembered the excitement of that day, the promise of something new and how it had felt that his life was starting over. He'd only been back a few times to visit her, had been too busy with his own life to think about the loneliness that had been his legacy to her.

The bedclothes felt dry to the touch. A closer inspection with the iPhone torch showed them to be uninhabited by insects or rodents. It would have to do.

Morning crept in like an unwelcome guest, the grey light filtered through dirty glass and illuminated the sorry state of the place. Teàrlach woke, momentarily disorientated in the bed that had been his since he had turned seven. His aunt's presence remained as a comfort, the last anchor to his childhood. Now she was gone as well, slipped away whilst he was abroad with the army. Guilt clawed at his insides as he dragged himself from the musty sheets. He'd never meant to stay away so long and now it was too late.

In the bathroom, he cranked the tap, flinching as it coughed up a stream of rust-coloured water. Teàrlach let it run until it turned clear, then brushed his teeth and splashed the sleep out of his eyes. As he splashed the water on his face, the cold shock brought a moment of clarity – and with it, a fresh wave of remorse. The door to his aunt's bedroom remained closed; he needed time before he could face seeing the remnants of her life. Why hadn't she told him she was dying? He could have been there for her at the end, held her hand one last time.

Teàrlach dressed, stared into his eyes in the bathroom mirror and counted the years evident in each new crease in his skin. Older, but not wiser. He needed to contact Dee and Chloe, but there was no phone signal at the cottage. The gnawing pain from his stomach wasn't due to his stab wound this time, merely a reminder that he should eat. The nearest shop was in Dervaig, some twelve kilometres along a winding mountain road across the backbone of the island. He locked the cottage door behind him and started driving.

Dawn had broken almost an hour ago and traces of mist still clung stubbornly to the road, thick enough in places to conceal deer and hiding the potholes that threatened to annihilate the car suspension. As he drew nearer to his destination, the pencil tower from Dervaig church stood out like an ICBM waiting to take the last few believers heavenwards. It waited patiently on a consecrated launchpad filled with the ghosts of failed astronauts. Teàrlach gave it a cursory glance as he drove by, turning off the road to park beside a small supermarket and a sign advising him it would be opening in an hour.

He grabbed his phone. Signal was back and there were emails waiting for him. He swiped to the first.

Hey, Teàrlach. David Webster sent the photographs from a place

called Dervaig on the Isle of Mull. There's only the one message
he sent from that email and I can't find any record of him locally,
so he's probably using an assumed name. I'm making my way
over later today, should make the 14:15 and be at Craignure at
15:15. Where should I head for?

Dee

He looked out of the windscreen at the centre of Dervaig
and wondered at the coincidence of finding himself at the
epicentre of Dee's email.

The second email came from Chloe.

Hi,

I can't find any mention of a Calum Donald either being missing
or being the subject of violent assault. Also, the fishing boat he's
meant to be on – the Morning Dew *– it doesn't show up on any*
shipping registers. I talked to my brother and he says any
commercial fishing boat has to have a basic level of certification,
so you've either been given the wrong name or our client Fraser
Donald isn't making much sense.

P.S. I'm coming over for the weekend so I can help with your
cottage. I'll take the train and let you know times.

Teàrlach read Chloe's email twice – it was unlike her to
want to travel anywhere, but he appreciated the offer of help.
There was an hour to kill and he could do with stretching his
legs. The road led around a corner, then straightened to pass
council houses with toy bikes scattered erratically on front
gardens. New builds faced over a sea loch, green gardens
covering the recent scars of their birth. A little further and he'd
left the small settlement behind. Here the road was bordered by

fields and trees – a scene so pastoral that he found it difficult to imagine that anyone here had a connection to Robert Jameson's death, even if their only misdemeanour was to take a dead man's camera.

Ahead of him stone pillars marked the demarcation of some estate, the road continuing through mixed woodland. Teàrlach turned back, returning leisurely to the centre of the village and the local shop. He arrived just before 9 a.m. to join a small queue of shoppers eager to purchase essential breakfast items, and they filed in as the door was unlocked. Teàrlach made straight for the sandwiches and soft drinks, grabbing a bottle of water and taking it to the cashier's desk.

'Cash or card?'

'Card please.' Teàrlach selected his credit card, touched it against the card reader as it spun to face him.

'You don't know a David Webster by any chance?'

The cashier took note of him for the first time, her eyes narrowing in suspicion.

'I used to live here – well, in Tobermory – when I was a kid. We were good friends, but I've lost touch. Last thing I'd heard he was living here in Dervaig, and as I was passing through...'

'David Webster?' She repeated the name doubtfully.

'Aye. Keen photographer,' Teàrlach added for good measure.

'He used to live here,' she responded. 'Only the David Webster I know died four years ago. He's buried in Kilmore Church, but I don't think he could have been your friend.'

'Why's that?'

'He was at least eighty. Don't think he'd have been at school the same time as you were.' She laughed at her own joke.

Teàrlach thought quickly. 'Has he any family here? Everyone called him Davy – maybe he was called after his dad? Any other Websters living locally?'

She narrowed her eyes at his continued questioning. Teàrlach was aware a small, impatient queue was lining up behind him.

'He lived on his own. No relatives I ever knew about. Sorry – maybe it was a family that lived here for a few years and moved away. Not everyone adapts to island life.' The last point was made for the benefit of her growing audience. She pointedly looked behind him. 'Next please.'

Teàrlach took his sandwiches and water and sat in his car. It wasn't that uncommon for people to adopt identities from a gravestone, but why go to all that bother just for a few photographs? At least one question had been answered – Chloe and Dee had been searching for someone still living. The only David Webster in Dervaig had lain in the church graveyard for the last few years.

EIGHTEEN
OTTERS

Sergeant Suzie Crammond stood on the foreshore as two police divers surfaced, giving a thumbs up to the remainder of their five-man team waiting on the pebbled beach. They began pulling on a rope, the divers slipping beneath the waves like oversized otters to assist with the recovery. Once clear of the water, they carried the corpse up to the first patch of rough couch grass, far enough above the high-water mark to ensure it wasn't going anywhere.

She expected to see John Stevenson's body but wasn't prepared for what followed. His corpse, white and bloated, was bad enough. What caught her unawares was the creel attached to his arm. Attached with metal jaws that gripped his arm to the bone.

'What the fuck is that?' She found herself pointing at the creel, at the newly cut ropes trailing behind the wickerwork basket like tentacles.

'That's what we'd like to know.' One of the dive team bent over John Stevenson's body and peered closely into the creel. 'It's been baited with something.'

Suzie took a few steps closer, saw a package close to John's outstretched fingers.

'Looks like he was trying to take it. Why would anyone dive to empty a creel?' Suzie questioned out loud. 'How deep was it?'

The two divers had climbed onto the beach, walking comically on their large, finned feet. It was the only source of humour there.

'About two metres where we found him,' one of the divers volunteered. 'And the creel had been deliberately anchored to the seabed. We had to cut it free to release him.'

They formed a circle around the corpse and his strange appendage, the five-strong dive team, Suzie and PC Clare Pringle.

'I've never seen a creel fitted with a spring-loaded bear trap before.' Clare stated the obvious. Everyone's gaze was fixed on the vicious metal teeth embedded in John Stevenson's arm. He hadn't stood a chance once that had closed on him.

'I've called Oban, they're sending out a detective and forensics to have a look,' the leader of the dive team advised. 'Whatever this trap was for, I think we can rule out lobsters.'

'We'll keep the beach closed down until they've been.' Suzie thought on her feet. "Clare and I will keep the beach off-limits.'

The two policewomen watched as the police RIB motored out of the rocky cove, the throttle opening once they were far enough away from the shore. In the ensuing silence, John Stevenson's sightless face stared with fixed horror at the passing clouds, sea pinks coming into flower like a tribute around his head.

'I'll get my jacket.' Clare volunteered and made her way back up the track to where they'd parked the patrol car.

Suzie didn't blame her. Two bodies in as many weeks. What had the Fort William detective said about death threats?

She had a feeling this wasn't going to be the accidental drowning she'd initially expected.

Sergeant Suzie Crammond sat in her airless office and replaced the phone on its receiver. She'd finished updating the DI from Fort William about the discovery of John Stevenson's body. He'd thanked her but was now in direct contact with the Oban police as John Stevenson's death was no longer being treated as accidental drowning – the baited creel alone provided sufficient cause for concern.

She'd wanted to retrieve whatever the package was that John Stevenson gave his life for, but the Oban team had laid claim to that. Frustrated to be excluded from a case on her own patch, Suzie attached the audio file she'd received from the Fort William police to an email and sent it off to the Oban detective detailed with handling the case, together with a reference to Tauth Wildlife Tours. She guessed how that was going to go. The audio they'd ditch as irrelevant to the fate of John Stevenson – he'd already be marked down as culpable homicide. No marks on the body apart from the jagged contusions on his arm where the steel jaws had clamped tight, a few contusions from being dragged over rocks and then pulled above the high-water mark with difficulty by the police dive team. There'd been enough salt water coming out of the corpse's mouth to make death by drowning a given from the coroner – his lungs were full of it.

She expected a response asking her to follow up on the Tauth Wildlife Tours outfit. True to form, her inbox pinged a notification from the Oban police tasking her with that action. Suzie read the rest of the email, noting they'd be analysing the audio file but didn't see what relevance it had.

It was too early for lunch and her two constables had taken the traffic radar to the only stretch of road on the island where it was at all conceivable to break the speed limit. That left her to do the donkey work. Before she left the office, Suzie copied the audio file to a memory stick. There was a marine centre on the high street, conveniently close to the baker's where she could grab a bite to eat and a takeaway coffee.

'Morning, Suzie, don't normally see you in here.' A young man stopped chalking up the number of seals spotted yesterday on a blackboard. There were spaces for whales, basking sharks, porpoises and otters. Suzie frowned with irritation – every time otters were mentioned she had flashbacks to Robert Jameson's brains staining the water in Fingal's Cave and the ready meal they provided.

'Morning, Wes. I was wondering if you could help me with something?' She opened her fist to reveal the memory stick.

'What's that?' The chalk stopped on its journey back to the blackboard.

'It's an audio file I want you to have a listen to – an underwater recording taken by a wildlife expert. Can you identify what's made the noise if I leave it with you?'

'Aye, of course. Where did it come from?'

'I can't say, apart from the fact it was recorded here – or a few miles south of here. It's an ongoing investigation, so I'm not able to provide any more information.'

'No, I understand. Leave it with me – we've a library of aquatic sounds so should be easy to ID it for you.'

'Thanks, Wes. I'll be back around lunch to pick it up.' Suzie dropped the memory stick into his open hand and made for the café.

Tauth Wildlife Tours operated out of a Portakabin located a few miles out of town. Suzie brushed croissant crumbs off her uniform as she climbed out of the patrol car, adjusted her cap to the regulation angle and tapped smartly on the cabin door. A handwritten sign advertised this was the office of Tauth Wildlife Tours together with a mobile number in case the office was unattended. The door opened before she had a chance to try the handle, and Suzie was face-to-face with Micky Chambers.

They stared at each other in surprise for a few seconds before Suzie broke the silence.

'Is this your business, Micky? Wildlife tours?' She asked the question with more than a hint of derision evident in her tone.

Micky Chambers was one of the island's more colourful characters. To say he had a chequered past would be an under-statement. Petty theft, joyriding, drunk and disorderly – at one point Micky had kept the entire Tobermory police team gain-fully employed chasing him around the island after he'd stolen a tourist's Lamborghini. You'd have thought nothing could be easier than catching a car thief on an island with a limited number of single-track roads, but Micky used to take part in the annual road race and knew every twist and turn as well as which forest tracks could be used as diversions. He was only caught due to the low-hanging suspension giving up the ghost on such unsuitable terrain.

'Yeah, well – I help out.' The shock of seeing the police was wearing off. 'You want to book a tour?'

The sergeant eyed him with contempt.

'Is your driving licence even valid? How long since you were banned?'

The smirk said it all. 'A year. I'm back to being legal – you want to check?'

'Yes. Who else is involved in this scam?'

He reached inside the cabin, came back with a wallet and produced a new photo licence.

'See? Nice and legal. No points on it.'

She flipped the licence, checked what he said was true. It still rankled with her that they'd only managed to ban him for a year for dangerous driving. Then he was let off with community service. Suzie nodded her head as she remembered he'd been serving with a nature conservancy outfit. That explained how he'd ended up here.

'This the same outfit you were doing community service with?' She pointed at the Tauth Wildlife Tours sign for clarification.

'Yeah. One of the blokes set it up and asked me if I wanted to help out. He appreciates my local knowledge.'

Suzie gave him a look from under her brows before handing back the driving licence.

'Well, I'm glad you've found something useful to do with yourself at last. Who else is involved with Tauth Wildlife Tours?' She tried the same question for a second time.

'Tom. Tom Churchill. He used to work for Scottish Nature. It's all upfront.' Micky adopted a hurt tone. 'We take people around all the wildlife spots, show them the wonders of nature.' He stopped talking as if realising he'd overdone it.

'Aye. All right. Does the name John Stevenson ring any bells?' Suzie noticed the panicked expression flit across his face before he could conceal it. Micky was never a good liar – which was why he was continually being arrested for a long string of misdemeanours. He couldn't lie to save his life.

'Yeah, he's some sort of sound recordist. We've been dropping him off at various points around the coast. More like a taxi service than a wildlife tour.'

'When did you last see him?'

Micky attempted an expression that showed he was thinking.

'Around two days ago, I think. We dropped him at Craignure with his gear.'

'When exactly?'

The thoughtful expression returned, making it look as if Micky was in pain.

'Hang on, I'll get the diary.'

He returned with a well-thumbed diary, turned the pages to the date in question.

'Here we are. Sunday 12th. Dropped him at the side of the road. He said he was going to hire a van and wouldn't be needing our services any longer.'

'Didn't like how fast you were driving?'

Micky looked at her askance. 'I always keep to the speed limits. Got a driving job now, so I can't afford to lose my licence, can I? No, I told him we were fully booked this week with a photography tour, so he got his own wheels.'

Suzie wrote in her notebook in neat longhand.

'He didn't leave any equipment with you?'

Micky shook his head. 'Nah, he took it all with him.'

'Can I see the vehicle you used to transport him?'

Micky reached inside, taking keys off a hook out of her sight. 'It's just there. Help yourself.'

Suzie took the proffered keys and triggered the door lock to a minibus parked beside the cabin. The inside was empty of any recording equipment or anything that might incriminate Micky.

'Why are you interested in the recording guy?' Micky asked with evident curiosity.

'Because his body was pulled out of the sea this morning. You'll let me know if there's anything you want to add – or if you're thinking of leaving the island?'

Micky wasn't that good a play actor that his shock wasn't real.

'He's dead?'

Suzie gave one firm nod of confirmation.

'Fuck!'

NINETEEN
PENCIL CHURCH

The grave was easy enough to find – one of the few stone markers relatively untouched by Mull's erratic seasons and still recognisable as Portland limestone. A sad bouquet of plastic flowers lay scattered around the headstone where a strong gust of wind had torn them out of the sunken aluminium grave vase. The colours had bled – reds had turned coral, greens celadon. Unbidden, the image of another grave flashed before his eyes: his mother's, in a sterile Glasgow cemetery. The memory of pink gravel, forever hiding her ashes and those of his younger brother, made his stomach lurch. When was the last time he'd visited? The realisation that he couldn't remember sent a wave of shame crashing over him, so intense he could taste its bitterness.

He straightened, took a photo of the inscription.

In loving memory of
David Webster
The sound of a bagpipe – without music, life would be an error.
1935 – 2020

Teàrlach puzzled over the words. No mention of family, merely an obscure reference to bagpipes. He checked the time – 10:00 a.m. Above his head the pencil church tower pointed towards cauliflower clouds drifting across a cobalt-blue sky. From this angle, it looked like a middle finger raised to heaven. He still had to try and talk to the missing fisherman's girlfriend – Siobhan MacNeill. The local police had shown no interest in looking for Calum Donald, and if his father refused to raise a missing person report, then that's how it would stay. Chloe had said the fishing boat his father said he worked on – the *Morning Dew* – didn't exist. So, either Fraser Donald was confused, or his son had been feeding him a pack of lies.

He settled back behind the wheel, started the engine and sat staring out over the estuary that nudged the small humpback bridge ahead of him. A pair of swans made noisy progress through the air, white wings sweeping litres of air with each beat so they could be heard even from inside the hermetic embrace of his car. What was he even doing here? The photographer, Robert Jameson, how could his death be anything other than accidental? Alone on Staffa, fallen from the cliffs and into the sea cave to be discovered by the first tourists of the season. The police had decided it was accidental – the only alternative was that he deliberately stepped off the edge and no one wanted to explore that possibility with a grieving wife. The missing camera gear was a mystery, as was whoever had passed his photographs off as their own – this David Webster whose grave lay the other side of the church gate.

Then the missing fisherman, Calum Donald. Teàrlach suspected he wanted to be missing, for whatever reason. Taking himself out of circulation until Siobhan's mother had calmed down and accepted their relationship. The local police had no record of Calum's disappearance, which made him question how real it was. As for Calum's father, Fraser... He'd admitted he had brain cancer, only had a few weeks left to live. It was possible that the man was confused, unable to think coherently. But why would his son deliberately put his dad through so much worry if he knew he only had weeks left to live? None of it made any sense.

He checked his phone and saw he had a signal. Dialled the office.

'Hi, Teàrlach.' Chloe's voice sounded cheerfully in his ear.

'Hi, Chloe. I've found David Webster – he's buried in the graveyard here in Dervaig. Died in 2020. I can't find any relatives, so it looks as if someone used his name when they submitted the photographs. See if you can find anything about him – looks like he was a piper by the inscription on his gravestone – I'll send you the picture.'

'OK. I've not found the fishing boat Calum Donald was meant to be crewing.'

'Aye, read your email.'

'I have found a boat with that name operating out of Florida but think we can discount that one.'

'Aye. Bit of a commute for him. I'm beginning to think Calum's disappearance is voluntary.'

'Anything I can do this end before I come over – did you talk to his girlfriend, Siobhan MacNeill?'

'No. Tried to last night. Her band were playing in Tobermory, but I couldn't get through to her dressing room. Can you find out where she lives? I'll doorstop her – see if she knows where Calum is. At least I can let his dad know he's safe before he passes.'

'Do you think Fraser's brain cancer explains why he's given us the wrong boat name?'

'Either that or Calum's not been entirely honest with his dad. Look, I'm staying at my aunt's cottage, and I'll need to spend a bit of time there sorting it out. There's not even any electricity and the place hasn't been touched since she died.'

'Sounds idyllic.'

Teàrlach's frown returned. 'Aye. Hadn't planned to stay there, but the hotel wasn't keen on having me since Fraser Donald almost died in my arms.'

'That's not surprising.'

'Can you text Dee with the address? My phone keeps cutting out, so it's not easy for me to make or receive any calls unless I'm in range of a mast. Here's the What3Words reference.'

He could hear Chloe's pen scratching on paper as she took down the details.

'We'll all be camping out there, so bring a sleeping bag.'

'You're really selling this to me!'

Teàrlach heard the amusement in her voice.

'Aye. I'll try and sort the place out before you arrive, but best you're both forewarned. Send me a text with this Siobhan's address when you find it.'

'Will do. Are we finished with the investigation into Robert Jameson's death, then?'

He hesitated before answering. Lucy Jameson had travelled to Glasgow asking for his help – he needed to have something for her.

'No. The least we can do is track down whoever has her husband's camera. I don't see how we can shed any light on the man's death. Like the police say, it's just an accident. Those cliffs are dangerous.'

'OK. I'll send you Siobhan's address when I find it. Anything else I can do?'

'I don't think so, Chloe. If I can think of anything, I'll be in touch.'

'OK. See you tomorrow.'

He sent the headstone snap and waited until it successfully uploaded, then headed over the humpback bridge and on towards Calgary. There was another grave waiting for him. The aunt who'd cared for him and done her best to repair a child even as his universe collapsed around him.

TWENTY

SIRENS

Sergeant Suzie Crammond returned to the marine centre in Tobermory. There was a small group of excitable Japanese tourists crowding the entrance, phones recording every detail with selfie sticks placing themselves firmly in each frame. She waited until they moved on before entering.

'Hi, Suzie. Wondered when you'd be back.' The same young man greeted her with a ready smile. She couldn't help but notice the smile slip as he handed over the memory stick.

'Where did you say this was recorded?' He appeared puzzled more than anything.

'I didn't,' Suzie replied. 'We're not sure, somewhere down towards Balmeanach I think. Have you identified what the noise is?'

One look at his expression was enough for her to lose any hope of the easy identification he'd promised.

'It's like nothing I've heard before. It sounds like singing more than anything else. Underwater singing.'

Suzie sighed in exasperation. 'That's what I heard. I was hoping you'd come up with something more tangible.'

'I can tell you what it's not. It's not whales, it's not sonar, it's

not porpoises or any aquatic mammal we have recordings of.'
He turned around, leaned over a counter and pressed a switch.
The room was filled with the sound of surf, muffled and remote
as if recorded from a distance. She could identify pebbles
rattling over pebbles, bubbles breaking as they surfaced and
under it all an ethereal music that was almost lost in the sound
of the sea.

'There!' The young man's excited shout startled her. 'Do
you hear it?'

Suzie inclined her head. 'What exactly am I listening to?'

'That's it. It's like nothing I've heard. We have a library of
marine recordings from the British Museum – they have
nothing like this. Weird, isn't it?'

Suzie had to admit it was weird. 'What about sound leaking
from a yacht? Some of them are like floating fibreglass caravans
equipped with sound systems. Could music be transmitted
through the hull and picked up by an underwater microphone?'

'Maybe. I don't know.' His face brightened. 'This bit, back
here.' He pressed a few keys on the computer, dragging the
audio file nearer to the end of the recording and pressed play.

Suzie made out a rhythmic mechanical throb and a metallic
scraping noise growing louder before the audio cut out.

'Is that a boat?'

'Fishing boat dragging a trawl net I'd say. That sounds like a
diesel engine and the regular swishing sound is the propeller.'

'So, you're saying he stopped recording when a fishing boat
turned up?'

'Looks that way.'

'OK. Thanks.'

She pocketed the memory stick and left the marine centre
more confused than when she'd entered. The sound of mythological sirens luring men to their deaths faded into insignifi-
cance now that a fishing boat had been identified as the last
contact John Stevenson had before drowning.

Suzie sat in the patrol car and considered her options. The Oban police were already investigating John Stevenson's death with a view to culpable homicide at the very least. By rights she should back off and let the detective and forensics scene of crime unit deal with the case. It would take her an hour to drive the twenty miles from Tobermory; longer if she met a campervan driver who'd never mastered reverse gear. Then what was she expecting to find that they hadn't?

The sergeant looked wistfully at the baker's front window and recalled with admirable observation the range of pasties and cakes displayed on the counter. The beach where John Stevenson's body had been unceremoniously recovered or a pasty?

What the hell, it was almost lunchtime.

TWENTY-ONE
CALGARY BAY

Teàrlach pulled into the car park overlooking Calgary Bay. The scene was exactly as he remembered – a large crescent of white shell sand meeting a turquoise sea. Further out in the bay a collapsing stone pier jutted out into deeper waters, the rose-coloured granite blocks contrasting with basaltic stone. He could have been in the tropics except for the bite in the wind and an enduring memory of how cold the water was. There were a few cars and campervans sharing the view, even a few brave souls hesitating at the water's edge before risking a dip.

Teàrlach's focus was in the other direction, inland towards a small cemetery almost concealed by encroaching woods. He walked back along the rutted track and crossed the quiet road to follow a grassy path that led to his aunt's final resting place. His memory populated the track with her funeral cortège: seeing himself positioned near the front with the coffin resting too lightly on his left shoulder for such a burden. Black-clad funeral directors shared the load, a rag-taggle of friends and neighbours made the final journey with heads bowed. The flowers consigned to the earth – the hollow sound of soil against wood.

Her grave was easy to find, one of the few recent markers in a graveyard full of ancient stones and muted birdsong.

He bent down, clearing the more aggressive weeds that grew like wildfire in the soft climate, and contemplated the simple stone inscription he revealed, still clean and sharp.

> *Remember me when I am gone away,*
> *Gone far away into the silent land*
> *Rosie Livingston 1956 – 2022*

The words blurred, so he had to wipe away tears with the back of his hand. Two years since her death, and this was the first time he'd been to see her grave since the funeral. The words came from 'Remember' by Christina Rossetti. He had a book of her poems, part of the bequest that he'd taken back to Glasgow which did little to replace the void in his heart. The rest of the poem had been about forgiveness, he recalled. Saying it was better to forget her and to be happy rather than always to remember and be sad. It was her final selfless gift to him, the last thing she had to give.

Teàrlach wiped away a stubborn tear. He'd not forgotten, how could he? But he had managed to shut away the pain-filled memory of the aunt who'd given this orphan a roof over his head and unconditional love when he had nothing left. Was this how to repay her – by taking the literal message her inscription implied and to forget rather than grieve?

The graveyard trees had no response to offer, save a gentle sigh as the salt-laden wind played with fresh new leaves. Teàrlach looked up at the sky, searched for the eagles who often flew silently unobserved over the heads of holidaymakers engaged in building sandcastles, or splashing in the cold Atlantic. They weren't making an appearance today, staying as reclusive as his emotions usually were. He stayed at the grave waiting for words to come, and when they failed to materialise, he touched the cold stone marker and said a simple thanks.

Everything on this island held memories for him. Teàrlach knew why he'd never been back. He saw himself and his aunt playing on that beach, caught glimpses of them walking past Tobermory shops, had seen himself heading up the hill to school. Now he was here he couldn't escape the pain each memory brought.

A call from Chloe broke his reminiscing.

'Hi, Teàrlach. Finally – I've been trying to reach you for hours.'

'Aye. Phone cover is fairly random here. What have you got for me?'

'This Siobhan MacNeill, the fisherman's girlfriend. She lives at Fiorlesk House – do you want the address?'

'No, it's OK. I know where the place is. Good work, thanks, Chloe. Anything else come in?'

'No, that's all I have. I'll take the train to Oban tomorrow and catch one of the morning ferries. Dee offered me a lift on her bike, but I'm not that brave.'

'Probably wise. Call me when you know what boat you're catching and I'll pick you up from the ferry.'

Teàrlach drove back to the cottage, resolving to face his demons head on. The place needed attention after two years; it was nothing short of a miracle that the house had remained watertight. He negotiated the road as it twisted and turned, clinging close to the cliff edge above Calgary Bay. There were ships far out at sea, fishing vessels or pleasure craft – it was impossible to discern from this distance and the road required all his concentration.

Fiorlesk House was just a few miles ahead. He'd driven past the estate enough times and glimpsed the outline of a large white house set some way back from the road. The rest of the estate was bounded by a high stone wall; originally built to keep out deer, it now served to deter tourists from prying.

Siobhan MacNeill's family once owned huge swathes of the island yet had managed to keep themselves almost hidden away. He knew of the family, anyone living on the island would have heard the name, but until this moment he hadn't made the connection between Siobhan and the big house up the road. He'd assumed Siobhan was merely one of the many MacNeills that lived across the island with more humble origins. Teàrlach drove past black wrought-iron gates, emblazoned with what he imagined must be the family crest, and down a treelined drive to park in front of the imposing Georgian façade that was Siobhan's home. How would the MacNeill matriarch take to a private investigator searching for the man whom she wanted kept away from her daughter at all costs? He pulled on a lever and a bell clanged from somewhere deep within the house, swiftly followed by the aggressive sound of what must be a large dog running towards the door and barking a warning. Teàrlach just hoped the dog was on a leash as the door opened.

TWENTY-TWO
DEERHOUND

The heavy door pulled open to reveal an Irish deerhound, straining away from the woman whose hand was wrapped around its collar. Her other hand gripped the door, which swung backwards and forwards in the ensuing struggle. Teàrlach saw hair the same steel grey as the dog, eyes as brown and untrusting.

'What do you want?' Her voice was clipped and impatient. 'Dusk! Sit!' The commands were issued to the dog, which completely ignored her.

Teàrlach switched his attention from the woman to the dog and back again. He had no wish to have the animal's jaws tighten around any part of his anatomy and its owner apparently had little to no control.

'My name's Teàrlach Paterson. I'm a private investigator.' He rummaged in his coat to produce a business card, only to hold it uselessly in the air as both the woman's hands were too fully occupied to accept it.

'Why are you here? Who asked you to come?'

Teàrlach had read that dogs grew to look like their owners, or was it vice versa? These two shared the same temperament.

'I'm sorry, could we talk without the dog?' He found he had to shout as the deerhound started another burst of barking. It gave every impression of wanting Teàrlach to start running so it could perform the job it had been bred for – chasing down fully grown deer and killing them with teeth locked around the throat. As if on cue the dog began snarling, revealing yellowed canines perfectly capable of doing damage to anything they locked onto.

'Dusk! Bad boy.' She shook the dog by the collar with no perceptible effect. 'I can't hear you. Wait here!'

Teàrlach had the impression he was being spoken to in the same imperious manner as the dog. The door closed, footsteps and barking swallowed up by the cavernous interior of the house. Standing on the porch, he could see flaking paint on the walls, evidence of rot in the window frames. The once grand house had fallen onto hard times. The garden was kept in check by a lawnmower cutting a swathe free of encroaching rhododendrons, their tree-like limbs contorting towards the building like fingers in a horror movie.

The door reopened without the fanfare of animal barks and scrabbling feet, startling Teàrlach when he turned to face the stern features of the deerhound's owner once more.

'Now, what was it you wanted?' She gave every impression that her time was being unnecessarily wasted.

Teàrlach handed over the business card still clenched between his fingers.

'I'm a private investigator. I was wondering if I could have a word with Siobhan?'

'Siobhan? Why do you need to speak to her?' Impatience gave way to incredulity.

'It's to do with her boyfriend, Calum Donald...'

'Don't mention that boy's name to me.' She had turned bright red and apoplectic with rage – to the point that she was struggling to breathe much less say anything else.

Teàrlach mentally ran through his first-aid training in case she was having a stroke. She strained at the door in a manner so similar to the deerhound that he wondered if the adage about dogs and their owners had more behind it than he'd given credence to.

'I'm sorry if I've upset you,' Teàrlach said lamely. 'It's just that Calum Donald has gone missing, and I hoped that Siobhan may have been able to help?'

The second mention of Calum's name was too much. Her teeth had by now clamped together with undisguised rage. If this had been a cartoon, he could reasonably expect to see steam issuing out of each ear.

'Is Siobhan in?' he asked reasonably.

'Don't you dare... don't you dare come here and mention that name!' Like a pressure cooker the words spat out with force. 'He'd be missing if he showed up here, I can tell you that! Now bugger off from wherever you came from, and don't you dare come here again or I'll set the dog on you, I swear.'

This time, the door slammed shut with sufficient force to leave flakes of paint pirouetting down to the concrete doorstep where they joined others to make an abstract image. The dog's bark returned, growing louder and encouraging Teàrlach to return to the safety of his car.

'That could have gone better,' he advised himself before following the drive back onto the road. Whatever else he might have learned from Siobhan, the woman he took to be her mother was obviously not taken with her daughter's choice of boyfriend. Fraser Donald's words came back to him as Teàrlach negotiated a blind corner, wary of meeting someone coming the other way. *They killed my son, Mr Paterson; or they have him prisoner.*

Dee stood on the ferry deck as the *CalMac Loch Frisa* made slow progress away from Oban pier. She shivered as the boat cleared the relative shelter of the harbour and turned into the wind.

She gave up looking for porpoises, irritated by the proximity of a pot-bellied smoker whose gaze repeatedly swept over her body, and made for the onboard café.

'Cappuccino please.'

'Do you want chocolate with that?'

'Aye.'

'You're a biker?' The guy behind the counter appeared slightly confused that the red-headed woman standing in front of him and dressed in leathers might be something other than she seemed.

'That's right.'

'What have you got?' He transferred his attention to her cup, shaking a metal container over it until the coffee surface was covered with a dark brown stain.

'Kawasaki Ninja 300,' Dee answered, reaching for the cup.

He held a card reader in readiness, and Dee placed her

phone against it until an electronic ping confirmed the transaction.

'Fast?'

'Fast enough.'

He nodded wisely. 'I'd kill myself on one of those.'

He looked more like a heart attack would get to him first.

'I'm careful.' She took a window seat, sipping at her coffee and watching the distant shoreline drift by as the boat made steady progress up the Sound of Mull.

Was she careful? Dee searched the lounge and regarded her fellow travellers. Tourists, delivery drivers with tankers or vans, commuters treating the ferry as just another leg of a journey they repeated every day. None of them gave the impression that they lived life on the edge. She used to work for Glasgow's most notorious gangster, a man who had left a trail of death in his wake. Now she was working for a private investigator and had only just avoided being murdered during their last big case. Were these the actions of someone who played it safe? Even riding the bike through Glasgow traffic or along Scotland's winding roads had more than an element of risk.

As did drinking the coffee, she decided, leaving half a cup to sway in sympathy with the ferry's rolling motion. Should she tell Teàrlach about her decision to look for her parents? She decided it was better to keep that news to herself – nothing might come of it now she was reduced to the lottery of a DNA match. She still wasn't convinced that it had been a good idea to start looking in the first place. Dee pictured the envelope left in her flat – maybe that's where it would stay.

The journey to the Mull ferry terminal at Craignure would take another thirty minutes. She pulled her laptop out of her backpack, opened it on the table and angled the screen away from any prying eyes. The ferry had its own Wi-Fi – too public for her to do anything really useful, but she could read up on the family accused of doing away with the missing fisherman.

Dee searched for the name in Chloe's email and entered it into her browser.

The MacNeills had their own Wikipedia page, which impressed Dee no end. There was a lot about the clan – how they used to own many of the Hebridean islands until the Jacobite rebellion. Her interest quickened when she learned that the Donalds from Tiree won a historic legal battle against the MacNeills which cost them their fortune.

Was this what the enmity between the two families was all about?

Dee made a note of the web page to show Teàrlach. If anyone knew how the locals felt about events that had happened generations ago, it would be him. She checked her emails and saw Chloe had sent her a What3Words location for Teàrlach's cottage – same as the WhatsApp text she'd sent earlier, only now she'd added some additional detail.

Hi Dee, Teàrlach asked me to mention the cottage hasn't been lived in for a couple of years and hasn't any electricity, so you may want to grab a sleeping bag as you'll be camping. Weather's meant to be getting worse! See you tomorrow.

Chloe xxx

She grimaced at the thought of camping out in a dilapidated ruin. There were other options available if it was as bad as Chloe made out.

The tannoy system chimed, announcing a stream of words in Gaelic, a language that had all but died out in the islands that had once been its stronghold. The instructions for drivers to return to their vessels were repeated in English. Dee leisurely packed her laptop away, strapped her backpack on and waited until the mad rush for the stairs had eased. Bikes would be the last off the ferry, and she was determined to enjoy the trip.

TWENTY-FOUR

ATLANTIC

The cottage was cute enough from a distance. Dee opened a sagging metal farm gate that blocked the track at the road, wheeled her bike through before lifting the gate back into place and sliding home the metal bolt to secure it. Teàrlach's car was parked at the end of the track, so she knew she had the right place.

The bike threatened to skate on loose stones, causing her to ride it like a beginner with feet poised to catch the ground. Teàrlach opened the door as she brought the bike to a standstill, grateful she hadn't suffered the indignity of falling sideways at the last turn.

'Made it then?' His smile was rare enough for her to do a double-take.

'Aye, although this track needs some attention.' She climbed off the bike, wiped the worst of the dust off her leathers with her gloved hands. 'And the roads – some of the potholes are big enough to swallow me and the bike whole!'

The view caught her attention, a stretch of deep blue sea until another island reared out of the water a few miles distant. Further out she caught sight of other islands, one shaped like a sombrero. Bracken encroached, held back by inquisitive sheep who'd stopped their incessant grazing to warily view this noisy new addition to their environment.

'Nice view,' she added eventually. It was a nice view; in fact, it was a stunning view. The breeze coming off the Atlantic tasted so pure it could have been bottled and sold.

'Come on in. I've been tidying the place, even managed to turn on the electric and find some gas.'

She followed him inside, not entirely sure what to expect after Chloe's warning. Apart from a musty smell, she couldn't find fault. There were signs of cleaning – kitchen surfaces were still drying and giving off a lemon scent; the floor carpet was criss-crossed with hoover brush marks. Every window and door had been flung wide open allowing the fresh air she'd wanted to bottle free access.

'Better than I thought it would be. Maybe I don't need a hotel after all.'

Teàrlach turned from the cooker he'd been coaxing into life and placed an old kettle on the newly lit hob with a satisfied smile.

'No internet I'm afraid. That's a step too far, although we used to have it somehow. Your room's in a bit of a state. I picked up new sheets in Tobermory – I can give you a hand...?'

'No, you're all right. Which room am I in?'

Teàrlach led the way to a small bedroom filled with book-cases and a desk which he'd been going through. Papers and files lay open in full view.

'Sorry. I'd just made a start.' He tried to pile papers up in a heap, causing a paper avalanche to layer the floor. A whistle sounded in the kitchen, increasing in pitch and volume as the kettle began to boil.

Dee dumped her backpack on a clear patch of carpet. 'It's OK. I'll deal with it. Where are the sheets?'

Teàrlach pointed to a package on the floor and left the

room. Dee made a start on making the bed, checking the blankets for mould – or worse.

'How was your trip? Found it all right?' Teàrlach's shouted questions drifted down the hall.

'Aye, it was fine. Quite enjoyed myself, to be honest. Bit of an adventure coming over to the islands.'

'That's good. I've not made much progress with the photographer or the missing fisherman. Maybe you can have a look at what the police have found, if you manage to get online? I've only instant coffee. Black. That OK?'

'Sure. Maybe we can pick up something to drink tomorrow?'

He reappeared in the doorway as she fitted the sheet to a mattress that smelt of mice, holding out a steaming mug.

'Thanks.' Dee's nose wrinkled at the musty smell. 'How long since anyone's slept here?'

'Two years. This used to be my aunt's room. Mine's the one next door.' A thumb indicated the next doorway down the hall.

'So, why's it been left like this for two years? Couldn't you sell it – or let it out as a holiday rental?'

'I suppose. I should have done something with it.' Teàrlach was being uncharacteristically hesitant. 'I don't know, to be honest. I just wanted to leave it until I was ready to deal with everything.'

She saw the grief etched on his face despite his attempt to appear cheerful. Dee remembered him telling her how his aunt had taken him in, treated him like her own after his mother and brother had died in the house fire his father had set. She'd been dead for two years and he'd dealt with it by trying to forget any of it had ever happened. A social worker had once sat her down after her failed adoption – an event that had hurt her more deeply than anything else in her life. She'd solemnly explained that what Dee was feeling was grief, and that it was perfectly normal for her to feel rejected and angry. There were five stages to grief, she remembered being told: denial, anger, bargaining, depression and acceptance. Teàrlach hadn't made it past stage one.

'Aye, well. You're here now, so this would be a good time to make a start.' She sipped her coffee, burned her lip on the boiling liquid and blew across her mouth in an attempt to avoid a blister. 'I can help – if you like? Seeing as how I'm here.'

'Thanks. I'd like that.' Teàrlach drank without any sign of being scalded.

An air of tension had descended on them both as if there were things waiting to be said but neither wanted to make the first move.

'I've began searching for my birth parents,' Dee started.

Teàrlach frowned. 'What – I thought you'd decided not to bother? Seeing they didn't want anything to do with you.'

'Aye, I did say that.' She couldn't miss the look of unease flooding his face and realised he felt that he'd overstepped the mark.

'It's just something I feel that I want to do. You know, now that I'm older. They're not going to be around for ever. If they're still around at all.'

'I suppose not.' Teàrlach shrugged.

'I'm not going to find anything for weeks. There's nothing in the paperwork – I tried Scotland's People. They'd have had a record if one existed.'

Teàrlach was struggling to process the information.

'Is there anything I can do to help.'

Dee shook her head. 'Thanks, but I've got it covered. DNA testing is the last chance saloon. I'm not really expecting to find a match.'

'What brought this on?' Teàrlach asked.

'I think being so close to death, you know? I felt – I thought it wasn't right that I could so easily die and never know who my parents were. Even if they were shite at it.'

Teàrlach's smile made her feel better.

'Anyway – we've a cottage to make habitable before the light goes. Another year or so isn't going to make any difference to me. Where's the cleaning stuff?'

One look at his face was all she needed.

'You haven't brought anything, have you?'

'I didn't think I'd be staying here – much less you and Chloe.'

TWENTY-FIVE
LARGE LAPHROAIG

They'd spent several hours trying to make the cottage more welcoming, finding any activity more acceptable than dealing with problem parents. Once the place had been tidied, and the worst of the stour swept out on a sea breeze, they both began to breathe more easily.

'Right! I'm hungry and there's no food in the house. I'll treat you to a pub dinner.' Teàrlach held his car keys high in invitation. The light was already fading outside, leaving the cottage to be lit by an insufficient number of working bulbs. The temperature was also dropping rapidly, with no working heating to take the edge off the cold.

'Let me grab my laptop. May be able to piggy-back on their Wi-Fi.' Dee looked questioningly towards Teàrlach before adding, 'They do have Wi-Fi here on the island, don't they?'

He looked at her in surprise before realising she was joking.

'Aye, and electricity.' His finger aimed at the overhead lampshade that was struggling to cast its light into the corners of Dee's bedroom.

They drove in silence back to Tobermory, Dee fully

engaged by the sight of the sun dipping westwards until Teàrlach turned inland and the Atlantic was finally lost from view.

He parked on the high street, facing out over the harbour. A few of the yachts moored at the pontoons had lights on, signs of movement onboard. Teàrlach locked the car, led the way to a pub on the waterfront and the sound of music increased as he opened the door.

'This will do us,' Dee made straight for a table next to an open fire, rubbing her hands in satisfaction at being in an environment she understood.

'What can I get you?' Teàrlach asked.

Dee scanned the bar from her seated position. 'I'll have a large Laphroaig – on ice.'

He could feel his eyebrows raising. 'Starting a bit heavy?'

She cooly held his gaze. 'With good reason.'

Teàrlach fetched the drinks and scooped up a bar menu. By the time he returned to their table, she'd already opened her laptop, hunched over the screen with a look of concentration.

'Slàinte Mhath!' Half the glass emptied down her throat before she lowered it to the table. She blinked back the tears leaking from her eyes. 'Needed that,' she explained.

Teàrlach sipped from his own half pint in response. 'Picked up a menu.' He held it until she took it out of his hand, scanned it and said 'fish and chips', then bent back to her screen as if he didn't exist.

He placed the order, looked around the bar for any faces he recognised. There were mostly locals in the bar, too early for the summer tourists or the fair-weather sailors that frequented the town once winter released its grip. A couple of guys caught his eyes, recognising the boy in the man and nodded over their drinks in acknowledgement of someone who was once an islander.

What was he now? No longer an islander, that was for sure. The town held memories, was achingly familiar, but this was a different life to the one he now led. He had changed since leaving here at eighteen – did everyone else he left behind stay the same?

'It's Teàrlach, isn't it?' The voice blindsided him, coming from behind as he'd been exchanging nods with a faraway table. He turned to face a guy whose features were mostly obscured by a black, bushy beard. He'd recognised the voice before seeing a face he knew from school.

'Mitch! Haven't seen you since we were both thrown out of here as kids.' Teàrlach grabbed the man's shoulder with real affection, pulling them together.

'Thought it was you. Then I saw the woman you'd come in with and had my doubts.' His head tilted in Dee's direction; she remained unaware she was the focus of attention, her head still buried in the screen.

'Oh, that's Dee. We work together.' Teàrlach wondered at his easy dismissal of Dee as merely a colleague. Another fact he was unwilling to face.

Dee looked up at a mention of her name, raised her glass in salute and the contents joined the rest of the measure.

Mitch stood in wordless admiration of the redhead by the fire, reluctantly dragging his attention back to Teàrlach.

'What are you doing here? Thought you'd joined the army or something. You're looking well, man.'

His hand impacted Teàrlach's back, the shockwave travelling down towards his scar and setting off a familiar ache.

'Aye, for a while. In the military police. Now I'm a private investigator in Glasgow.'

'A PI?' Mitch exclaimed. 'Taking pictures of illicit affairs and stuff?'

'Nothing so exciting. Here, can I get you a drink?'

'Twist my arm if you like. Pint would be lovely.' He indicated the pump beside his elbow.

Teàrlach ordered a pint, and another single for Dee as she waved her empty glass in his direction.

'So, what brings you here?' Mitch asked. He lifted his pint, and the ready conversation came to a halt.

'I've been asked to look into Robert Jameson's death – on Staffa.'

'Lucy asked you?'

'Aye – not that there's much I can do for her.'

Mitch gave Teàrlach a cryptic look from over his pint glass as it tipped more beer down. 'That's not what you used to say about her.'

Teàrlach felt a blush starting to colour his cheeks.

'No. This is purely business – and doing her a favour following her man's death. It's the least I could do.'

'Right enough. It was a shock, hearing Rob had died. Couldn't believe it – he knew his way around Staffa. Still, what a place to go, eh?'

'What are you doing with yourself?' Teàrlach was anxious to move the conversation away from discussing Lucy or her man.

'Forestry. Could never work in an office or factory – or out on the boats. It's been good. Plenty of freedom, no one breathing down yer neck.'

'Talking of boats, you don't know Calum Donald – from Tiree? He was crew on a boat called the *Morning Dew*?'

'Why are you asking?'

'His father, Fraser, asked me to try and find him. Seems he's gone missing?'

'I don't know anything about that.' Mitch sipped his beer and developed a sudden interest in the football, turning away to view a TV mounted in a corner of the pub.

Teàrlach's eyes narrowed. Mitch was clearly uncomfortable with the direction the conversation was taking.

'You know him, though?' Teàrlach pushed.

'Aye, as well as anyone else that drinks in here regularly. Don't really know him that well.' He took the opportunity to take a drink himself, hopeful eyes observing Teàrlach from over the rim of his pint.

Two plates of food were being laid on the table, Dee beckoning him over in case his detective capabilities were failing.

'Oh, that's your meal. Don't want to keep you. It's been good catching up – and thanks for the drink.' Mitch made to go and Teàrlach laid a hand on his arm to stop him.

'Calum's dad isn't doing too great. He's in hospital, in Craignure. He may not have much time left and I promised to find Calum for him. Is there anything you can give me that would help?'

Mitch seemed conflicted, eyes darting from side to side. He took another deep drink from his glass.

'Look, I don't know much about what's going on.' He'd leaned in, almost whispering. 'There's bad blood between him and some people. He'd be clever not to show his face around here if that's true, ye ken?'

Teàrlach knew all right. 'What about the woman – Siobhan MacNeill?'

Mitch's eyes opened wide. 'Keep it down, man. She's one of *the* MacNeills. You don't want to be poking around there, not if you've any sense.'

Teàrlach puzzled over the man's obvious disquiet. From what he'd seen of Siobhan's home, they were a family in decline. They might once have had considerable influence, de facto rulers of this and other islands, but that was ancient history. Their house had that air of genteel decay he'd seen with other once-proud families as fortunes ebbed away. Her mother had been unpleasant but hardly enough to strike fear into the heart of someone like Mitch. He was built like a bearded tank – from the size of his biceps alone, he likely wrestled trees out of the ground without needing any machinery.

'I need to speak to Siobhan, ask her if she had any news of him. They were engaged to be married I'd heard.'

'You hear lots of stuff, some of it's true, some less so.' Mitch stood up, shrugging off Teàrlach's arm as if it was a feather.

'His dad's dying, Mitch. Can't you just tell me how I can speak to Siobhan? I tried to have a word at the concert here yesterday but couldn't get through to the dressing room.'

Mitch looked at his pint, then back to Teàrlach as if weighing up a particularly difficult decision. The pint must have swung it as he turned his head to the back of the bar, away from the band whose noise covered his words.

'I saw her go into the back room, where the pool table is. You'll find her there. Just don't tell her I told you.'

Teàrlach joined Dee at the table. She nodded enthusiastically at him. 'Great fish and chips. I can see why people live next to the sea!'

'When we finish, do you fancy a game of pool?' he asked.

'If you don't mind being humiliated in front of your old friends, aye. I'll play you.'

TWENTY-SIX

POOL

Dee had watched the exchange between Teàrlach and the bearded giant, catching quick glimpses from above her laptop screen. She knew instinctively when she was being discussed, even though she didn't hear a word of the conversation above the noise of the band. The bearded guy made no secret of his interest in her, fixing her in his sights with a familiar intensity. If she hadn't been so disturbed by what she'd discovered on Oban's police servers, she might have found her admirer a worthwhile diversion.

As it was, her screen had shown nothing on the missing fisherman, Calum Donald – or Robert Jameson apart from a note stating death by misadventure. Dee had a strong suspicion the Oban police had taken the easy way out opting for that result. With Robert Jameson's death called an accident, there would be no need for any further investigation, another box ticked and case closed. She could sympathise – he was on his own when he fell, as far as anyone knew. He slipped, lost his balance, ended up dead. Teàrlach wasn't going to be able to spin the guy's death any other way, however much he wanted to impress Lucy.

She beckoned Teàrlach over when the plates of food

arrived. The bearded guy looked like he wanted away, and she hadn't had her second drink. Dee closed the laptop, listened to Teàrlach offering to play her at pool with half her attention.

'There's another reason I want to play pool.' Teàrlach leaned forward. 'The missing fisherman's girlfriend is through there, and I need to speak to her.'

Dee stopped eating her chips as she considered his words.

'This is the girlfriend whose mum wants him dead?' Dee cut another piece of cod, knife crunching through the batter and fork impaling a bite-sized morsel.

'Aye, except I think this story is blown out of all proportion. I've drawn a blank with everything else, this Siobhan is the only person I can think of who'd be able to give me a lead.'

'I don't know,' Dee managed between chewing. 'Her mum sounds a piece of work. Is her daughter going to be any different?'

Teàrlach frowned in response. 'Aye. I need to speak to her, though. I was at her house earlier and her mother threatened to set the dog on me.'

'You *are* Mr Popular.'

'Come on then, the pool table awaits.' He stood, encouraging her to follow.

'Maybe leave me to talk to her,' Dee suggested.

Teàrlach gave a tight smile. 'Aye, that might work.'

TWENTY-SEVEN
NUDGE IT

The game was just finishing as Teàrlach and Dee entered the back room. A TV screen showed a silent football match, Teàrlach's eyes squinting as he tried to make out the teams displayed in small font. Siobhan MacNeill was lining up a cue, a yellow ball close enough to the corner pocket for a glancing nudge to send it in. He recognised the other girl from the band, the one who'd played cello. There were three guys who could have made up the rest of the band, he'd paid little attention to them on the night, but the young man who scowled at them as soon as they entered the back room was new.

The yellow obediently fell into the pocket and the white rebounded off the cushion to come to a halt in line with the black. It was a simple shot, and the other girl dramatically threw her hands up in the air. 'Jesus, every fucking time!'

Siobhan gave her a sweet smile, then efficiently dropped the black without any fuss.

'Table's yours, if you want it.' She held the cue out for Dee.

'You not wanting a match?' Dee asked.

'I've had enough, thanks. You guys have it.'

Teàrlach rummaged in his pocket for loose change and

Siobhan laughed, aiming her hip at the side of the table followed by the sound of cue balls making their way to join the rack in the ball return.

'Just nudge it for the next game,' she explained.

'Thanks,' Teàrlach replied.

'You're welcome.' She turned away, picked up a jacket left slung on a chair together with a clutch bag. 'I'm going to the loo, meet you outside.'

Teàrlach exchanged a look with Dee, then started setting up the table as Siobhan and her entourage exited into the main bar. The scowler waited until last, following them out without a word.

'I'll be back in a minute,' Dee announced. 'Don't start without me.'

Women's pub toilets all follow the same blueprint. A few cubicles with large enough gaps underneath to check that the occupant hasn't collapsed in a drunken heap; large well-lit mirror above the sinks to re-apply makeup; space enough for five or six women to gather together and talk without inhibitions.

This toilet was empty, except for one stall. Dee occupied the second cubicle, waiting for the sound of flushing before making her move. When her cue sounded, she stood next to Siobhan at the mirror, exchanging a quick smile.

'You're Siobhan, aren't you?'

The woman switched her attention from applying lip gloss to focus on Dee's reflection.

'Aye, sorry, I don't recognise you – do you follow the band?'

Dee shook her head. 'I'm working here. Looking for Calum Donald.'

Siobhan stopped and turned to face Dee directly.

'Why are you looking for him? Who sent you?' She replaced her lip gloss in her clutch bag, her eyes narrowing with anger.

'I'm working for Calum's dad.' Dee held her arms up to pacify her. 'He's dying. He wants to know Calum's OK, that's all. He asked me to look for him.'

'How do you mean he's dying?' Siobhan said suspiciously. She looked towards the door, either to make a run for it or worried that someone else was going to come in at any moment.

'He's got terminal brain cancer. He's been taken to the local hospital.' She decided to leave out the bit where he'd collapsed at Teàrlach's feet. 'All he wants is to know Calum's safe – that's all.'

Siobhan's face screwed up; tears filled her eyes.

'That's awful. Calum doesn't know anything about this. It's not fair.' She opened her clutch bag again, returned to the mirror and patted her eyes dry. 'I can't speak to you here; someone might come in.'

'How is Calum? Is he in danger? We can help him – and you if you're in trouble.'

She panicked, pulling the strap of her bag over her shoulder and giving once last check of her reflection in the glass.

'I can't say anything.' She stopped with her hand on the door, listening for anyone coming. 'Tell Fraser he's OK. I'll try and get him to see his dad before... before it's too late.'

Siobhan quickly opened the door, and it pulled shut behind her. Dee was left staring at her own reflection, her eyes troubled and mouth twisted in confusion. Siobhan had given every indication of being happy and carefree until she'd mentioned Calum's name. Then her reaction – what was she frightened of? Dee returned to Teàrlach, patiently standing by the pool table with cue in hand.

'Well?' he asked.

Dee checked behind her before replying. 'She says he's OK,

but she's frightened about something – and whatever it is, it's not Calum.'

'Is he going to see his dad, in hospital?'

'She said she'd tell Calum, but she was anxious. Mentioned it might be too late.'

'Too late for what?' Teàrlach said impatiently.

'Maybe for visiting his dad? She ran off at that point. I wasn't going to chase her through the pub.'

Teàrlach frowned. 'I need to know where Calum is. Is Siobhan still here?' He dropped the cue on the table and rushed out without waiting for an answer.

'I think they were ready to drive off home,' Dee shouted after him.

He returned after a few minutes, a troubled look still etched on his face.

'Couldn't see them. You sure Calum's OK?'

Dee nodded. 'Siobhan's been seeing him as far as I can make out. They hadn't heard that his dad was sick – that came as a shock. I believed her when she promised to take Calum to the hospital. I don't see there's much more we can do?'

'No, suppose not.' Teàrlach grabbed two of the balls, gave one to Dee.

They started at opposite sides at the head of the table, lined up their cues and simultaneously hit the balls against the end cushion. Teàrlach's returned first, bouncing back off the head rail to come to a halt five centimetres from the cushion. Dee's ball made more leisurely progress until drifting to a halt against the edge of the head rail.

'I start,' she announced.

Teàrlach realised he was going to lose before Dee had taken the first shot.

TWENTY-EIGHT

UNDERWATER

Dee surfaced from a troubled sleep, blinking away the confusion whilst she struggled to identify where she was. The sound of pots being scrubbed in the cottage kitchen had woken her. Teàrlach must be taking this housecleaning seriously.

She reached for her laptop, then cursed when she remembered there was no internet here. Her phone was on the pine bedside table where she'd dropped it last night, too pissed to do anything other than climb between the new sheets of his aunt's bed. The disturbing thought that she might have died here was quickly put to one side. As suspected, there was nothing at all – no data, no phone signal.

Dee entered her password, checked her searches for whatever had been found whilst still in range of the pub's Wi-Fi last night. It was much like fishing, she thought, baiting a few pots, dragging a net through the dark web and seeing what she might have ensnared. Her search had brought in some data, though – the Oban police server had regurgitated emails from Tobermory police, referencing a body found with an arm trapped in a creel. The case wasn't directly of interest – Teàrlach only wanted information that related to either the Staffa photographer

Robert Jameson, or missing fisherman Calum Donald. She started to hone the search parameters on her program to avoid spurious hits, then opened the emails out of curiosity.

The first one was from Sergeant Suzie Crammond, from Tobermory police. She'd attached an audio file that she'd received from a DI James Corstorphine based in Fort William, together with a statement from the dead guy's partner stating he was doing a wildlife survey and recording underwater sounds. The attached was the last recording he'd made before being found near the Eas Fors waterfall.

Dee made a note of his name – John Stevenson – and the preliminary note of a fatal accident enquiry with a review scheduled for next month. One comment from his partner's statement grabbed her attention '*Threatening posts on social media.*' She opened the file listing a series of death threats made directly to John Stevenson's Facebook page. She read his posts, nearly all were concerned with environmental issues – the widespread use of neonicotinoids in farming; radiation leaks at Faslane, microplastics in drinking water. Recent posts were all concerned with the destruction of the seabed around the Hebrides by trawling and scallop dredging. Photographs showed the before and aftereffects – a rich environment with crabs, lobsters, seaweed and then an underwater wasteland with telltale tracks and broken shells. The attached audio file was unusual enough for her to focus on. Dee turned up the laptop volume to counter the noise Teàrlach was making in the kitchen and pressed play.

All she could hear at first were the muted bubbles and roar from surf, accompanied by the rattle of small stones being carried by the tide or washed out to sea. Then she heard a faint song coming through the sound of the sea, so weak she thought she imagined it. There was a melodic content to the sound, otherwise she'd have dismissed it as a freak of nature – some natural utterance from the ocean that merely sounded human.

The hairs on the back of her neck stood up as the sound came more strongly, calling to her to follow the song into the water. Dee had heard of sirens, dismissed the thought of mermaids entrancing sailors to their deaths as pure fancy – but then she remembered how she'd felt as the night mist had concealed the loch where Tony Masterton had died, the knowledge that something unspeakably evil had been coming for her. Her finger stopped the recording, and she took a minute to shake off the feeling of dread that had once more returned long after she'd consigned that night to oblivion.

There was a second email, thankfully without any attachments this time. The same sergeant had given details of Tauth Wildlife Tours, the company that John Stevenson had been booked with. There was a response from the Oban detective handling the case, asking her to talk with them and see if they knew anything about his movements over the last week.

She sat in bed, laptop on her knee and tipped her head back to stare at the ceiling. This case had nothing to do with Teàrlach's enquiry, yet here was another death happening within twelve days of one another and both individuals were keen conservationists. John Stevenson was critical of the trawler fishing industry; Robert Jameson had complained that the puffin's natural food source – the sand eels – were being fished to extinction. Both men drowned, alone and without any witnesses to the event.

There was a polite knock at her bedroom door. Teàrlach's voice sounded through the wood. 'You want a coffee?'

'Aye, I'm just getting up. Be with you in a bit.'

The sound of a tap coughing water into a kettle followed. She grimaced, looking at the glass she'd managed to fill from the same tap late last night. It looked more like tea than water and had the same peaty aftertaste as the whisky she'd consumed. Outside the window the weather seemed to be brightening, fat cumulus clouds sailing stately through a powder blue sky like a fleet of exotic ships. The view should have been calming, a rural idyl, but she felt on edge.

'Found this on the Oban police server.' Dee turned her laptop around for Teàrlach to view. They were sat at an old wooden table in the cottage kitchen, mugs of instant and rashers of bacon and eggs being quickly demolished as soon as they were served.

'Nothing here about Calum Donald or Robert Jameson?' Teàrlach's head moved towards and away from the screen in an attempt to bring it into sharper focus.

Dee bit back the comment forming about him needing his eyes tested.

'No, but it's a bit of a coincidence that the island has years without an accidental death and here's two in the same few days – and have a listen to this audio.' She stood beside him, pressed the audio file play button and the kitchen was filled with the submerged sound of the sea.

'Play that bit again.' Teàrlach struggled to find the stop button.

Dee obliged, taking the audio back to where the singing could first be heard.

'Sounds like Siobhan MacNeill, from the group – Deò,' he added after seeing Dee's puzzlement. 'How?' Teàrlach waved his hands around in confusion. 'How can she be singing underwater?'

'That's not all.' Dee held a hand up for Teàrlach to continue listening. The distant throb of an engine and propellor churning the water grew louder until the audio cut off.

'That was the last recording John Stevenson sent back to his partner in Fort William before he was found. The local police sent it to the Tobermory sergeant in case they could shed any light on it.'

She could see the gears engaging as Teàrlach processed the information.

'Two wildlife enthusiasts, one a photographer and then another recording underwater sounds, and they both die accidentally within days of each other.' His hand reached for an imaginary beard.

Dee imagined what he'd look like if he allowed the dark stubble to colonise his chin.

'And in both cases, they had gone on record criticising the fishing industry.'

A beard would suit him, she decided. A beard and a haircut.

'Whoever has Robert Jameson's camera lives in Dervaig, or at least sent his photos from there. I wonder if they have any connection to this John Stevenson?'

'And what did he record that was so important that he met with an accidental death?' she added.

Teàrlach sat deep in thought.

'Have the police started looking for Calum Donald?' he asked quietly.

'Not that I could see, but I need to find somewhere with internet so I can check on a few things.'

Teàrlach stood, leaving most of his coffee untouched. 'There's a café at Calgary with Wi-Fi. That road also goes past Siobhan MacNeill's family house – I wouldn't mind another look as we drive by.'

'And Dervaig?' Dee prompted.

'We go there next. It's a large enough island to keep secrets, but too small to hide two possible murders.'

TWENTY-NINE
MISSING

Siobhan slipped out of her family home with the practised ease of a multiple offender. Her brothers had both left whilst it was still dark, their attempts at stealth defeated by slamming the front door shut with such force that the entire house quaked in response. Her mother wouldn't be stirring for another hour at least. Only the dog noticed her leave, raising a heavy head from front paws and giving a languid swish of tail as if to wish her good luck – dark brown eyes non-judgemental.

Calum would be waiting for her in the holiday cottage up the hill, keeping out of sight so her mother couldn't try to stop them. Siobhan carried the smallest overnight bag, toiletries and a change of underwear and her money. On previous visits she'd managed to take enough to fill a suitcase, taken bit by bit without attracting any suspicion.

Why did her mother have such an aversion to them being together? Siobhan had broken the news to her a month ago, and instead of the expected encouragement, she reacted as if she'd seen a ghost and point-blank refused to accept their relationship had any chance of success.

He's not suitable. No career. He's never going to amount to

*anything. You can do better. He's not worth it. It's just something
that will blow over, he doesn't really love you.*

When that approach had failed to make her change her
mind, her brothers had been recruited to battle.

*Calum's an OK bloke, but I don't think he's right for you.
Calum? You can't be serious? Why not wait – the band's doing
well – there's no need to rush into anything.*

Why were they being so mean? Her mother had no reason
to dislike Calum. There was an absurd historical enmity
between their families going back generations, but that was all
ancient history now. Unless there had been something personal
between her mother and Calum's dad? Siobhan dismissed that
idea out of hand – every word her mother had to say about
Fraser Donald was to denigrate and criticise him as being
beneath contempt.

Her mother had also spoken with an almost visceral hatred
against Calum once she realised Siobhan was not going to be
swayed. It made no sense, neither to her nor to her brothers who
reluctantly sided with their mother to keep the peace. As a
result, she'd had to act alone and in secret. Keeping their relationship quiet from both families, hiding her liaisons from the
rest of the band and most difficult of all – pretending to have
finished with Calum and acting as everything was normal.

But today, all that would change. She had her car; the ferry
was booked, and she and Calum were going to leave the island
that had become their prison to start a new life on the mainland.
By the time either family knew where they were, it would be
too late – they'd be together and both parents would either
come around to that fact or she and Calum would never see
them again.

A pang of guilt hit her at the thought. Not so much at the
loss of her own family but for Calum and his sick dad. She'd
have to tell him.

With the handbrake released, the car freewheeled down the

drive, silent except for the crunch of gravel under tyres. Siobhan started the engine as the drive neared the road and turned towards Calum's temporary home. She'd be seeing him soon. The excitement almost made her dizzy – the two of them leaving this island, following their hearts and beginning afresh.

She'd tell him on the way to the ferry, explain this red-headed PI had cornered her in the pub toilets and she'd not believed her – thought she'd been put up to it by her mother as another sick ploy to flush Calum out after bad-mouthing him to everyone she knew on the island. It was a good excuse for not telling him immediately.

She approached blind corners with more care than usual. Even a small collision could be enough to make them miss the boat. The route up to his holiday home was up a rough track on the right. She sped up, ignoring the handwritten sign advising a 10mph speed limit, otherwise the drive wheels would lose grip and she'd never make it up. She stopped at a gate, opened it – there was the cottage ahead. She let the gate swing shut, jumped back in the car and drove the last fifty metres up to the newbuild. Calum would have seen the car, would be carrying suitcases out of the back door.

She'd say they could stop at the hospital for ten minutes. It was on the way to the ferry; they could spare the time. Calum could see his dad – if he was really there – tell him they were making a life together and explain how they could both come back to visit him properly once they'd found jobs and a place to stay.

Relieved at the thought of unburdening herself of an omission she'd felt guilty about ever since meeting the redhead, Siobhan turned around the final curve to the back of the cottage.

But Calum wasn't waiting there. The door remained shut.

He was probably still packing. Reassured, she ran to the door, let herself in and called out.

'Hurry up, Calum. We have to be at the ferry in an hour.'

The house was silent. No suitcases lined up at the door ready to be carried to the car.

'Calum?'

Adrenaline flooded her bloodstream, making her heart pound in her ears. Her hand sought balance on the nearest wall, the fight or flight reflex stultified with neither action being immediately required. Siobhan instinctively knew he wasn't there. She searched the spartan interior in a panic, hoping her initial feeling was wrong.

His bed had been slept in recently, his bags still unpacked. There was only the one thing missing, the most important treasure of them all.

Calum.

THIRTY

HAPPY FAMILIES

Siobhan returned to the family home in a state of near panic. Had Calum gone to her house despite the warning from her mother for him to never set foot there again? She'd have set the dog on him for sure. How could he have just disappeared when they had planned this day for weeks?

Her mother waited in the kitchen.

'Come back, then – have you?' The words dripped with sarcasm.

She was sitting at the table, toast cooling in a rack surrounded by pots of marmalade and jam. A glass teapot still had sufficient tea for another cup. Siobhan silently helped herself, filling a cup before trusting herself to answer.

'Have you seen Calum?'

Her mother winced as if she'd been wounded. She scowled in response, buttered a slice of toast and added a thick layer of marmalade.

Siobhan was tired of playing this game.

'Have you seen Calum?' she asked again, taking advantage of standing over her mother.

'No.' Her mother answered emphatically. 'I've not seen the

useless boy.' A smile played around the edges of her mouth. 'Has he left you? I always said he would. You should have listened to me.'

Siobhan felt the rage building inside her. The dog lay at her mother's feet, its eyes watching the interplay between mother and daughter as if it had seen this episode hundreds of times before.

'Have you said anything to him? Where is he?' Her mother knew something, she was sure of it.

'I wouldn't waste my breath on him.' She bit unconcernedly into the toast, teeth crunching the burned surface with evident satisfaction. Her eyes lit on Siobhan's with a hint of amusement.

'He could have gone straight to hell as far as I'm concerned.'

Siobhan struggled to keep it together.

'Why do you hate him? What has he ever done to make you like this?' She asked the question that had been there from the first time she'd met Calum, almost three months ago.

They'd been listening to a band in the pub on a cold February night. She and her two brothers, Duncan and Finlay, together with a bunch of mates. Siobhan was now something of a minor celebrity – her own band, Deò, had been booked for Celtic Connections in Glasgow. Everyone was convinced that a world tour was in the offing, recording contracts would follow, TV appearances, money for a big house on Mull. Everyone except Siobhan.

She was the one in the family with a level head and retained a realistic if slightly cynical view of life. A view in which a reasonably proficient clarsach player with an OK voice might play a few gigs but was never going to make it professionally. Besides, she knew the rest of the band would eventually go their own ways – off to university, take jobs that offered a living wage, move to the mainland. This was just a dream.

Duncan was the eldest of her siblings. Built like a rugby full-back, he'd taken to fishing as if born to it. Unimaginative, he took the first job that was offered to him – and with their father's boat lying idle since his death, it was a no-brainer. He took after their dad, quiet, thoughtful, kind. But he had his own problems, mostly concerning his mental health and the belief that he was somehow subject to madness.

Finlay was as different to Duncan as a sibling could possibly be. Small and wiry where his brother was tall and broad; sly and malicious where Duncan was straight and honest. Siobhan thought he had more growing up to do than any of them. He was also the one who took most after their mother, always seeing the worst in people.

She was the last of their MacNeill clan – an afterthought as far as she was concerned. Her mother fought with her from the beginning, laying down rules where her brothers had been allowed to run free. She was expected to help around the house with cleaning and cooking where Duncan and Finlay were there to be fed and looked after. Sometimes, she felt her mother didn't even like her at all – held a lifelong grudge against her for the sin of existing. She didn't take after either parent. Maybe that was her problem.

The band playing that night were shite. No surprise when the landlord paid in free drinks. They'd started all right – covers played well enough to be recognisable and sang along with, but as they consumed as many drinks as they could during the gig, the inevitable musical decline happened. It was part of the fun really – the band and the punters were all in on it. On the rare occasion, musical brilliance occurred as inhibitions were shed and previously unheard-of chords and harmonies spontaneously came into being. This wasn't one of those rare evenings.

Calum had been stuck on Mull. February ferries were notorious that way, and like any experienced islander he found a bed for the night and made for the bright lights of Tobermory. Attracted by the sound of a band, he'd ended up talking to

Siobhan and her brothers, then Siobhan alone when the music made anything other than one-on-one conversation impossible.

Does anyone know when they fall in love? Siobhan could place it around the point when the drummer fell off his stool and Calum sat in his place, hitting the drums with rhythmic precision if little skill. By that time of night, it didn't matter. Impressed by his musical prowess and seeing how well he'd been getting on with Siobhan, Duncan had offered him a job on the boat.

The universe turns on moments such as these, and Siobhan found herself swept along on a current over which she had no control, caught in the same flow as Calum. Two hapless sailors clinging on to each other with the same disbelief this was happening.

Then her mother met Calum for the first time a month ago and she looked as if she'd seen a ghost.

'Where are you from? Whose family? What's your dad's name?' The questions had been more interrogative than polite chat, each answer met with a more intense questioning.

'What the fuck was all that about with your mum?' Calum had asked.

Siobhan now waited for an answer.

THIRTY-ONE
MORAG

If looks could kill... Morag MacNeill ruminated as she chewed reflectively on her toast. Siobhan stood over her, hands clenched into fists. She'd always been the difficult child – headstrong, ruled by emotions, clever. Too clever. Cleverer than her brothers, although that wouldn't have been difficult. They took after their father.

Her daughter would wait there all day for an answer. She added stubborn to the list of personality traits, along with talented, pretty – and in love. Definitely in love – and that was a problem.

'Sit down.' The dog looked up at Morag from its reclining position on the floor with such confusion that she almost laughed. Almost.

Siobhan took the furthest chair she could at the other end of the table. She was, Morag knew, making a statement. Putting the distance between mother and daughter into physical terms. So, she'd finally found the courage to ask the single question that had been burning a hole in her since Calum had turned up that day in March.

Morag remembered she'd been in an unusually good mood.

The first real sun of the year, warm enough to hint at a summer that winter had erased from memory. A downpayment on a promise that the seasons do change. Eventually.

Her husband, Jack, had died a year ago, the previous winter. Ambushed by a cough which turned into covid, then into antibiotic resistant pneumonia and he was gone. No fanfare, no long farewell. Just gone. The family he'd left behind reacted like he was a player suddenly removed from the stage, hunting around for clues as to why he was no longer there. She felt cheated, more than anything. Deprived of their golden years. He'd finally admitted to himself he was getting too old to put out to sea – her partner of almost forty years. Beaten by time when the sea and seasons had been unable to tame him.

The children had coped in their own ways. Duncan committed it all to his diary, the written words expressing confusion and loss. His worry that he wouldn't live up to the role of breadwinner as his dad would have wanted. Forever pulling up short under his father's critical gaze. She used to regularly read his diaries, when he was a lot younger. Seen his young soul outlined in simple words and tortured cursive handwriting. Recognised the madness he tried to hide, recognised the same tides that pulled at her – that had led her astray.

Finlay dealt with it like a spoilt child. Angry that his dad had been taken, not knowing who to be angry with, so he took it out on everyone. Angry and calculating what inheritance would be left now the money had been reduced from an already low level to a laughably small amount. Except that there was nothing to laugh about.

Siobhan had taken it worse of all.

Siobhan had shed tears at the funeral service. Real tears. She should have put the rest of them all to shame. That omission could be pardoned, given enough time, but Siobhan would never be able to forgive her now.

'Well, are you going to tell me or just stare into the distance as if I'm not here?' Siobhan's angry shout made the dog's ears prick up.

Morag sipped at her tea, wishing it was something stronger. Even cyanide would be preferable.

'I was your age, once,' she began.

'Oh, for fuck's sake!'

'Young people forget that this is what they become,' Morag continued, unfazed by her daughter's outburst. 'You see wrinkles and infirmity.' She stared at her own hands, curled them backwards until the skin folded into waves. 'You can't imagine there's a young woman inside this tortoise skin.'

She had her attention at least. Siobhan's shaped brows curled down towards her fine, chiselled nose. His nose. Morag had recognised it as soon as she had been placed into her arms, red-faced and indignant at the rough medical handling as airways were cleared, umbilical cut.

Morag's breath left her body like Jack's last breath. Ragged and laboured, reluctant and final.

'You can't go out with Calum because he's your brother.' She lowered her head. There – she'd done it. Said the words that should never be said.

'What do you mean? He's not... How can Calum be my brother?'

Morag faced her daughter's accusative eyes, saw the intelligence that she'd admired in her father – that keen intellect so loving of art and music and, once upon a time, of her.

'Fraser Donald is your father,' Morag said simply.

Siobhan was shaking her head in denial. 'That isn't possible. How?'

'How do you think?' Morag asked quietly, wondering if Siobhan could see her as she was then, young and impetuous, skin pure and smooth, so very alive.

'No! You're making this up for some warped reason of your own. You never wanted me to be happy!' Siobhan's face expressed horror, turning to hate as she realised how manipulative her mother was.

'I'm sorry. I really am.' Morag surprised herself how badly she felt on Siobhan's behalf when it was her own sorrow that should have taken precedence. 'I was young. I thought I was in love – we both did.'

She saw them both, two lovers wrapped in each other's arms when the world was so much younger. If she could only go back. But the past could only ever be visited in her memories. Fraser brushing her face with his fingertips saying he couldn't leave his wife, *we're both married – we made vows*.

She hated him for his cowardice. Hated herself for the choices she'd made. Hated the daughter she carried from a husband she no longer loved. Siobhan would be Fraser's so he had no choice but to stay with her, no matter the truth of it. It had been her last roll of the dice, and he'd looked at her in sorrow, explained how Siobhan couldn't possibly be his.

Why should her daughter have the happiness she was denied?

'I hate you!' Siobhan spat the words at her.

Morag bowed her head in contrition. She deserved no less.

THIRTY-TWO
MURDER

Siobhan's house had offered no clues as they cruised slowly past the driveway gates, only reinforcing what he'd said about the family having fallen on hard times. Ivy clung to stone pillars supporting iron gates that sagged under the weight of years. The house itself could only be glimpsed through a tangled forest of rhododendrons, strangling the life out of any native plants.

'She's somehow involved in all this,' Teàrlach was speaking his thoughts out loud. 'We just have to understand how.'

'What do they do? The family?' Dee sat in the passenger seat, quieter than usual. She stared at the changing view, lost in her own thoughts.

'Originally made their money in the slave trade. Shipped manufactured goods from Glasgow to Africa, slaves from Africa to the Caribbean estates, sugar back to the UK.'

'Not still doing that, are they?'

Dee's face was so earnest that he had to laugh, then immediately felt guilty for finding anything about the family's history at all amusing.

'No, not sure what they do now. Live on investments I

guess, like most of the landed gentry.' He mused on her question for a while as he negotiated the blind turns on the single-track road hugging a cliff edge.

'Whatever money they once had must be long gone.' He quietened as his childhood memories returned.

Calgary Beach came back into view, the blue sky and spring sunshine turning the sea into a glorious shade of aquamarine. Where the white sand met the water, it looked like a tropical paradise, the last view those cleared from the land would have remembered in their new homes in Canada and the US – or those driven to the other side of the world to Australia and New Zealand. There was little difference to the slave trade, he realised. Landowners treating the poor like cattle, black or white alike treated with the same complete disregard for a shared humanity.

The café was closed. Like many of the businesses on the island which relied on the summer tourists, it lay mothballed and waiting for the return of the holiday home or camper migrants.

Teàrlach waited for an oncoming refuse truck to pass. 'We'll find something in Tobermory.'

'I need to find internet, otherwise I'm no use to you.'

'I wouldn't have put it as strongly as that.' He glanced at her expression, saw she wasn't being receptive to his comment.

'We'll find something. I swear the phone and internet follow the tides here – one moment there's a connection, the next moment it's gone.'

Teàrlach sped as fast as the road would allow, following the twists and turns towards the white tower of Kilmore Church that stood like a beacon at the edge of Dervaig.

'We in *Lord of the Rings* territory now?'

He had to laugh and was gratified to hear Dee joining him – her uncommonly dour mode forgotten if only for a moment.

'Aye, it's a bit like that.'

The church slid from view as they rounded a headland, then reappeared as the sun's rays fell on the white paint throwing into sharp relief against the blue sky. The road led around a pub before making a tortuous route upwards to cross the island's backbone, a telecoms mast planted on the nearest summit. Dee was now too busy with her phone as it entered into the range of 4G to engage in any more conversation, leaving Teàrlach alone with his thoughts.

Coming back to the island had been more traumatic than he'd imagined – returning to the place that had been his home as he grew from troubled child to almost a man. He missed his aunt more than he'd ever let himself realise; her presence was there in every place he went, her absence a wound as painful as the phantom knife in his side. There was so much he wanted to tell her, so many questions he needed to ask. Now it was too late.

'Still nothing on the police server about Calum, but there's been a development on this John Stevenson case.' Dee's quiet voice broke into his thoughts.

'What's it say?'

She looked at him with an expression so serious and unlike her usual cavalier attitude that he pulled into the first passing place.

'It's become a murder investigation.'

THIRTY-THREE
CHLOE

Chloe was on the train to Oban, rattling through Glasgow's urban outlands and making for the west coast. Her carriage was almost empty – a combination of travelling in the middle of the day and outwith any holiday season. She decided to continue working, reaching for the files she'd lifted before leaving the office and started to look for any connection between the dead photographer and missing fisherman. They were both based in Tobermory, that colourful port that served duty as Mull's largest town. Robert Jameson living with his partner in a tiny, terraced house high up above the harbour, whilst Calum Donald rented a guesthouse room facing out over the bay. His landlady had said she hadn't seen Calum since the day he was meant to have gone missing – she checked her notes – 7th April.

That was close in time to Robert Jameson's fall from the Staffa cliffs – 6th April. She read a news bulletin stating a drowned body had been recovered yesterday. John Stevenson, underwater sound recordist. Teàrlach had installed in her a strong distrust of coincidences, and these three events happening within days of each other on an otherwise quiet and incident-free island felt to her like they were connected.

Chloe settled back in her seat. Glasgow had been left behind and she started to breathe more easily as mountains and forest filled the view. She began drawing what links she knew connected the three men on the island, starting with a single circle on her notepad in which she added Robert Jameson and John Stevenson. She titled it Drowned, then thought for a while, then renamed it Nature Recording. A second circle she titled Missing and Calum Donald's name had sole occupation of this separate circle. The diagram mocked her with its simplicity and lack of any overlap. She found she was scratching her nose in concentration, rifling through the files in case anything else suggested itself.

Geography – Robert was from Mull, John from Fort William, Calum from Tiree. The only connection was the Isle of Mull where they were based during the time of the incidents – excepting Robert Jameson of course who died on the lonely and isolated island of Staffa.

Motive – here she drew a blank. If their deaths and Calum's disappearance were anything other than accidental, what possible reason was there?

Relationship – key to every investigation she'd helped with. What linked these three men? Did they even know each other?

What was missing? Chloe searched the landscape for inspiration. In the distance, she could make out a few intrepid walkers braving the changeable April weather as they trudged along the West Highland Way towards Fort William. Shadows chased across the mountains as cumulus clouds played hide and seek with the sun. Highland cattle watched her speed past with bovine unconcern, flicking their horns in irritation at the first flies.

History – what background did they have? Could they have met at university, did they have hobbies in common?

All Chloe's two Venn circles could tell her was that she was either missing a key part of the puzzle or these were isolated incidents with no common factors. She closed her notebook in disgust. Maybe Teàrlach and Dee had found something – in which case she could look afresh at her diagram. Until then, she may as well enjoy the view.

As the train approached Oban, Chloe caught her first sight of Loch Etive and the small yachts taking advantage of the weather. Her brows creased in thought as she recollected Dee's email that had arrived earlier that morning. The body that had been recovered, John Stevenson, his last recording finished with the sound of a boat. Calum was a fisherman, working from a boat that didn't exist according to marine registers. Robert Jameson's death, if it wasn't accidental, meant someone had arrived on Staffa on their own boat and left the same way after Robert's fall.

She opened her notepad, drew a large circle to encompass the three disparate cases and titled it Boat. Chloe had no idea how these deaths were related, but she was now as sure as she could be that a fishing boat connected everything together. They just had to work out how.

THIRTY-FOUR

SAM

Sam waved goodbye to the other photographers with an air of relief. He'd been cooped up with them for six days and decided to forgo the last day of the pre-booked tour. The minibus gave one last toot on the horn, and they all headed south in search of seals or otters or golden eagles – frankly Sam didn't care anymore. The ferry back to Oban was due in thirty minutes, and he was looking forward to meeting his partner and having another attempt at making both the campervan holiday and his flagging relationship a success.

He spent the time idly scrolling through the pictures he'd taken, viewing them on the small LCD screen. There were some good shots of Iona Abbey, although the grey sky had rendered the architecture two dimensional and monochrome. The golden eagle snaps were simply that, and not particularly good snaps. The bird, large as it was, remained an insignificant dot in the centre of the frame. Magnification resulted in so much pixelation he could be looking at a mutated sparrow by the time the image filled the screen.

He sighed, looked down guiltily at the aluminium case by his feet. It had been an impulse. What did he need with another camera? Sam rationalised the purchase in strictly financial terms. His fellow passenger on the tour, the corpulent character that he'd instinctively disliked, had offered to sell him his camera for cash at well under its true value. Sam had thought he was the target of some elaborate joke, had even explained that the lenses alone must be worth a few thousand, but the offer had been genuine.

'I can't really get on with it. Too many controls and options. I'm happier with my previous camera than all this technology.'

'You're selling it for a thousand?'

'Cash.'

Sam had spent last evening considering the guy's offer. A quick search on the web had convinced him he could turn an instant profit selling it on, maybe double or triple what he wanted in payment. He had £500 still in cash and there was a bank on the sea front with a cash dispenser – a rare enough occurrence for Sam to take it as a sign. It happily regurgitated £250 last night, then another £250 this morning. They'd completed the transaction as the ferry terminal came into view, Sam lifting the aluminium case out of the back of the minibus under the relieved face of his fellow passenger. He gave Sam the impression of someone who'd made a Faustian pact with the devil and managed to turn it around.

Struck with the sudden realisation that he may have been had, Sam hastily opened the case to check the contents. It was all there – top of the range Canon with remote, telephoto, macro and standard lenses, charger, spare SD cards. He'd struck gold!

An influx of passengers joined him in the queue as a CalMac ferry made slow progress towards the jetty. Car doors slammed in the lines of traffic awaiting boarding, staff heading towards moorings and traffic control. He shut the case, leaving a closer inspection until he was on board.

The stream of vehicles leaving the ferry began as soon as the boat had come to a halt, and Sam waited for the foot passengers to make their way down the covered walkway. A woman with tight black braids caught his eye, unusual enough to stand out from the crowd. She carried an overnight bag and files under her left arm. He idly considered whether she might be a solicitor, or estate agent. They exchanged a glance as she drew near, as if she'd been aware of his casual observation.

Lawyer, Sam decided. Anyone with that look of troubled preoccupation had to be a lawyer.

His queue started moving up the pedestrian ramp, and he forgot all about her. Ensconced in the on-board lounge, Sam began looking at the camera in detail. He was surprised to see the previous owner's photographs hadn't been deleted, feeling a vicarious thrill in searching the library in case it showed anything other than wildlife. In that regard he was disappointed. There were also a few shots of the sea and fishing boats, so he wasn't the only one to find artistic value in the subject matter, but his interest was raised when puffins showed up on the monitor. The trip out to Staffa had been cancelled and nowhere on their travels had they been anywhere near puffins. They were good shots as well, far better than the locations he recognised from travelling the length and breadth of the island. It was almost as if the first photographs were happy accidents, well exposed, sharply focussed, imaginatively framed. Maybe he'd managed a trip out before joining the minibus tour?

They were all amazing photographs except for one shot of puffins awkwardly flying in to land. The camera must have panned out in a hurry to catch the birds as they approached. They may have been the first birds to return to the small island, and fortuitously the sun had made a rare appearance to illuminate their bright colours. Bright orange beaks and feet almost glowed out of the screen. The shots were good enough to be taken for publication in a magazine.

THIRTY-FIVE

FISH'N'CHIPS

Chloe checked her phone – 3:20 p.m. She hadn't received any acknowledgement from Teàrlach – not entirely surprising considering he had complained about the lack of a signal around the island. Craignure offered little in the way of diversions whilst she waited, a few shops, tourist information and a couple of cafés. A mostly blue sky suggested the weather would remain dry for an hour at least, so she explored the small port, wrapping her jacket close to overcome the chill April wind blowing inland off the sea.

Now that the ferry traffic had left, the village returned to peace and quiet as the shops waited for the next arrival. Chloe wondered what it would be like to live in a place like this, subject to its own tidal system of passengers making their way to and fro in synchronicity with the large CalMac ferries. She had felt a sense of isolation as the ship departed, a feeling of being abandoned and no longer connected to the larger mass of humanity on the mainland. The thought troubled her in a way she couldn't articulate.

Teàrlach's car horn alerted her to his arrival. Dee sat in the passenger seat, strangely subdued and only able to give a faint smile of welcome.

'Was your trip OK?' Teàrlach asked.

He gave the impression of being distracted, worry etched on his forehead. Had something happened?

'Aye. All good.' Chloe saw Teàrlach noticeably start to relax. 'How are you two getting on?'

She climbed into the back whilst Teàrlach stored her bag in the boot and slammed it shut.

'Slightly surreal,' Dee responded. 'Teàrlach's cottage has been frozen in time – still is freezing, so I hope you've brought your woollies.'

'I'll crank the heating into life when we get back,' Teàrlach joined the conversation. 'And I'll pick up some things: bedding, food—'

'And wine.' Dee interrupted. 'I hope you don't mind sharing a bed?' She glanced over her shoulder as the car pulled away from the kerb.

'No. Whatever. Any port in a storm.' She'd picked an appropriate metaphor at least.

'You can have my bed, Chloe.' Teàrlach searched for her in the rear-view mirror. 'Just need to find more sheets for you. I'll be OK on the settee.'

Chloe watched as the island slid by her windows, the shoreline briefly joining the road. Old hulks had been abandoned, timbers blackened with age and supporting each other in their last moments, waiting patiently for time and a storm to provide the final coup de grace.

'Have we made any progress on the photographer and missing fisherman?' Chloe was keen for an update – hard facts to fill in her prototype Venn diagram.

'Dee's found something of interest on the police server. There's something strange about the deaths, especially the one we're not paid to investigate.'

'Is this the body the police divers recovered?' She opened her notebook in readiness.

'Aye,' Teàrlach replied. 'They found him with his arm stuck in a creel underwater.'

'Stuck in a steel trap,' Dee interjected. 'If he hadn't left a pile of clothes on the shore, no one would have thought of looking for him there. Good way of disposing of a body actually,' she added thoughtfully. 'Hey, we could have fish and chips on the way. There's this neat little silver van parked up...'

'God, Dee.' Chloe could feel a gag reflex coming on and had to stop speaking until it passed. 'How can you talk about that and then suggest we all eat fish and chips?'

'Have to eat,' she replied, untroubled by Chloe's outburst. 'Besides, he wasn't fish food and the cod they sell here are mostly from Norway and Greenland, not off the bloody pier in Tobermory.'

'We're going to be there anyway, it's on route,' Teàrlach broke in. 'It's not a bad idea, cooking at the cottage is going to be tricky until I've bought more gas. We can bring you up to speed with what we've been working on.'

Chloe settled into the back seat. A heron high-stepped delicately along the nearby shore, focussed on its own meal. Ahead of them the road twisted along the coast and towards Tobermory. When she caught site of the colourful buildings along the sea front, she instantly relaxed. How could anything dark and dangerous exist in such a pretty place?

THIRTY-SIX
VENN

Teàrlach opened the cottage door whilst Dee and Chloe were collecting the shopping and luggage from the car. The light was already beginning to fade, the western sun having been submerged in a bank of dark clouds massing ominously on the sea's horizon as night approached.

'Well, this is cosy.' Chloe stared at the cottage with an expression that gave lie to her words.

'Will be once I manage to get the heating to work.' Teàrlach gave a wry smile and led the way inside, flicking a light switch and still surprised that a bulb lit up on command.

Dee brought up the rear, struggling with two laden shopping bags. 'Probably something to do with the wood burner not being used for two years.' She dumped them on the kitchen table, pulling out the two wine bottles that had advertised their presence with the unmistakable sound of glass on glass.

'This will help.' She went in search of glasses, then started washing them once they'd been found.

'Sorry, Chloe.' Teàrlach had noticed she was still standing in the doorway. 'This will be your room.' He led the way down the corridor to his bedroom, wishing he'd cleared out the mementos from his childhood. 'This will only be for a couple of days. Thanks for offering to help, it's not going to be much of a holiday for you.'

'Don't worry about it,' she responded, dropping her bag on Teàrlach's bed. 'I've brought the files – not that there's much in them. What do you want me to do, now that I'm here?'

It was a good question. They were in a cottage, perched on the edge of an island in the Inner Hebrides, with Dee missing the internet and no easy way of finding out what was going on...

'I made a start on looking for anything linking the two deaths – Robert Jameson and John Stevenson.' Chloe was waving her notebook at him.

Teàrlach shook his head in admiration. Chloe was like a dog with a bone, not letting go until she'd extracted every last morsel of nourishment.

'Let's go back to the kitchen, at least there's a table there.'

Dee had her back to them, watching the sky stain red. She turned when they came in, and Teàrlach saw she'd made a start on the wine.

'Some view you have.' Dee gestured to the worktop surface where an open bottle was keeping two empty glasses company. 'We should make a toast, now we're all together.'

Chloe was happy to join in, filling the two glasses and passing one over to Teàrlach. They looked at him expectantly.

Teàrlach held his glass, debated what to say.

'Are you going to make a toast or stand there looking at it all night?'

He engaged with Dee, saw the laughter had returned to her eyes. Chloe stood next to her, happy just to be there.

'Here's to us.' Their glasses met over the table and Teàrlach drank, the red wine efficiently cleansing the greasy aftertaste of a fish supper.

Chloe opened her notepad to show two circles drawn independently of one another, a larger one containing everything.

He struggled to read her writing in the dim kitchen light, making out Nature and Missing as the labels for the smaller circles, then read the names written inside.

'What are we looking at, Chloe?'

'This is a Venn diagram. I was looking for anything that connected the two deaths and the missing fisherman.'

'And?' Dee questioned with interest.

'And this circle,' Chloe pointed to the large circle drawn around her page, 'this is the only common factor linking all three cases.'

Teàrlach exchanged a look with Dee.

'This is the boat. Calum worked as a fisherman; Robert needed a boat to get to Staffa and so would anyone else if he was killed there. Then John Stevenson's last recording was of a boat.' She sat back with an air of satisfaction.

An hour later and Chloe needed to find a larger sheet of paper. Circles filled the sheet: one for each of the dead men and one for Calum Donald – but now Chloe was adding more.

'The fishing boat links Calum and one was also recorded by John Stevenson,' she intersected both character's circles with a new one marked Boat. 'Recording equipment, camera and sound gear, belonging to Robert Jameson and John Stevenson – not sure what significance that has, if any.' Another circle linked the two men. 'And Calum was engaged to Siobhan MacNeill, whose voice was recorded by John Stevenson under the water.'

'Is she meant to be a bloody mermaid?' Dee was already eying up the second bottle with an expression that suggested she shouldn't have stopped at two.

'I'm only putting down the facts,' Chloe replied tartly. 'And her voice links Calum and John.' Her pencil completed another circle.

Teàrlach was looking at six circles with very little overlap between them.

'Not sure that this helps all that much, Chloe,' he said tentatively.

'If there's a boat connecting all these events, it will. That's what we're missing – otherwise it *is* just a coincidence that both men died within days of each other.'

'Aye, OK. We'll do more work on it. Siobhan's holding something back, I'm sure. John Stevenson had been receiving death threats and something made him dive to that creel.'

'Death threats?' Chloe asked. 'Are we investigating his death too?' She poured another glass of wine before Dee finished the bottle.

'I was looking for any updates on Robert Jameson's death or Calum Donald's disappearance and found this.' She selected a file containing photographs copied from Oban's police server.

Chloe moved in closer to examine the steel jaws at the mouth of the creel.

'That's not normal – is it?'

'No. Someone went to a lot of trouble to make sure anyone putting their hand inside wasn't ever going to be taking it out again. What we don't know is what's in the package he died trying to retrieve from inside the creel.' Teàrlach reached for the wine bottle only to discover it was empty.

Dee took that as her cue to open the second bottle, poured a measure into Teàrlach's glass and generously refilled her own.

'I'm working on it,' Dee spoke as her glass made steady progress towards her mouth. She took a swig and continued as soon as she'd swallowed. 'Forensics are taking their sweet time in raising a report. I'll check in again tomorrow.'

Chloe's pen hovered over her diagram. 'You think his death is connected to our two cases?'

He shrugged. 'Lucy's convinced that her husband was murdered on Staffa. It looks like an accident to me, but if there's anything connecting Robert Jameson and this John Stevenson, then we may have to take her concerns more seriously.'

'Or if there's a connection between either of them and Calum Donald.' Chloe was drawing another, tenuous link on her notebook.

Outside the window the last light had leached from the sky, leaving a pitch-black world beyond the meagre reach of the cottage lights. Teàrlach took stock of the information they had on the three men – it wasn't anything like enough.

'OK. Tomorrow I'll have another try at talking to Siobhan. She's the only one who's likely to know what's happened to Calum. We should be able to solve this case at least. As for Robert Jameson, unless we track down whoever has his camera, I can't see his being anything other than a tragic accident.' Teàrlach watched as Dee sunk another glass of wine.

THIRTY-SEVEN

SECRETS

Teàrlach had opened up about his time growing up in this small cottage. He'd kept Chloe company until almost midnight, telling her about his shock at finding himself at a primary school with only seven pupils and one teacher. She could imagine him, a wee Glasgow boy suddenly immersed in a completely different world where school trips were by boat to the other islands, often cut short when approaching storms threatened.

Now Teàrlach was crashed out on the couch in the small living space. Dee's bedroom light had gone off at 10 p.m. and Chloe sat at the desk in Teàrlach's old bedroom feeling wide awake.

Chloe decided to spend the hours idly going through Teàrlach's bookcase. For the most part they consisted of action books – spy thrillers and crime paperbacks. She smiled at the thought that his reading material might have influenced his choice of career – the military police and then becoming a private investigator. At least he was consistent. She'd studied computer science in Glasgow, could have done well if it wasn't for getting involved with drugs. And then the pregnancy.

She rarely thought about the abortion. It was still too painful for her. That life was behind her now, thanks in no small part to Teàrlach. If he hadn't found her...

Her parents had asked him to look for her. She'd dropped out of their lives, had stopped all communication and they had imagined the worst. Except they couldn't imagine how rapidly her life had deteriorated – to the point she was selling her body for the next fix. After losing the baby, she'd hit rock bottom, and she'd attempted to take her own life but managed to fuck that up as well. Toes barely touching the floor when the rope stretched under her weight and leaving her dancing for hours until he found where she lived and broke down the door. She owed him more than could ever be repaid. Taking her in, cleaning her up, keeping the circumstances of her discovery to himself so her family remained ignorant of the truth.

Her hands reached for a large paperback copy of *Lord of the Rings*. The pages were well-thumbed – this must have been one of Teàrlach's favourites. She tried to reconcile what she knew of the serious private investigator with him reading about hobbits and elves and failed. The title page had an inscription, and she moved it closer to the desk lamp to read writing so faint it had almost disappeared.

To our darling boy, happy xmas, Mum and Dad xxx

Chloe's eyes moistened. This must be one of the few mementos he still had from his parents. She flicked through the pages, intrigued to see what else she could find, and a single sheet of paper fell out onto the desk.

Chloe held a handwritten note, reading the words with guilty interest before the meaning hit her square in the chest.

Darling Teàrlach,

I know that one day you'll be back to collect this book because it means so much to you. This is a cowardly way of reaching out to you, but I couldn't bear to tell you myself – not when I know how much you'll be hurt by what I have to say.

Your father contacted me, told me he wanted nothing more than to be back with your mother and bring the family together. He can be very convincing, and in my heart, I wanted nothing more than for you all to be happy again.

I told him where your mother was staying, in the sheltered flat. I thought she'd be safe there, if anything happened. I could never imagine he'd do what he did.

You know I love you dearly as if you were my own child. I can never forgive myself for being so stupid, but I was trying to do the right thing. I was trying to make it all work out for you all.

I take the knowledge that I'm responsible for their death to my grave. I know I don't have long left myself and I've made sure I'll never be a burden to you.

I hope you find it in your heart to forgive me, Teàrlach. I love you so much.

Your aunt Rosie

Chloe carefully re-folded the paper and held it tight in her fingers, undecided what to do next. Should she replace the note back where she'd found it? Teàrlach was unlikely to open the book for a while, maybe for years. She had no right to interfere, yet the thought of his finding this when he was still emotionally vulnerable made her uneasy. Chloe followed her instincts and hid it in her overnight bag before putting the book back on the shelf. This was one small thing she could do for him – there was nothing to be gained from him reading this letter. It would only bring him more pain.

THIRTY-EIGHT
STORM

Sergeant Suzie Crammond was off duty. Her shift had finished four hours ago and Tobermory had been entrusted to PCs Clare Pringle and William Aitkin. Her feet were up on the sofa, mug of tea and open packet of biscuits in her lap. Normally, she'd be enjoying a large glass of Prosecco, but it was a Saturday night – and unlikely as it was for the small tourist town to erupt in a riot, the recent discovery of the drowned sound recordist had unsettled her. Her fourteen-year-old daughter curled up companionably at her side, the TV shining a spotlight on ambitious American moms and their diva dancing daughters.

She treasured these rare moments of calm, a lull before the next inevitable hormone-fuelled swing changed her daughter from sweet love to feral hate. The TV show washed over her, young girls strutting athletic dance moves and pouting redly for the camera and fame. Off stage, their mothers displayed steely resolve, so the bitchiness only showed in their eyes.

Rio ostensibly watched the show for the dancing and to cheer on her favourite, but Suzie knew her interest was on the unwritten dialogue powering each unscripted comment from the moms. It was an education, of sorts. A glimpse into another, more exotic version of adulthood far removed from their Inner Hebridean home. As exotic as her name.

They'd chosen Rio after deciding that's where they'd be going for the big holiday – the one they'd painstakingly saved for over two long years since the wedding. Brazil remained an unreachable dream when Rio arrived, unexpected and unplanned. Her tiny pink fingers clutching at life and a future where anything was possible – including her husband taking fright at becoming a dad when he still had a life to live.

She wondered what her ex-husband would be doing now. Drinking in some Glasgow bar, making eyes at some lass stupid enough to see anything worthwhile in a serial loser. Two more years and he could stop paying maintenance, unless Rio carried on to university. Not much hope of that – neither parent had excelled in academia.

The wind had stepped up a notch, rattling the windows like a poltergeist. That was another reason for staying off the alcohol – this was the sort of night when ships came to grief. She could only hope no one was stupid enough to be out in weather like this. It wouldn't be long before Rio's easy acceptance of a night in with her mum became an anathema. What then? Her imagination crawled the few streets of the town, searching for Rio in the wind and rain.

Suzie extended an arm, hugged Rio close and wished life could just stay as it was forever. She'd have given anything for that moment of shared love to stay. But Rio was growing older, would need to make her own mistakes and learn to live with them. And she'd be left alone, like an island. There was a fragment of poetry she half remembered from school 'no man is an island' – they got that wrong. We're all fucking islands, every single one of us.

The phone rang, as she knew it would.

'Suzie Crammond.' She took her mobile through to the

kitchen, away from the nasal tones coming out of the small TV speakers.

'Sarge. Sorry to disturb you, but Siobhan MacNeill's just been into the station.'

She waited for PC Aitkin to get to the point.

'She's a bit upset,' he added. 'She says that Calum Donald has gone missing, and she thinks her brother, Duncan, may have something to do with it.'

Suzie remembered the private investigator telling her he'd been asked to look for Calum. Calum's dad was still in no fit state to provide a statement in the hospital.

'Is she there now? In the station?'

'No, ma'am. I told her there wasn't much we could do. Not right away. I said we'd require her to make a statement, but when I returned with the logbook, she'd already left.'

'Where is she now?' Suzie held her impatience in check.

'I don't know. She didn't say anything else – just went back out into the storm.'

THIRTY-NINE
SUZIE

Suzie drove around Tobermory, searching for Siobhan or her car. It was almost 10 p.m., and the streets were deserted apart from those making a pilgrimage along the wind-swept sea front from one pub to another. She'd driven to the station and interrogated PC William Aitkin about Siobhan's visit. The storm had almost reached its zenith, catching the small police station and the higher streets of Tobermory full on. There'd be trees and power lines down for sure. It wasn't a night to be out and about – not if you had any sense.

'She was in a bit of a state, to be honest. Seemed to think that Calum Donald had gone missing and was in some kind of danger.' He'd delivered a synopsis of the message he'd provided over the phone in a laconic Somerset drawl, the final syllable dragging on forever.

'What do you mean by "state"?' she'd asked.

He'd given her question his full consideration before venturing an opinion.

'She was borderline hysterical. Said Duncan had done away with him or some such nonsense. I don't think that family are the full shilling.'

'And you let her go out in that state on a night like this?'

He'd shrugged. 'Had to man the station. No telling what could happen in a storm – ships at sea, trees down. I couldn't just go chasing after her.'

Not when the station had central heating and remained dry. The cynical thought that he'd make certain progress in the ranks returned.

'And you've no idea where she was going?'

He'd shrugged and added helpfully, 'Could have gone anywhere.'

'Did she have her car?'

'Don't know. The wind was making too much noise to hear if she drove away. Is there a problem?'

Suzie had left him in disgust, driving slowly around the town in case Siobhan had run off into the night.

She found Siobhan's car parked facing the harbour, and climbed out only to stagger in the face of strengthening winds powering in from the sea. The car was empty. Struck with a premonition, Suzie clasped a white metal railing and swept her torch along the exposed beach below. The tide was almost fully in. Salty foam sprayed her face as a massive wave reached the stone wall, She could feel the force of the impact through the soles of her feet. If Siobhan was distraught enough to take her own life...

Suzie dismissed the thought before it fully formed. She couldn't imagine another death on the island, not in such quick succession. Turning her head to face out of the wind, she made for Siobhan's most likely refuge.

The pub was packed. Not just the usual regulars but every sailor who'd sought shelter in the harbour had gathered in Tobermory's favourite watering hole. Suzie had to push her way past the press of bodies to get inside. She forced her way to the bar, flashing her warrant card at visitors who took exception to her queue-jumping.

'Have you seen Siobhan MacNeill?' She had to shout at the barman to be heard.

A finger pointed to the back room where the younger folk hung around the pool tables. She nodded her thanks and forced her way to the back of the pub, breathing a sigh of relief as the crowd thinned. Siobhan sat at a table, working her way through a row of shots to the enthusiastic cheers of her friends.

'Siobhan, can I have a word?'

Her friends quickly melted away into the corners, leaving the two of them as the centre of attention.

'Can we talk outside?' Suzie asked. The thought of the brewing storm made this an unwelcome prospect, but she needed privacy.

'There's nothing you can't say to me here,' Siobhan's words slurred in response. She stared belligerently into Suzie's face as if she was the reason for all her problems.

'I'm only here to help.' Suzie caught the sound of derisive laughter from the onlookers. She ploughed on regardless. 'You said Calum has gone missing. What can you tell me?'

Siobhan raised her head from a contemplation of the row of shots. Red rimmed eyes peered bleakly out of wrecked mascara.

'What can you do? The policeman in the station couldn't even be bothered to get off his arse. Calum could be out there, needing help!' Siobhan's voice edged towards hysteria.

'If you can tell me what has happened, where you last saw him. What makes you think he's in trouble?'

An air of silence descended upon the pool tables. Suzie faced down the curious onlookers. 'Get on with your game, this is a private conversation.'

She was met with a sullen response, but the volume level returned to a high enough level to afford them some privacy. Suzie leaned in close enough to smell the alcohol on Siobhan's breath.

Siobhan hesitated, then clearly decided she had nothing to lose.

'We were both planning to go away together, this morning. We'd arranged it weeks ago – ever since my mum and Calum's dad said they were dead set against us getting together. I went to pick him up early this morning and he wasn't there. His bags hadn't been packed. I've looked everywhere. Something's happened to him, I know it has.'

Siobhan grabbed a shot and downed it before the tears could start again.

'Could he have changed his mind?'

Suzie was met with a look of contempt.

'That's what my mum said – amongst other things. He loves me. We love each other.' She spoke with the conviction of youth.

Suzie thought of her own man, his declaration of love and how gullible she had been at that age.

'Men change their minds,' she said simply.

'Not Calum.' Siobhan started toying with the next glass. 'We both wanted the same thing. Away from here.'

'Tell me where he was staying. I'll have a look first thing tomorrow and I'll make sure everyone keeps an eye out for him. He couldn't have gone to see his dad in hospital?'

Siobhan's head jerked up. 'How do you know about that?' Her expression veered from surprise through to hope in the space of a second.

'I was called in when he collapsed on Thursday. He was taken to Craignure Hospital.' Suzie grabbed at the most likely scenario with a sense of relief. 'I'll call the hospital now, see if he's there or has been to visit since this morning.'

Siobhan's hopeful expression remained locked on her as she made the call, turning back to fear as she relayed the news that he hadn't made an appearance.

'Look, I'm sure it's nothing to be worried about. What's the address?'

Siobhan gave her the holiday let details. 'He's cleared everything out. I thought he might be in here.' She looked around her in the hope that Calum might still miraculously appear.

'Look, Siobhan. I'll send a constable out to the holiday let this evening. I bet that's where he is. Why don't you go home and I can contact you there if we find him?' She viewed the number of empty glasses with concern and made a swift calculation. 'Is there someone who can drive you?'

'I'm not going home,' Siobhan said in a tone that indicated she wouldn't be swayed. 'I'll stay here in case he turns up.'

Suzie engaged with her combative stare and decided not to push. 'If that's what you want to do. Just don't do anything stupid – will you promise me that?'

'I'm not driving anywhere if that's what you mean.'

She gave a sharp nod. 'We'll see if we can find him.' Suzie made to stand, then returned to a sitting position. 'One last thing – when you spoke to the policeman on duty, you said something about Calum's disappearance being Duncan's fault. What did you mean by that?'

'Nothing. He's just been behaving weirder than usual. They're good mates, he wouldn't do anything to harm Calum.'

Suzie had the strong impression that Siobhan was trying to convince herself more than anything.

'I'll be in touch tomorrow – or tonight if we find him. Try not to worry.'

Suzie could feel Siobhan's gaze on her as she left the pub. She couldn't leave Rio alone for long – not on a night like this.

FORTY

GULLS

Dee left the cottage at 7 a.m., an hour after dawn and light enough for her to make careful progress up the rough driveway with the bike threatening to slide at any moment. Teàrlach had been awake, sat nursing a mug of coffee on the settee. He'd asked her if she'd slept OK – he didn't look as if he'd slept well at all. Shutting the metal gate behind her, ears tortured by the protesting screech of a metal bolt, she kept a watchful eye out for sheep who sensibly preferred to sleep on a dry road rather than wet grass.

Tobermory remained mostly asleep, the nine hundred or so inhabitants easily outnumbered by the gulls colonising the sea front as the weather worsened at sea. The birds vocalised their displeasure at Tobermory's tardiness with their repeating unmusical klaxons, circling the front like noisy feathered alarm clocks. Only the fishermen stirred, small boats being prepared at the old stone pier in the middle of the town for the day's salty harvest.

Dee set her bike onto its stand, removed her helmet and locked it to the bike. She shivered in the morning air, a touch too fresh for a habitual city dweller, and opened her laptop. Teàrlach was right – there was a free internet signal. She needed a coffee and somewhere warm to park herself.

A light went on in the building she had mistaken for the ferry terminal, followed by a sandwich board being taken out and placed in front of outdoor seating. Dee needed no further encouragement. Minutes later, she was out of the wind in a warm café table where she still had internet.

The police server displayed the latest reports. The first one to catch her eye was a report that Calum Donald had been listed as a missing person last night. She copied the detail, with the PC's name who was on duty at Tobermory police station – a PC William Aitkin. Siobhan MacNeill's name was mentioned as having raised the report. If she didn't know where he was, Teàrlach wasn't going to have much success interviewing her.

Dee was aware of someone walking towards her table and saved the latest reports on her hard drive to look at in private. Her screen now showed an innocent graphical representation of data download. A young waitress stood with a pad ready to take her order, wearing an expression that spoke of wanting to be anything other than a waitress in a small town café.

'You travelling on your own, then?' the waitress asked.

Dee switched her attention from a slowly rising count of gigabytes downloaded to see the waitress looking over her shoulder at the screen.

'Aye, touring the island. Lucky you open so early – I was in danger of freezing to death outside.'

They both stared at Dee's screen.

'Is that a game?' The waitress was at most eighteen. Her bored eyes locked onto Dee's.

'Sort of.' Dee saw a younger version of herself in the girl's eyes. A mask of ennui to cover the lack of experience, adopting a world-weary persona to face a confusing world.

'Just doing some work,' Dee added vaguely.

The interest in the girl's expression faded along with the mention of work.

'Can I get you something?'

'Full Scottish breakfast and coffee please.' Dee glanced over to the entrance as a couple entered. The waitress left her to deal with new customers.

Dee confirmed the waitress was too busy to come back to her table for a while and opened the data packages. There hadn't been any developments on Robert Jameson's death. It looked like he was going to remain an accidental death – the coroner had nothing to add to that. Her eyes opened larger when she opened the investigation into the sound recordist.

Forensics had provided a write-up on the mysterious package that he'd died trying to reach. It was a battery-operated Dictaphone, the sort of device used to take audio notes for transcribing into print. It had been sealed in PVC plastic to keep it waterproof and left playing the same recording over and over until the batteries had run down.

She made a start on the coffee and the breakfast. What possible reason would anyone have for putting an audio recording underwater? Then she realised the only person ever likely to be able to hear such a thing was the underwater sound recordist the trap had caught.

Dee read on. There were additional notes about the death threats made via social media. The police were convinced they were sent from John Stevenson's hometown of Fort William, but only based on the information they'd gleaned from the sender's profile which Dee felt was almost certainly fake.

There was a section on forensics inability to find any fingerprints or DNA evidence on the actual device which Dee skipped, until she reached a copy of the recording. She popped a single AirPod in and pressed play.

The now familiar sound of a woman's voice singing underwater played in her ear. Dee listened intently, screening out the random sounds of the ocean until she was certain. She was listening to Siobhan MacNeill's voice. Was this what had lured the sound recordist to his death?

The waitress arrived to clear her plate away, then frowned when she saw how much had been left untouched.

'I'm sorry, I'd thought you'd finished.'

Dee came back to reality with a jerk.

'Aye. All done.' She gave the waitress her plate.

'Was everything all right?'

Dee had lost all interest in breakfast and half the meal remained untouched.

'Yes, lovely. I'm watching my weight,' she improvised.

The waitress nodded unhappily in shared misery and left her alone once more.

Dee stared out at a quiet island town as it slowly awakened, switched her view to the sea and distant mountains and wondered who would go to the trouble of designing such a trap to catch the only person capable of discovering it.

FORTY-ONE
THE DEAD

Teàrlach stood in the open doorway, looked out across the sheltered waters of the bay and felt as if the last twenty years had never happened. Nothing much had changed from when he'd first arrived here as a young boy – the same view of the outer islands; the same sounds of birdsong and sheep; familiar smell of bracken and salt on the air. Chloe was active in the kitchen, hunting for pots and plates. He could imagine his aunt was still there with him, making breakfast or taking out a freshly baked loaf; saw himself exploring the foreshore, swimming in the freezing sea. The fiction provided comfort in the same way morphine dulls the senses. An escape from harsh reality.

But nothing ever remains the same. The land had grown new homes and new scars; the sea now home to salmon farms and microplastics. His aunt now gone, like the generations of people before her, and her only legacy the four stone walls at his back, an abandoned grave and his fading memory of her.

Dee had left the cottage as soon as it was light enough to do so. She'd been monosyllabic in response to his greeting, likely still worrying about the wisdom of tracking down her parents. He'd listened to the sound of her motorbike being erased by distance whilst he wandered down the pasture to linger on the view, judging the day was set to be overcast and threatening a storm. Teàrlach returned inside to find Chloe frying up a breakfast.

'I'm making bacon and eggs,' she announced as he entered. 'Assume you want some?'

'Aye. There's coffee as well.' Teàrlach reached for a cupboard only for Chloe to indicate the cafetiere already full on the kitchen table.

'Call yourself a detective,' she said scornfully.

Teàrlach gave a wry smile in response, poured them both a cup.

'So, what are we going to do about the missing fisherman and the two drowned guys?' Chloe's tone was businesslike as she spooned the contents of a frying pan onto two plates.

'The dead can wait.' Teàrlach picked up his cutlery, cut into a rasher. 'I want to prioritise the search for Calum Donald, the missing fisherman.' He thought of the young man's father, dying in a hospital bed in Craignure; the way he'd spoken as if he knew his son was already dead. Siobhan had claimed to have seen Calum recently – had promised Dee that she'd tell him about his father and the urgent need to visit him in hospital, but he'd heard nothing since Friday evening. Something wasn't right and Siobhan's family were involved, one way or another. Fraser Donald only had so long left to live, and his son was still missing. His sense of urgency increased with each passing hour Calum remained undiscovered.

'What can I do? I may be on holiday, but I'd rather be doing something useful.' Chloe's chin was raised in defiance.

'OK. This is what we've got.' Teàrlach prepared to count each relevant piece of information on his fingers.

'He's alleged to have gone out fishing on the *Morning Dew* first light 6th. There's no record of any commercial fishing vessel with that name operating anywhere in Scottish waters. That's our first problem.' Teàrlach folded down his thumb.

'Hang on, my notepad's here.' Chloe jumped up from the small table, returned with a notepad and pen and started writing.

'Fraser Donald told me the skipper assured him that everyone returned to shore, but he had a suspicion that something happened on the boat that the crew are covering up.'

'Who's the skipper? Do we have any names for the crew?' Teàrlach folded a finger to join his thumb.

'I can't find the crew from a boat that doesn't exist. Fraser Donald says he talked to the skipper, so he knows who he is, but I'm doubting what he's told me.'

'You think he's making this all up for some reason?' Chloe puzzled from the other side of the table.

Teàrlach shook his head. 'He wasn't lying to me, I'm as certain of that as I can be.'

'So, what's going on with an imaginary boat? It's not that easy to fake a boat's name – my brother confirmed you need transponders and licences if you're fishing commercially.'

'I think it was real, for him.' He hurried on before Chloe could interrupt. 'Fraser Donald's brain cancer – his memories can be affected; his grip on reality is no longer as it was. He may have simply muddled up the name of the boat.'

'Is there another way of finding out what boat he was on?'

'We just ask fishermen at Tobermory. It's not that big a place that they don't all know one another. Then we talk to the skipper and crew to find out when Calum was last seen.'

'What about his girlfriend, the one in the band. Siobhan...' Chloe turned back a few pages of her notepad.

'Siobhan MacNeill,' Teàrlach prompted. 'Dee spoke to her Friday night in the pub. She said she'd tell Calum to see his dad but then broke down in tears saying something about it not being fair.'

'She knows he's alive then?'

'She thinks he's alive,' Teàrlach qualified. 'But her family want her to have nothing to do with him and, according to Fraser Donald, the mother would rather have Calum dead than move in with her daughter.' A second finger folded to join his thumb.

'But Siobhan's not saying that?'

'Dee didn't get that impression, no. She ran off before Dee managed to get much out of her.'

"Then we need to talk to her again.'

'That's proving more difficult than you might think.' Now only his little finger remained extended.

'Is that everything?' Chloe's pen made a forceful jab at her notepad.

'Everything except what I think is Siobhan's voice appearing on the underwater recording of a drowned wildlife researcher, yes.' Teàrlach's left hand had turned into a fist. 'We need to talk to Siobhan, or her brothers.

FORTY-TWO
FINN MACCOOL

Dee had outstayed her welcome in the small café, her table hastily vacated for the next influx of customers. She stood undecided in the street, wondering whether to go to another part of the island where she might be able to tether her laptop to her iPhone, or try another café. It was almost 9 a.m.

She made for her bike, then caught sight of a red bench at the side of the café almost hidden from the street and facing out over moored yachts. It was private, still in range of the pier Wi-Fi, and the laptop had sufficient charge left. Dee parked herself on the bench, flipped the lid open and continued with the task she'd began inside.

The investigation into John Stevenson's death was being treated as a murder enquiry, that was clear from the initial report. How was this related to the cases they were there to investigate? Dee struggled to make a connection between the photographer's plunge off Staffa's high cliffs, the missing fisherman and now this sound recordist. There had been death threats made on social media – she could make a start there.

Dee cursed under her breath at the time it took to do the simplest of tasks using the resources at her disposal. If she'd stayed in her flat, this would have only taken a few minutes. A seagull landed at her feet, considered joining her on the bench. They entered into a staring contest – Dee's green eyes fixed on a single round black pupil suspended in a pale-yellow iris. The bird broke contact first, haughtily strutting away in search of more agreeable company.

She shivered in an onshore wind, cooled on its passage across the Atlantic to numb her fingers sufficiently for the blood to have retreated deeper under the skin. This was a crazy place to try and surf the internet. John Stevenson's social media pages were easy enough to find and he'd made them available for public viewing. Dee read through his posts, reading more concerns about environmental issues. He'd only begun to concentrate on the destruction of the seabed over the last few months, hence the before and after photographs of widespread habitat destruction and laying the blame at indiscriminate scallop dredging and prawn trawling. The government's own environmental protection agencies were roundly condemned in his posts, as were the trawlers operating in so-called protection zones. Apparently, the coastal waters surrounding the Hebrides were protected in name only and trawlers could operate with impunity.

He'd managed to piss off both the Scottish Environmental Protection Agency as well as the local trawler fishermen. Only one of those was likely to want him silenced for good. Dee read the screenshots of threats attached to the police file. They were the usual poison pen outpourings from people too scared to put their real names down. One poster in particular had been high-lighted by the detective working the case, calling himself Finn MacCool. Intrigued, Dee began to research the character.

Finn MacCool was a legendary Irish warrior/hunter who led a band of Irish warriors known as the Fianna and created the Giant's Causeway. Finn first came to prominence after catching and eating the Salmon of Knowledge. He also possessed a magic thumb.

She raised an eyebrow. Whoever Finn MacCool was, he identified with being a fisherman. Now the difficult part, trying to find the real identity behind the online name. Dee first tried a search of anyone using that name on other social media platforms. There were too many for her to search in any depth, but the ones she found hadn't posted anything that related to fishing. Next, she tried looking for any connection between Finn MacCool and the Isle of Mull. This time, the search came back with a positive match, but disappointingly enough the result was only another mythological mention connecting an area of Mull's west coast known locally as the wilderness, to Ireland's Giant's Causeway and two feuding giants. Then Dee spotted a mention of Fingal's Cave on Staffa as being one of the few places where remnants of the giant's stone causeway that connected Scotland to Ireland still remained. It was too much of a coincidence for her to ignore, yet instead of supplying any insight into the three separate cases, she'd only managed to add another layer of complexity.

Whoever this Finn MacCool really was, Dee needed to find him. The Oban police had taken his personal details straight from the social media profile he'd created along with his name. She had no trust in his stating he lived in Fort William, but discovering who lay behind the avatar was not an easy task. There were layers of encryption and safeguards built into the social media platform specifically designed to keep people like her out. If she was working from home, with a concealed IP address and fast internet, it could take her weeks. Sitting on a freezing bench with the slowest internet known to man made the job impossible.

She replaced black leather gloves over her dead fingers, stowed away the laptop and climbed back on her motorbike.

Tobermory sea front had sprung into life during the time she'd spent huddled over her laptop. Locals heading for the bakery and Co-op; the first tourists angling cameras to catch the best view; tradesmen starting their day. A police patrol car passed her as she headed out of town, the driver taking undue interest in the redhead dressed in black leathers. Dee ignored him, flicked the indicator and turned sharp right at the small roundabout at the top of the hill out of town.

Teàrlach's cottage was an hour from here, along a road that swept a sinuous path across Mull's volcanic backbone. In normal circumstances, she'd enjoy the ride, take in the distant mountains and glimpses of sea, but not today. She was failing at finding who wanted the sound recordist dead, hadn't tracked down the photographer passing off Robert Jameson's photographs as his own, and had come up against a brick wall in finding her own birth parents. Her mood was starting to mirror the dark clouds gathering ominously on the horizon and closing in towards the island.

FORTY-THREE

THE SEARCH FOR CALUM

Sunday was meant to be Suzie's day off, but she'd spent breakfast talking to PC Clare Pringle with the growing conviction she was deserving of her surname.

'No sign of Calum Fraser at all?'

'No, ma'am. Someone's been there, the bed's been slept in, but the place is empty.'

'And you've tried his mobile again?'

'I don't have any signal here. I'll try again when I'm in range of the transmitter mast – it's blocked by these hills around the holiday cottage.'

'All right. Thanks for trying. Keep an eye open for him, you know what he looks like?'

'Yes, ma'am.'

Sergeant Suzie Crammond put down her radio. Rio was still in bed upstairs and wouldn't be rising until ten or eleven at earliest.

The missing fisherman was really starting to worry her now. Him and Siobhan MacNeill who still hadn't returned home – not that her mother was expressing any concern. There was one angle left for her to try: the private investigator hired by Fraser Donald. She had his number on her mobile.

'Teàrlach Paterson, how can I help you?'

'This is Sergeant Crammond from Tobermory police. Have you had any success looking for Calum Donald?'

'No, he's proving a difficult man to find.' There was a pause on the other end of the line, the sound of a kettle whistle dying down as someone switched off the hob. 'Are you looking for him now too?'

'Siobhan MacNeill reported him as a missing person.' Suzie wondered how much she could trust the PI. 'It's too early for that, but she's concerned enough to raise an official report. I thought we might try working together, share what we know?'

'Yes, I'd be happy to help any way I can. His father doesn't have long as I understand it, so the sooner we find him...'

'Exactly. What do you know about his disappearance? Any idea where he is?' She asked more out of hope than any expectation the PI would have anything of use.

'There's not much I can tell you. He was last seen leaving on the *Morning Dew* at dawn 6th April according to Fraser Donald. I'm going to try and talk to Siobhan MacNeill. She's seen him recently and knows where he is.'

Suzie's heart sank at the mention of the MacNeills' name. She'd hoped for better news. All the PI had managed to do was to implicate the MacNeills even further in Calum's disappearance.

'Has anything happened?' the PI interrogated her down the phone.

She bit back the response waiting on her tongue. She might need his help if this went on much longer without Calum being found.

'Siobhan MacNeill's really worried. If you hear anything, you'll let me know, on my number?'

There was a pause as Teàrlach processed this information.

'Aye, if we come across him, I'll call you immediately. And if you find him, you'll let me know?'

'If that's not going to cause me any problems.' An image of Calum's dead body appeared in her imagination, caught in seaweed.

'I know how to be discreet, sergeant. We all want the same thing – Calum's safe return.'

It was less than a day since Calum had officially been reported missing. No one would expect her to raise his disappearance as a problem this early. She gazed out of her windows at the black clouds gathering on the horizon like a foretelling of what was to come. The PI had first mentioned Calum was missing on the Thursday, four days ago. If he didn't turn up by Monday, she'd have to escalate the search.

FORTY-FOUR

THE TWISTIES

Siobhan cautiously opened one eye in case she was still suffering from double vision. The interior of the *Dealt na Maidne* wheelhouse remained in focus. Opening her other eye brought no return of last night's unsettling visual gymnastics. The twisties – her mind reminded her of the word gymnasts use to describe losing all reference of body position when executing rolls and turns in the air. She'd been suffering from something similar when she left the pub last night. Attempting the difficult task of placing one foot in front of the other without falling over as everything around her cartwheeled, flipped, twisted and turned. Tobermory's pavements had tilted like the sea, sending her first in one direction and then another so she walked like a sailor back on dry land.

That thought had given her drunken mind an idea of where she could lay her pounding head, and she'd set course through the storm and uneven seas towards her brother's fishing boat. Her steps had veered dangerously close to the pier edge and the churning sea below, continuously making adjustments to keep close to the pier wall, relative shelter and safety. How she made the transition from bucking stone pier to fishing boat without being thrown into the sea was nothing short of a miracle. The crucifix Duncan had insisted be attached to the inside of the cabin mocked her for her unbelief.

Siobhan felt as though she'd been on a long sea voyage. The night had been spent on the wheelhouse floor, a pile of nylon rope supplying the most uncomfortable pillow she'd ever had the misfortune to experience. There were times when the boat threw itself around like a rodeo steer, desperate to shake off the mooring ropes holding it tight to the stone pier. She would have thrown up if she had anything left in her stomach – instead she lay there with the certain knowledge that death would be better than this.

Now morning had arrived and the storm had exhausted all efforts at dislodging the small fishing boat, leaving it rocking on a large swell. She attempted to stand, leg muscles complaining after hours in the one position, curled up like a newborn baby in an effort to conserve heat. Holding tight to the wheel, Siobhan levered herself upright and ignored the pulsing headache reminding her how much she had to drink last night.

She threw open the door, grateful to breathe air untainted with diesel fumes, and looked out on Tobermory. Even without the benefit of sunshine, the wee town managed to look cheerful – like a stone rainbow facing the harbour. The rain had stopped, for the moment, although leaden grey clouds threatened more.

Siobhan had searched all of Calum's usual haunts without success, finishing up in the pub where they'd both first met. No one had set eyes on him for days – not unexpected as he'd deliberately hidden himself away in the holiday home. She wondered again at his reasons for lying low. He'd said it was so they could be together, yet there was something bothering him. Had he fallen out with Duncan and Finlay? He wasn't working with them anymore.

Her brothers had been on her side before starting to echo their mum's warnings that Calum wasn't suitable. She felt like they were treating her as farm breeding stock – searching for a sire to strengthen the family line. Initially, they'd been left bewildered by their mother's desperate attempts to break up the relationship. Now her mother had come up with the preposterous statement that they were related. Half-brother and half-sister. Had her brothers been told the same thing? None of it made any sense – unless her mother was going mad?

Siobhan shook her head to clear it, then immediately wished she hadn't. She waited for the blood to stop pounding before climbing up to the pier. It must be around low tide, the pier was two metres higher than it had been last night. A set of rusty metal ladders set into stone provided the only route, her feet slipping on lower rungs still wet with green slime. Feeling like she'd conquered Everest once safely back on solid land, she stood next to a pile of creels and took stock.

She'd been to the police – they were a waste of space, especially that one from Dorset or Somerset or wherever who'd been on duty. The sergeant hadn't called with an update, but at least she had taken Calum's disappearance seriously. Siobhan had a pang of regret that she'd mentioned Duncan's name to them, but her brother had responded strangely when she'd asked him if he'd seen Calum – and she knew him well enough to know when he was lying. Duncan was covering up something, she was sure of it, but even suspecting him of doing anything to Calum was surely just a product of her imagination. They were good mates, after all. Calum hadn't been to Tobermory or someone she'd met last night would have seen him. Why would he take off like that? Had he heard about his dad? It was the worry of not knowing where he was, whether he was safe. Siobhan found she was unable to think clearly, spending every moment puzzling over his disappearance. Something the sergeant had said last night had haunted her – *men change their minds*. Had Calum changed his mind?

The horrifying thought that Calum might be her half-brother returned. She'd dismissed her mother's statement out of hand – the whole idea was mad. But what if it was true? Siobhan shook her head in disbelief, triggering another pounding ache from deep within her skull. Yet still the nagging doubt persisted as a means of explaining Calum's sudden disappearance. If he'd been told the same thing...

She didn't believe it. She couldn't believe it. But Calum, what if he'd been told the same story? Would he respond by leaving her? No, he'd never do that. He'd talk to her and they'd both laugh at this last, desperate attempt to keep them apart. Wouldn't he?

She couldn't return home, not after what her mum had told her. She looked along Tobermory's sea front, hoping for a glimpse of Calum. Only the colourful buildings mocked her with their cheerfulness. He wasn't here – she'd looked everywhere.

The Co-op was across the road, as much a central hub as anywhere on the island. Siobhan stocked up with enough food for the two of them and drove back to the holiday cottage. It would be empty until this coming weekend. She had nowhere else to go and this was the only place Calum would come looking for her.

She drove back to the holiday cottage, climbed into the bed with his scent still lingering on the pillows and pulled the covers over her. There was nothing else to do but wait for Calum to return.

FORTY-FIVE
ISLA

Teàrlach heard Dee's motorbike long before the screeching gate bolt advertised her arrival. They'd brought two kitchen chairs outside to take advantage of the rare April sunshine, Chloe beside him nursing a mug of something hot. Dee crept down the track, wary of each loose stone that threatened to send the bike skidding.

He waited until she'd removed her helmet before quizzing her. 'How did you get on?'

'Let me put these inside.' Dee entered the cottage, returning with a third chair and placed it next to the others so they sat companionably in a row. The cottage provided some respite from the onshore wind, raising white horses on the bay.

'I've not had much luck.' Dee shook her head to free her red curls and they caught the sun like a beacon. 'The sound recordist they dragged out of the sea, John Stevenson, is now a murder enquiry. The package he was attempting to retrieve had a recording of a woman singing in Gaelic. Sounds like Siobhan's voice. It sounded like it had been recorded underwater – I could hear muffled waves and the sound was distorted somehow. Gave me shivers when I heard it. The police must have thought along the same lines as I did – that it had been put there deliberately to attract his interest. Whoever did this to him knew he was the only person likely to be able to hear it and must have known he was working in that area.'

Teàrlach nodded absent-mindedly. He caught Dee's eyes narrowing and gave her an encouraging smile to continue.

'The police have a person of interest they're looking for, a Finn MacCool. Not his real name, it's a handle he uses on social media. He's the guy who's been making death threats on John Stevenson's posts.'

'What had John been posting about?' Teàrlach asked.

'All his posts relate to environmental issues, but recently he's been concentrating on the damage done to the sea floor by indiscriminate trawling and dredging. I looked up Finn MacCool – he was meant to have been a giant with a penchant for magic salmon – in other words, a fisherman. And he ripped up a causeway between Mull and Ireland with the only stones still standing on the west coast on Mull, the Giant's Causeway in Ireland and, get this – Fingal's cave!'

'And this John Stevenson was found on the west coast of Mull...' Teàrlach started.

'And Robert Jameson in Fingal's Cave,' Chloe added.

'Except, apart from the tenuous link from someone using a mythological giant's name and these stories – how does this move us any further forward?' Teàrlach neatly summed up Dee's concerns.

She raised her head to stare into his eyes, seeing something in his expression that caused her to frown.

'I'll be able to find who this Finn MacCool really is, but it will take weeks of painstaking hacking to get there. We'd be better to let the police track him down and concentrate on finding Robert's missing camera and this Calum Donald.' Dee regarded them both with a quizzical expression. 'Has something happened whilst I've been away?'

Teàrlach felt Chloe tense next to him.

'Chloe found something – clearing out my aunt's papers. I'll get it.'

There was an envelope on top of the papers strewn over the kitchen table. He picked it up with the same care he'd handle a live grenade.

'Here.' He passed it to Dee, saw her spot the New Zealand stamp and her frown intensified as she pulled out a photograph.

'OK, so she's a pretty wee thing. What's the problem?'

'She's my daughter.'

If tumbleweed grew on the island, this would have been its cue. As it was, the wind sighed as it played with couch grass and gorse – a soft moaning as Dee processed the news. He risked looking at her. Dee's attention was focussed on the photograph of a young girl, three or four years old, smiling shyly at the camera.

'How? I mean, why? Didn't you know?' Dee glared at him in anger.

'Read the letter,' Teàrlach replied tersely. He expected her anger – any orphan would have the same reaction to a parent abandoning their child.

Dee fetched a folded letter from inside the envelope, opened it out and held onto the edges to stop the wind carrying it away.

Dear Teàrlach,

I'm sorry that I haven't been in touch sooner. When you left, we'd decided that was it. We gave it our best shot, but we both knew it was never going to work out for us. I promised myself that I'd never contact you again, even after I found out I was pregnant. As you can see, I returned to my parents' home in NZ and I've made a good life for myself here. I met a guy, Jeff, I think

*you'd like him. We're getting married in February, and we both
think it would be good for Isla to meet her dad.*

*I don't have any address for you except this one, and I'm hoping
your aunt will forward it to you. I don't want any money or
expect you to take any part in her life. We couldn't live any
further apart! She's named after one of your Scottish islands, I
thought you'd like that.*

*If you can come and visit, we can find somewhere to put you up.
I'd like to see you again, and Isla should have the chance to meet
her dad.*

I hope you're keeping well and doing fine.

Love,
Tessa xxx

'When was this sent?' Dee asked, looking closely at the post-
mark. 'Two years ago. You never saw it?'

Teàrlach shook his head. 'It must have arrived around the
time Rosie – my aunt – died. It could have been the medics who
cleared post away from the door, left it on her table.'

'How could you not have seen it?'

Teàrlach brushed his hair out of his face, stared over the bay
to the smaller island opposite. He knew Staffa was hidden by
the bulk of the island, another five kilometres distant.

'I'd just come back to civvy street when I received word
from the police. They'd been trying to reach me for days. I
made the memorial service by the skin of my teeth, had so much
to organise.' He remembered being in a state of shock, unable to
process her death and desperate to get away from the island.
The cottage held too many memories – it was always something
he was going to attend to but managed to put off. Until now.

'What are you going to do?' Dee replaced the letter and photograph back in the envelope, handed it to Teàrlach.

'I'll have to contact her. Let her know I was never given the letter. And go and see my daughter.' He looked into Dee's eyes, saw the hurt and felt as if he'd betrayed her.

'That would be best – for your daughter at least. She'll be older now.' Dee stood. 'I need the loo.'

They both saw the tears forming in her eyes and with unvoiced agreement pretended they hadn't.

'We'd better clear up these cases then, before you head off to the other side of the world.' Chloe found refuge in practicalities.

'Aye. We'll give Dee a minute, then head into Tobermory – see if we can find this fishing boat and crew.

Teàrlach slipped the envelope into his jacket, next to his father's letter. The weight of these two pieces of paper felt crushing, each one a world of unresolved emotions. He'd barely come to terms with his father's final words, and now this – a daughter he never knew existed. The revelation left him reeling, struggling to process one life-altering truth, let alone two. His chest tightened as he tried to imagine how he'd face either of these challenges, when each one alone felt overwhelming.

FORTY-SIX

GAELIC

They arrived back in Tobermory just after 2 p.m., and parked up facing the harbour filling with yachts. Dee imagined some sort of regatta was underway but had spotted the fish and chip van was open for business and her mood instantly improved.

'Anyone else want a fish supper?'

Teàrlach shook his head. 'I need to talk to a few fishermen, see if anyone knows about this boat that Calum is meant to have returned from.'

"I'll go with Teàrlach.' Chloe shot her a critical glance as if accusing her of prioritising her own needs ahead of a visibly shaken Teàrlach. He threw Dee the keys.

'Won't be long – just need to talk to these guys on the pier. We'll see you in a bit.'

Dee watched them from the front seat. She was putting on a brave front – the disclosure that Teàrlach had a child was still reverberating inside, for reasons she couldn't pin down. It wasn't that they were an item, or ever would be if Teàrlach had his way, but she held a flame for him and the news had just doused it. Even that made no sense when she analysed it. Teàrlach was completely in shock and struggling to take in the fact that he was a dad. Of course, his own past would have come back to haunt him – especially living in the cottage where he'd grown up.

She shrugged, made for the chip van and placed an order. Teàrlach and Chloe were on the end of an old stone pier which served the small fishing fleet, talking to the crew on a lobster boat. Creels were lined up waiting for the next expedition, a smell of fish hanging in the air. Nobody seemed anxious to put out to sea, if anything more boats were coming into the relative shelter of the natural bay.

Her order was called, and she took the takeaway back to the car, then fastidiously wiped her fingers clean of grease. Bored with the constant activity in the harbour, she opened her laptop and saw an announcement had come in from the benign virus she'd placed in *Scottish Birdwatcher* magazine. Her finger paused above delete. The search filter was only looking for Robert Jameson's photographs and she'd covered that angle already. Out of interest she read the response, thanking a Sam Topping for his enquiry but gently admonishing him they'd already received exactly the same photograph from someone else.

His email address revealed several hits placing him as a teacher in Birmingham. Why would he send the same shot twice? He must have known they'd see through any change of alias when receiving a duplicate submission. The sun was threatening to break through the thick cloud cover, throwing distant hills into colour when the light hit them. The darker clouds she'd spotted earlier were massing in the west, any sunshine wouldn't last for long.

Dee sent another response, purportedly from the magazine and requesting he send any other material they might consider for publication. A geo-tracker went with it – at least she could find where this Sam Topping was.

Teàrlach and Chloe returned to the car. His mood had

improved considerably in the last ten minutes, there was even the trace of a smile.

'Have you found anything?' Dee asked.

The smile expanded as he turned sideways in his seat to face her.

'Yes. Several things. The first is that Fraser Donald gave us the correct boat name, but out of habit he translated it into English. The *Morning Dew* is *Dealt na Maidne* in Gaelic. That's it moored against the pier.'

Dee followed the direction of his finger where two fishermen were pulling mooring lines tight.

'He might have given us the right name in the first place.' Chloe's complaint came from the back. 'I spent hours looking for a non-existent fishing boat.'

'Not his fault. Hardly anyone speaks Gaelic here. It will be normal for him to translate eveything into English, including the boat name. Important thing is, we've found it.'

'Did you ask them about the missing guy – Calum Donald?'

Teàrlach gave Dee a look that suggested he'd found her question insulting.

'What do you think? They both said Calum worked as crew, but neither had seen him since they returned from a fishing trip on the 6th.'

'Which ties in with what his father told us,' Chloe confirmed.

'No idea where he may be?' Dee persevered.

'Neither struck me as being very keen to talk about it. The big guy especially.' He stroked his chin, peering through the windshield at the two fishermen. 'I've seen the smaller guy somewhere, just can't place him – not whilst he's wearing bright yellow oilskins and wellies.'

'Did you get their names?' Dee was beginning to feel like she was running the investigation.

'They were too busy. Said there was a storm coming and

they had to batten down the ship – basically told us to bugger off so they could get on.'

'I'll do a search on the fishing register,' Chloe volunteered. 'Know my way around it now.'

Dee's computer chimed.

'You have internet here?' Chloe asked. 'I can't get a signal.'

'Tether to your phone, there's good 4G,' Dee replied absent-mindedly, opening up a map and watching where a red dot blinked Sam's location. 'Right. Someone else has uploaded the same bloody puffin photograph to *Scottish Birdwatcher*, and I can track him live.'

'Where is he?' Teàrlach spoke with genuine interest, his problems put aside for the moment.

'Inverness.'

'Is this the same guy – David...'

'Webster,' Chloe added. She'd opened her notepad, adding details as they spoke.

'No,' Dee corrected. 'This time, he calls himself Sam Topping and he's real. I've had a quick look – he's a school-teacher in Birmingham.'

Teàrlach started the car, reversed into the main street. 'How do you feel about heading to Inverness and finding this guy? The least we can accomplish is to return Robert's camera gear to Lucy.'

'And we may find out what happened on Staffa.' Dee needed time alone. This offered her the perfect excuse.

'Let's get back to the cottage. You take off for Inverness or wherever this guy is and we'll do some digging around this fishing boat and crew.' He exchanged a serious look with her before releasing the clutch. 'Take care. We don't know how dangerous this Sam is – I don't want you to take any unneces-sary risks.'

Her green eyes glinted in challenge. 'Me?' Her voice sounded less innocent than she'd tried for.

FORTY-SEVEN

Siobhan recognised the redhead from the pub on Friday night. She had her face buried in a fish supper, sitting in a car and staring out over the harbour, but her red hair made her difficult to miss. She'd said Calum's dad was dying of brain cancer, that he'd asked her to look for him. Hadn't she said she was working for Calum's dad? Siobhan tried to remember verbatim the brief exchange in the pub toilets. None of it made any sense – Calum never said anything about his dad being seriously ill, but now the police sergeant had confirmed it.

Her brothers were working on the boat, and she desperately needed to talk to them in case they knew where Calum was. Her mum's words were still fresh in her memory – '*Fraser Donald is your father.*' What an absolute bitch, trying anything to stop them from being together – even to the extent of such an obvious lie. Why was she so desperate to stop her having her own life? Did she think she'd stay in that crumbling mansion to look after them all when her mother was too old?

Siobhan threw caution to the wind, marching purposefully towards the pier until she saw the two people talking to Duncan and Finlay. The serious-looking guy was the same man who'd been playing pool with the redhead on Friday. The woman he was with was new. She changed course, crossing back over the road and entering a shop selling trinkets to the tourists.

Standing in the large shop window, hidden by toy highland cows and model ferry boats, Siobhan could spy on them unseen. They didn't spend much time talking, it looked like Duncan was giving them short shrift and they walked back along the pier and joined the redhead in the car. So, there were three of them! Were they all working for Calum's dad? They weren't police, she'd swear to that. The car reversed into the street, headed away out of town and Siobhan made for the boat.

'Have either of you seen Calum?' She almost had to shout above the wind. Her brothers were busy stacking the last of the creels onto the pier, roping them together and tying them down to mooring rings set into the stonework.

'Calum?' Finlay repeated with a typically blank expression fixed to his face.

'That's what I said.' Her patience was stretched to breaking point.

'No idea.' Finlay returned to the creels, threading another rope through and passing it to his older brother.

'What about you, Duncan. Have you seen Calum today?'

'Not today. Isn't he in that holiday cottage?'

She picked up at this revelation. 'How did you know about that?' She spoke more sharply than she'd intended.

'Oh, he told me he wanted some time off. Said he was staying there instead of his lodgings.' He spoke offhandedly, concentrating on the job in hand.

Siobhan thought they'd decided to keep the holiday place quiet, just between the two of them. He'd left his lodgings a week ago, taking the holiday let at a knockdown price so they had somewhere they could be alone. Somewhere they could plan a future together without anyone interfering. Something surprisingly difficult to do on an island.

'He's not there.' She viewed her eldest brother with suspicion. There was something he wasn't saying. Duncan was the worst when it came to lying, it was a technique he'd never managed to master without flagging his lie with a myriad tells. In this case, it was his inability to meet her eyes, pretending that the creels required his full attention.

'You sure you haven't seen him?'

'What is it with everyone looking for Calum?' Finlay interrupted. 'We just had two weirdos asking the same question.'

'The guy and the woman?' Siobhan quizzed.

'You been keeping an eye on us?' Finlay turned inquisitor.

'Saw them from over the road. I've seen the guy before – he was with a redhead who was asking where Calum was. She said she was working for his dad.'

'Fraser?' Finlay queried.

Siobhan nodded. Duncan was doing his best to stay out of the conversation, spending more time on his creels than she suspected was strictly necessary.

'Did they say who they were?'

Finlay dug around in a pocket, produced a business card which he offered to his sister.

'Gave me this. I was going to chuck it.'

Siobhan read the card. Teàrlach Paterson, private investigator. The address was in Glasgow. Her heart sank. If Fraser Donald had called in a team of private investigators, then this talk of his having terminal cancer might be real after all. It would certainly explain why he was desperate to see his son.

'What did you tell them?'

'Told 'em to fuck off,' Finlay replied with relish. 'Said there's a fucking storm coming and we had work to do. They left after that.' His face expressed satisfaction in how he'd dealt with that problem.

'So, neither of you have seen Calum today?'

'No. He should be here helping out. Lazy bastard!' Finlay took delight in cursing their hired help.

'I've not seen him today either.' Duncan finally met her eyes.

He was telling the truth.

'Where's he gone?' Her question was met with unconcerned shrugs.

The wind changed direction, feeding straight through the stacked creels and playing an eerie and discordant tune on the tightly wound netting. The sound reminded Siobhan of a horror film. A premonition of danger manifested in the raised hairs at the back of her neck. She had to find Calum. Something was wrong, something was very wrong.

Dee boarded the ferry heading back to Oban with a sense of relief. The CalMac staff were still debating whether the boat would be able to dock in the strengthening wind when it hove into view around a headland, leaning to one side as it fought against the elements and making straight for the pier. Traffic and passengers disgorged with even more alacrity than usual, making for solid land and security. There followed a short hiatus before the crew allowed the queues to board, waving everyone on with half an eye on the worsening weather.

The short crossing back to Oban was completely different to the stately voyage she'd taken just two days ago – this time, the ferry pitched into large waves as soon as it entered open water, the hydraulic stabilisers working overtime to reduce the ship's roll. Dee spent the time on board feeling slightly nauseous, her only entertainment observing customers at the café attempting to walk back to their tables without spilling most of their drink.

She left Oban after 6 p.m., facing a challenging hundred-mile trip to Inverness. The storm that had threatened them out at sea had made landfall. Random gusts of wind played with the bike as if it were a toy, throwing Dee off balance and causing her to veer across the road. She kept a wary watch for stray branches and other detritus, adding to the stress of biking in such adverse conditions. The trip should take her around two and a half hours, assuming no major delays, and she planned to arrive in Inverness a little before sunset.

One advantage of fighting the wind on her bike was it allowed her little time for introspection. No quiet moment to consider the stalled hunt for her parents; no space in which to face Teàrlach's having a daughter he'd never known about. No time for her to try and understand why she felt as if she'd been abandoned yet again, and why that bothered her so much. She felt angry more than hurt – and then cursed herself for feeling angry – for feeling anything at all. The storm of emotions inside mirrored the weather, unexpected gusts threatening to throw her, squalls of heavy rain leaving the road slick and treacherous.

By the time she reached Inverness, she was more exhausted than anything else. A Travelodge hotel sign came into view, and she pulled into the car park with relief. A fresh wall of rain was heading towards her along the cold, grey waters of the Moray Firth, and she made a dash for reception before the latest deluge hit, ricocheting off the glass doors as they closed.

Her room looked out over the sea. The receptionist had made that sound like a major selling point when she handed over the access card, pointing the way to the lift and wishing Dee a pleasant stay. Now she stood with her nose almost pressed against the rain-smeared glass window trying to make sense of the view. A bathroom towel wiped away the worst of the water that had soaked into her hair and down her neck. At least her leathers had kept the rest of her relatively dry. A full-size bath beckoned – there were bottles of bubble bath, shampoo, conditioner. The mini bar held vodka, wine, chocolate. If she had a religious bone in her body, she could have sworn she was being tested.

Reluctantly, Dee ignored bath and bar and opened her laptop. There was Sam Topping's location, less than a thirty-minute drive from her hotel. Zooming in on Google maps, she saw Sam's geolocator was in a mobile home park. She cursed, hearing a squall of rain lash against the windows. A mobile home could mean he'd be off again tomorrow, and she had no wish to spend the day chasing a moving geolocator all around the Scottish Highlands – especially in weather like this!

She had no choice and sent a quick text to Teàrlach to let him know where she was and that she was about to check in on a mobile home. She checked her top jacket pocket where a tin of pepper spray reassured her with its presence, before fitting her helmet and headed out again.

There was still some residual daylight left, struggling to pierce the dark clouds shedding bucketloads of rain onto the car park tarmac. It was coming down with such force that she could hear it ricocheting off her helmeted head. A gloved hand swept a small tsunami off the bike seat before Dee straddled it and keyed the engine, taking the road towards Culloden and the campsite she'd pinpointed. If ever there was an evening for visiting the site of a brutal massacre, this was probably it.

The caravan park was easy enough to find. Low wooden picket fences enclosed areas of short-cropped grass. Caravans and campervans lined up in military precision ready for inspection; tents were banished to a corner where their lack of orderliness would be less displeasing to the suburban aesthetic. A few floodlights caught the rain in their beams, highlighting paths leading towards a central toilet and washing block.

Dee killed the engine, flipped the bike onto its stand and checked her mobile. Sam's computer was still broadcasting a location. She walked towards a row of campervans and stopped at the one identified by her app. It was a holiday hire – nobody else would have emblazoned the bodywork with Highland Coos and heather, much less added the signwriting announcing to the world this was a Midge Tours van. The lights were on, curtains drawn. Dee transferred the pepper spray to her right fist and banged on the door.

Curtains twitched back from the windows, and two startled faces peered out at her. Their expressions turned to shock at the sight of Dee's motorbike paraphernalia, then to curiosity as she removed the helmet and revealed her face.

'Is one of you Sam Topping?' Dee had to shout above the torrential rain.

'Who are you?' The voice from inside was muffled, but she managed the gist of it.

'Can I come in? I'm getting soaked.'

Dee had little choice but to wait whilst the two men held an urgent whispered conversation. After what felt like an age, the side door slid open sufficiently for them to speak face-to-face.

'I'm Sam. What do you want?'

Dee's grip on the pepper spray lessened. This Sam looked as dangerous as a poodle, his mate likewise.

'I'm a private investigator,' Dee replied. The statement still sounded strange as it left her lips, even after a year in the job. She could see that she'd only added to their bewilderment.

'I've come from the Isle of Mull. You were there, recently. Is that right?'

The two men exchanged a look, Sam shrugging his shoulders in response to his partner's accusative glare.

'Yes, but what's this about?'

Dee relaxed, as best as she could with freezing water making steady ingress between her neck and the rest of her body. That bath was waiting.

'I'm investigating the death of a wildlife photographer, and you have his missing camera. Can we discuss this out of the rain?' Dee took a purposeful step towards the open door.

The two men retreated, leaving just enough space for Dee to climb inside. They stared at her in silence as she dripped water on the floor. Her attention flicked to a camping table holding two plates of food and two glasses of wine.

'But he was fine when I left yesterday lunchtime.' The one who'd identified as Sam appeared in danger of having a nervous breakdown. 'And he sold me his camera – I didn't steal it.'

Dee was as mystified as his partner.

'What happened? You told me he wanted to sell it.' His partner's shock was turning to anger.

She began to piece it together.

'Who sold you the camera?' She spotted an aluminium flight case on the floor. 'Is that it?'

Sam nodded unhappily.

'I don't know his name. We were on the same wildlife tour, and I left before the week was up. He asked if I wanted to buy his camera, said he couldn't get on with it. I didn't know he was about to die.' This last statement was aimed at his partner. 'He wasn't in great shape – overweight and sweaty and his breath stank. But he didn't look like he was dying.'

'What tour were you on?' Dee focussed in on the specifics.

'Tauth Wildlife Tours. They run a week photography course. How did he die?'

Dee had the right camera but the wrong guy. She thought on her feet.

'How much did you pay, for the camera?'

'A thousand. Cash. The lens alone is worth—'

'This is what we'll do. I'll transfer you the money – if this is his camera – and we'll forget you ever had it. How's that sound?'

'That's fair, Sam,' his partner urged. 'We don't want any involvement with this man's death.'

'Show me the camera,' Dee commanded. 'I want to see the puffin photograph you sent to *Scottish Birdwatcher*.'

'How can you know about that?' Sam was recovering from the shock of her appearing out of the blue.

'Doesn't matter. I'm a PI, that's what I do. We can involve the police if you want to be done for handling stolen property?'

'No, no. I'll show you the photo.' Sam hurriedly opened the case, searched through the photographs and showed Dee the shot she'd seen before.'

'OK. What's your sort code and account number? I'll transfer the money over to you now.'

She left before they could fully process what had just happened, the aluminium flight case strapped into her top box. Neither of them looked in any mood to finish their meal; she only hoped the wine wouldn't go to waste.

FORTY-NINE

FINLAY

Finlay was driving them home in time for tea, after they'd made sure the *Dealt na Maidne* had been secured to the pier with enough ropes and fenders to survive the worst a storm could throw at her. The harbour was relatively well protected against the elements, but they weren't the only sailors adding more lines to their boats as the wind began to howl across the bay like a banshee. They'd stacked and roped the creels together, but the wind had little to work with – creels were more holes than anything else.

'When's your car going to be fixed?' Finlay was tired of becoming the family taxi, even after one day.

He slammed his car door shut and watched his brother making a slow exit. Slow, like everything he did.

'I'm not sure. I may need your help with something.'

Finlay didn't like the sound of that, tinkering with engines and mechanics. That was Duncan's speciality.

'Can't the garage fix it?'

'Not this time,' Duncan said enigmatically.

Finlay stared at him for a moment in surprise. Being enigmatic was a first for him.

'Talk about it later. It's time for tea.'

They found their mother sitting at the kitchen table, their evening meal not even started.

'What's up, Mum?' Finlay had seen the dead look in her face as they walked in. His brother had taken one look and carried on to the lounge where a TV started blasting out the weather forecast.

'Have either of you boys seen Siobhan?' Her voice lacked its usual sharpness wherever her daughter's name was mentioned.

Finlay picked up on the change in tone.

'Why? She gone out?' he asked flippantly.

'We had a disagreement.' His mother was uncharacteristically hesitant. 'She left yesterday morning, looking for Calum.'

'Saw her earlier – we've been securing the boat against this storm. She probably went to the pub,' he added helpfully.

'Probably with her musician friends.' She managed to imbibe the word musicians with poison.

'Why don't you call her?'

His mother shot him a look that suggested he was the imbecile of the family. 'She's not picking up.'

'I'll try.' Finlay bent to his phone, keyed in Siobhan's number and waited until it switched to voicemail. 'Hey, sis, where are you? You going to be here for tea otherwise Duncan and me will eat your portion.'

He looked triumphantly towards his mother as if having solved a great conundrum. They both switched attention to the windows as a particularly strong gust shook the frames. Even the dog stood up from its habitual position at his mistress's feet, ears pricked up in response to the unusual violence being inflicted on the building.

'I'll make a start on tea. No knowing if the power will cut off tonight. Shouldn't be surprised if the electric lines are brought down by a tree or something.' She stood with some difficulty as if she'd been frozen in the one position for too long a time.

'Go on with you!' She shooed him out of the kitchen. 'How am I meant to cook with you getting under my feet?'

Finlay left her to it. She was in one of her moods and anyone within range was liable to suffer from the edge of her tongue. Duncan had settled in for the night, ensconced in the seat that had been their dad's, eyes fixed on the TV news. Finlay knew he was waiting for any reports on Robert Jameson's death. He stood waiting to see if there had been any update on the sound recordist. Duncan was lucky the police hadn't interviewed him – he couldn't tell a lie to save his life. That private investigator though, and the woman with him. They could be trouble.

He'd heard they were staying down the road, in Rosie's old cottage. She used to be the detective's aunt, so he'd been told. Nothing remained a secret for long on an island – and that was their biggest problem. Married affairs were one thing, death was something else entirely. Sometimes, keeping quiet was the best thing to do.

He entertained the idea of driving to Rosie's cottage, disabling the PI's car so they'd be stuck for days. The garage wouldn't open until Monday, and then there was no guarantee they'd send anyone out. Finlay dismissed the thought as soon as he had it. Doing something like that would only get the guy's interest – and he didn't look stupid from what he'd seen.

No. Best bet was to lay low and continue as if nothing had happened. Duncan was already following that mantra, although in his case it was because he lacked the imagination to do otherwise. Fishing, drinking, rugby and TV. Round and round day in, day out until he turned into his dad and ended up the same way.

They all thought Finlay was a deadbeat, a no-hoper. He smiled thinly to himself, standing unseen behind his brother's back. He'd show them. He'd show them all.

FIFTY

TESSA'S LETTER

Chloe waited in the cottage kitchen for the kettle to boil, a task that took ages on the old gas cooker. It really belonged in a museum, along with most contents of this house. She'd left Teàrlach going through the papers in his aunt's desk – something he should have done two years ago when she died instead of abandoning the place. What was he thinking? At the very least he could have gone through her personal effects, saved what needed to be saved and calling in a firm who specialised in house clearances.

They'd heard nothing from Dee since she left on the last ferry. The island was now all but cut-off due to the storm sweeping in from the west, and judging by the look of the weather outside, things weren't likely to be getting any better soon. The sky had turned an ominous shade of black, bringing the day to an early close. If anything, the wind had picked up since they'd arrived back from Tobermory, moaning through the roof tiles like a wild animal in distress.

Teàrlach remained closeted in what Chloe thought of as Dee's room, the bed covered in papers and photographs as he searched for any other mention of the child and his ex-girlfriend. This wasn't going to be something he could easily post-pone, unlike the cottage and his aunt's personal effects. For someone so ready to take on other people's worries and prob-lems, he really had a blind spot where his own life was concerned.

The kettle eventually whistled submission, and she poured the decidedly brownish water into a cafetiere until the coffee stained the water a darker shade. She tentatively sipped a freshly poured cup, found it tasted OK and took one through to Teàrlach.

'Coffee?'

He sat on the bed surrounded by the memories he'd been so desperate to avoid. There were photos of him as a young boy, his small hand gripping his aunt's with such force she could see the muscles in his forearm tensing. He appeared like a shadow, always close to her side, looking up to check she was still there. None of the photographs scattered around appeared to show him any older than twelve or thirteen, as if he'd been frozen in time when adolescence kicked in. Chloe wondered what the story was behind that omission of his older years.

'Thanks.' Teàrlach took the proffered cup and sipped without checking the taste. 'I never knew she took so many photographs.' His arm swept to encompass the bed and its contents.

'Did you find anything else from your girlfriend and the kid?' Chloe instinctively felt on safer ground discussing this latest revelation than raking over his childhood.

"No, there was only the one letter from Tessa.' He slumped in on himself, his mood matching the darkened view from the cottage window. 'She would have thought I didn't want anything to do with her – or Isla.'

'I'm sure that's the last thing she'd have thought.' She spoke decisively although the words sounded hollow in her ears.

He stared out at the stormy sea, whipped into foam tipped

waves. The view of Ulva had been all but obliterated by rain, heading inland and starting to drum on the roof and glass with increasing ferocity until they may have been alone in the dark.

'I hope Dee made it to Inverness before this weather hit.' She changed the subject in an attempt to shake him out of the melancholy evident in the slope of his shoulders.

Teàrlach checked the time. 'She'll still be on the road. Should make it there by eight. With a bit of luck, she'll have made it before the worst of the storm. It's only just making land-fall now.'

The rain increased in volume as if in confirmation of his pronouncement, hard gusts blowing sheets of water against the glass. Chloe wondered if they were far enough away from the shore or whether that was the sea thundering against the side of the cottage. When the lights flickered, she swore in a panic.

'It's OK.' Teàrlach sought to offer reassurance. 'This cottage has been here a few hundred years. It's seen worse than this.'

Chloe nodded in acceptance, then wondered how much worse.

'I've got a signal, on my phone.' She spoke in wonderment, staring at her screen and seeing phone and data were both showing.

'Goes like that sometimes,' Teàrlach commented. 'Weather like this the signal should drop off entirely, but every now and then it's stronger. Maybe they up the power or something to cut through the storm?'

Chloe heard the conjecture in his voice. People would be reliant on their internet and mobile phones in weather like this. She spared a thought for those at sea, shivered in sympathy. No wonder the fishermen they spoke to earlier were taking every-thing that could be blown overboard and tying them to the immoveable stone pier. It also explained the sudden influx of yachts into the relative safety of the harbour. No one in their right mind would take a boat out in conditions such as these.

'I'll search for the owners of that boat, now I've some internet.' Chloe left him to it, perched on the edge of the bed. There was something indescribably sad about Teàrlach sat amongst the detritus of his past. Something best left for him to deal with on his own. In any case, there was little she could offer in terms of support.

Chloe returned to the fishing boat registration site, painstakingly entered the Gaelic words in the search bar, *Dealt na Maidne*. The response took a while, only a circling arrow giving her any confidence that her laptop was still connected. The result came back: Duncan MacNeill. Her eyes widened as she recognised his registered address was the same as Siobhan's – the same house Teàrlach had visited two days ago.

FIFTY-ONE
SHADOWS

Dee needed that bath. The rain had turned to sleet on the way back from Culloden, giving her no choice but to take the roads slowly in case the tyres lost grip. It was better to be pummelled by freezing rain and a cold wind than to risk coming off the bike. Cold water had managed to find its way through her leathers, running down from her neck and up from her gloves. She'd emptied an entire bottle of bubble bath, and now sat gently soaking in a purple chemical concoction that claimed to be highland heather.

Her foot casually operated the hot tap, adding to the overall heat until the overflow gurgled its displeasure at such wanton waste of resources. She flicked her foot sideways, and the flow stopped. The only sound came from rain impacting the hotel windows; caught in random gusts of wind, it battered the glass in waves. Nothing would entice her to go out again tonight.

The guys in the campervan were innocent of any wrongdoing, she was certain of that. Sam had known he was getting a bargain, and the adage if it looks too good to be true had proven accurate. Hence his ready acceptance of Dee's financial offer. That was an expense she'd have to square with Teàrlach, but she hadn't wanted to spend any longer arguing for the camera – not with the weather threatening to wipe her off the road on the way back to Inverness. She'd have to let Teàrlach know there was a corpulent photographer with halitosis travelling with the wildlife tour company. Only he knew where the camera came from, but that could wait.

The room mini bar was calling to her, and so far at least she'd resisted that temptation. There were too many problems needing a solution to try for oblivion – not that the meagre collection of miniatures would take her far along that road. There was a Toblerone though, and she'd not eaten since the fish supper on Tobermory. She decided to test herself, see if she could open the mini bar without taking any alcohol.

Dee climbed out of the bath, towelled herself dry and dressed in the white robe and slippers she'd discovered in the wardrobe. She checked the doorstop she habitually carried was securely wedged, took a bite of triangular chocolate and shut the fridge door on the bottles inside with less regret that she had expected.

With drink off the menu, for the time being at least, and with a storm outside and no other diversions, Dee eyed the camera in its aluminium case.

The guy who had the camera, Sam, was right enough about the value. She'd checked a few prices on camera sites and the contents of that case were worth almost three times what he'd paid – possibly even more if the other lenses were at the same eye-watering prices. Dee opened the case, held the camera in her hands. It only took a few seconds before she'd located the battery compartment and the memory card. Dee frowned as she remembered not packing a card reader in her laptop case and shut the battery door in disappointment. There were leads bundled in the aluminium case, including one for a Mac. The frown was replaced by a smile as she connected the two devices together and pulled data off the camera.

The most recent photographs were random shots of an old church, sea birds on a beach, seals on rocks, a sunset with a group of people and a minibus and what may have been an eagle in grey clouds. The only thing they shared was an impulse to consign them all to the bin. Dee's interest picked up as the quality of shots dramatically improved – these were the puffin photographs she recognised as being taken by Robert Jameson. Nearly every shot was perfectly composed and sharply focussed, just the odd one where it looked more like a random snap as the camera moved position. There was one long-distance photograph of a small fishing boat heading towards the camera. She magnified the image, zoomed in until red pixels outlined the cabin roof. It was too far out to make the name of the boat, but that looked like the same vessel Teàrlach and Chloe had been to see in Tobermory.

Dee pursed her lips as she tried to remember what the boat at the stone pier had looked like. She was sure the wheelhouse roof was red, same as this one – but maybe that was common with fishing vessels? The random snaps attracted her attention. They'd been taken at the same time as the fishing boat and puffin photographs, she could make out puffin burrows and Robert's shadow on one of them. Robert's shadow and another. Several days elapsed without any recordings and then the quality of composition declined as a less experienced photographer took over.

She double-checked the date and time of each shot. The one with two shadows was the last photograph Robert Jameson had taken. He wasn't alone when he died.

FIFTY-TWO
HALITOSIS

Teàrlach tidied up the paperwork and photographs, finding nothing more from his ex-girlfriend, Tessa. She had been his first, true love. He could picture her now: her bright smile, finding the good in everyone. Her infectious enthusiasm for life had captivated him, but she'd seen what he was too blind to realise – a man too haunted by his past. She'd made the right call. Even now, he held people at arm's length. The closer anyone came, the more distance he instinctively wanted to put between them. Dee's face appeared in his memory like a reprimand, a clear message from his subconscious that didn't require a therapist's insight.

The storm had reached the stage where the windows had begun to shake in their frames, accompanied by the electric lights dimming at regular intervals. He gave his aunt's bedroom a last cursory glance before shutting the door behind him. Chloe was bent over her laptop at the kitchen table, notebook at her side.

'Hey, Teàrlach. Have a look at this.' She angled the screen towards him.

A website displayed a list of boats and their registered

owners, he scanned the list until hitting on *Dealt na Maidne* and its owner, Duncan MacNeill, Fiorlesk House.

'Now that *is* interesting.' He ran through the earlier encounter at Tobermory pier, saw the two fishermen in his memory – one well-built, the other more of scrawny teenager. He remembered now where he'd seen the boy before.

'The younger guy, he was with Siobhan when Dee and I were playing pool in the pub. Thought I'd seen him somewhere before. He must be her brother.'

'That's not Duncan,' Chloe interjected. 'The bigger guy is Duncan. I've found his picture in the local press.'

She reclaimed the laptop, opened a saved tab displaying a group of rugby players. One of the props was named as Duncan MacNeill. The resemblance was unmistakable.

'OK, so Siobhan's brother owns the boat.' Teàrlach stroked an imaginary beard. 'And employs the scrawny guy and Calum as crew. He wouldn't do that if the families hated each other?'

His question was met with a shrug.

'We've only Fraser Donald's word on that – and he's not the most reliable witness.' Chloe read an incoming email from Dee with interest.

'I'm not so sure, Siobhan's mother certainly had no love for Calum. Almost set her dog on me when I mentioned his name. Strange behaviour when her daughter's sweet on the boy.'

Chloe hadn't heard a word he said.

'Dee's recovered the camera, says you owe her a thousand pounds because she had to buy it off some guy in a campervan.'

'What? Has she questioned him – he must be the last person to have seen Robert Jameson alive. She can't just let him go on his way!'

'She has his name and address. Says here he's a teacher in Birmingham, but he didn't get the camera from Robert; he never even set foot on Staffa as it was closed until forensics and the dive team had finished up. Dee said he bought it off a corpulent tourist on a photography tour.'

'Has she given us a name?'

'No. The campervan guy didn't mention his name, just his halitosis.'

'Fuck's sake!'

'She did give the name of the tour company – Tauth Wildlife. The tour should finish up today, but Dee said if the ferry's cancelled, he's still likely to be on the island.'

Teàrlach checked his watch, half eight. It was pitch-black outside, the wind and rain conspiring to take the cottage apart.

'Where are these Tauth Wildlife people based? I may be able to track the guy down.'

Chloe searched the web, came up with a telephone number.

'You could try ringing them?'

Teàrlach wrote the number down in his notepad, checked his phone still had a signal.

'Before you do that, there's more from Dee.'

'What else?' Teàrlach was impatient to start searching.

Chloe filled the screen with the photograph Dee had attached.

It took him a while. The scene was the same as the other puffin photographs, but the picture was slanted, as if taken in a hurry or by accident. Robert Jameson's shadow was in full view – and there beside it was another shadow.

'He wasn't on his own.'

'That's the same conclusion Dee came to.' Chloe selected the other photograph Dee had attached to her email. 'She also sent us this, taken an hour before that one.'

It was a view of the sea. A fishing boat had rounded the edge of Staffa, keeping a healthy distance away from the rocks. It was too far away to make out anyone on board or the boat's name. The red wheelhouse and blue paint looked familiar, though.

'That looks like Duncan's boat – the *Dealt na Maidne*!' The details were added to his notepad. 'I need to talk to him.'

'Are you going to the police with this?'

Teàrlach shook his head.

'We don't have anything but conjecture at this point. A second shadow; what could be Duncan's boat. Not enough to involve the police. If that *was* Duncan's boat, and the rest of the crew were on board, then someone's going to know what happened on Staffa.'

'And they'll know how Robert's camera came to be sold to some tourist on a photography tour,' Chloe added helpfully.

'Aye. Tauth Wildlife and the crew of the *Dealt na Maidne*.'

A heavy gust violently shook the kitchen windows, causing them both to stop talking.

'You sure this cottage is going to survive the night?' Chloe asked.

'Sure. It's been through worse than this.' Teàrlach spoke with more conviction than he felt – that last gust of wind had rippled through the roof tiles with such force it would be a miracle if there was a roof in the morning.

'First though, I need to speak to Tessa. It will be coming up morning in New Zealand, I'll have to explain I've only just seen her letter.' He made for his bedroom, turning back to pass comment over his shoulder. 'If she's still on this number.'

He could feel Chloe's eyes on him until he closed the bedroom door shut. The information from Dee had set his mind whirling – Robert's death was looking less like an accident and more like a murder. But who would have wanted him dead, and why?

Teàrlach set these thoughts to one side. Tessa had always been an early riser, and the time in Wellington, New Zealand was approaching 8 a.m. He sat on his bed, surrounded by the posters and memories of adolescence and prepared to make the most difficult call of his life.

FIFTY-THREE

UNDELETE

The storm swept through Inverness with a vengeance, leaving a trail of uprooted Sitka spruce across a swathe of the Highlands in its wake. Dee had drawn the curtains against the risk of breaking glass and had taken to the hotel bed, feeling the entire building shake in response to the more violent gusts. The room TV had offered little in the way of diversions, so she spent more time looking at the photographs downloaded from Robert Jameson's camera. There wasn't anything there that warranted his death, merely wildlife shots of birds. Even a close look at the backgrounds failed to reveal anything that may have been contentious – apart from the final shadow showing Robert hadn't been alone when he plummeted to his death.

Teàrlach and Chloe could deal with that – and the fishing boat she'd seen in one of the final frames. If her email had made it through.

In the corner of the room the mini bar mocked her willpower, offering a panacea she'd welcomed many times before. The fight had become personal, a question of honour.

'I'll have a drink when I want to – not when I need to.' She'd repeated this mantra several times in the last hour, and the worry gnawing at her mind was for how much longer she'd be able to resist the siren call.

Dee needed a diversion.

She prepared to pack the camera away in its aluminium case and then tried one last thing. Dee had a data recovery tool on her laptop, able to rescue deleted files off a hard drive even after formatting – as long as it hadn't been overwritten with new data. The SD card was reconnected via the camera umbilical and Dee ran the software. There was time to make a cup of coffee from the granules and whitener left in her room. One sip was enough – the rest of the cup went down the sink.

A chime from her laptop announced the task had completed. The results displayed as a graphical table showing sectors recovered, sectors overwritten. Sam hadn't taken any pictures since buying the camera, but whoever had taken it from Robert Jameson had deleted a number of photographs. Dee's interest quickened as she investigated, cursing those files recently overwritten by the photographer on the tour whose skill contrasted starkly with Robert's.

When she viewed those photographs that were still recoverable, they showed Siobhan artfully draped over a harp. They looked like publicity shots, but Dee's eyebrows raised as the harpist flirted with the camera – discarding clothes until she was semi-naked in the final shot. Her imagination filled in what the overwritten photographs might have contained.

Duncan MacNeill was Siobhan's big brother and had a fishing boat that looked very much like the one in the photo heading towards Staffa. She checked the deletion date: 6th April. The day Robert had fallen to his death.

Both Duncan MacNeill and Calum had a motive for killing Robert Jameson if he'd tried more than taking photographs. Had Siobhan asked Robert to destroy the photographs of her? Would

Duncan or Calum have gone so far as to murder Robert? And how was Teàrlach going to explain this to Robert's grieving widow?

FIFTY-FOUR
BABY KIWI

How was it even possible that the cottage had 4G on a night like this? By rights, the rain alone should have been enough to absorb what little radio signal reached this part of the island. Yet there it was, a 4G symbol at the top of his phone screen and a notification advising him Tessa was now on WhatsApp. How would she react to him contacting her two years after receiving her letter? He sat on the bed, springs complaining loud enough to be heard above the sound of wind and rain, took a deep breath and made the call.

He could feel his heart pounding and deliberately slowed his breathing in an attempt to calm down. The call picked up.

'Tessa?' Teàrlach heard his voice quiver, betraying his nerves.

'Is that you, Teàrlach?' A disembodied voice answered with incredulity from the other side of the world. 'Jesus, I thought you were dead.'

'No, still here.' Teàrlach hurried to make his excuses. 'Look, I'm sorry I didn't get back in touch. I've only just found your letter. It was left in a pile of paperwork here at my aunt's house. She died – around the time your letter was delivered.'

Tessa remained silent for so long that he took the phone away from his ear to check there was still a connection. Some words issued tinnily from the speaker, and he pressed it against his ear again.

'Sorry, didn't catch that. There's a bit of a storm blowing outside – it's a miracle I can even get a signal.'

'I said I'm sorry to hear that. I know you two were close.'

Teàrlach was only beginning to process how close he and his aunt were. At her funeral, he'd been in battle readiness – all efficiency and speed and keeping a lid down on his emotions as he dealt with everything. Except he hadn't been that efficient. Leaving her cottage untouched; relying on the solicitor to handle all the paperwork; refusing to grieve because grief isn't for soldiers.

'Aye. It came as a bit of a shock. I'd only just finished my commission – came back to the news that she'd died. I wasn't expecting it,' he added lamely. As if death issued handwritten invitations months before any visit.

There was a respectful pause.

'So, you're a dad,' Tessa said brightly, neatly putting a line under Teàrlach's grief. 'She's a bright little soul. Talks non-stop.'

He didn't know what to say. The thought occurred to him that those genes hadn't come from him. The photograph of his daughter lay on the bed in front of him. He searched the girl's features for any signs of his own, struggled to imagine her being real.

'Do you like the name, Isla? I thought she should have something of you and Scotland. I want to be open with her, when she's old enough. Tell her that you're her father. Would that be all right?'

'I guess.' He struggled to imagine a wee girl being told her real father lived on the other side of the planet. 'What does...' Teàrlach wracked his brains for Tess's husband's name and drew a blank. 'What does your man think of it? Not being the dad.'

'Jeff's good. He's a real sweet bloke and he loves Isla to bits. I think you'd like him.' Her Kiwi accent had become more pronounced as she relaxed. 'Can you come over and see us? I'd like you two to meet.'

'I'd like that, aye.' He wondered if that had been a wise thing to say. What if Jeff resented him, what if Isla took against a strange man who claimed to be her real dad? The last thing he needed was for another child to have a fucked-up life because of something he'd done.

'We've a spare room, no trouble in putting you up.'

Teàrlach felt events were running away with him.

'I'm not sure when I'll be able to get away.'

He applied the brakes, heard nothing but static.

'Listen, the kid... Do you want me to pay something towards her? I never knew you were pregnant.'

'That's because I never told you.'

He felt there was more being said in the silence that followed.

'I'm sorry. I mean, I'm sorry about us – about how it didn't work out.' *And I'm sorry that I never knew you were pregnant.* He wondered why she'd never told him – had taken a flight back home after they'd broken up and never been in touch.

'We were different people then,' Tessa said quietly. 'You wouldn't have wanted a child, or to settle down. It was never going to work with you being sent abroad, catching a few days together when you were on leave.'

Teàrlach heard the truth of it, considered arguing against it. *Let it ride.*

'It's what *I* wanted, Teàrlach. Maybe it was selfish of me to have Isla, but she'll be all right. She's the best thing I ever did, and Jeff loves her.'

'I'm glad you're happy, Tess.' He *was* glad. He'd been as

much in love as he'd ever been with her. This bright, bubbly Kiwi and her lust for life had even managed to turn Glasgow technicolour for him. The strength of that emotion had been overwhelming. They say people fall in love – Teàrlach had kept on falling and was fearful of the drop and the consequences of hitting the ground. He'd been the problem all along.

'I can hardly hear you,' Tessa complained through the static. 'Did you say you've a storm cos all I can hear is wind and rain this end.'

'Aye. It's pretty mad out there. Look, I'll arrange a date to come over and see Isla – and you guys of course. I'll call you when I'm back in Glasgow – OK?'

'OK, Teàrlach. It's been good to hear your voice again.'

'You too. Bye. And give my love to Isla.'

'I'll do that. Bye, Teàrlach.'

He stared at the phone screen after the call had finished, processing what had been said, what hadn't been said. She didn't want to rekindle any sort of relationship, he was sure of that – not now she was married. Teàrlach had the disconcerting feeling that he'd just been split in two, the original him and a version who has a child. What was Isla like? Did she look like him at all? He stared at her photograph, tried to imagine her two years older.

Was there anyone less suited to being a dad? It was a question that had haunted him ever since he'd stopped being a child himself. The answer had always come back as no. Not with the childhood he'd experienced. What was that poem? The one by Wordsworth, the most saccharine of the English Romantics with his lonely clouds and hosts of nodding daffodils. He'd never have written lines like that in Scotland, with its gales and daffodils with their sodding heads decapitated by a force 9.

The child is the father of the man. He'd know the truth of that soon enough.

'Teàrlach! Have a look at this!' Chloe's shout cut through

the storm as she flung open his door. 'Dee's found something on Robert Jameson's camera.'

FIFTY-FIVE
REVEALING

Teàrlach followed Chloe back to the kitchen, waited patiently for her to open the files sent by Dee. Her interruption had come as a relief, taking him away from thinking about Tessa and a life that might have been – and a daughter he never knew he had.

'What's she found?'

Chloe began showing him the photographs of Siobhan, starting with the young woman playing on her clarsach until he asked her to stop the slides.

'These were on Robert Jameson's camera?'

Chloe nodded.

'Shit!' He felt as if he had the world's problems on his shoulders. A daughter in New Zealand, a friend whose husband had a string of photographs depicting a woman in considerably less clothing than usual.

'Do we know why he took these?'

'Dee thinks they were shots for her album cover, or to promote the band. At least, they started off that way.'

'Do they get any more specific?'

'No. She said the next batch of shots were overwritten by whoever had the camera next.'

'These are bad enough,' he commented.

'That's not all,' Chloe opened Dee's email, pointed to the time the files were wiped. 'Someone deleted these photographs around the time Robert died.'

'Could have been Robert,' Teàrlach mused out loud. 'Maybe he needed space for more bird pictures.'

Chloe gave him a look that expressed how unlikely she thought that scenario was.

'More likely whoever's shadow that was made him do so – or deleted them after he'd fallen to his death.'

'Where's that shot with the shadow again?'

Chloe opened another file, displayed the accidental snap of a tilted landscape, puffin burrows and two shadows standing close to one another.

'We can't identify anyone from a bloody shadow!' Teàrlach's exasperation was heartfelt.

He'd promised Lucy he'd try and find out what had happened to her husband. All along he'd been convinced that Robert had missed his footing and fallen accidentally. Now the camera had been found, the sequence of events had taken a more menacing turn.

'Let's try and think this through.' He sat at the table. Chloe's pen stood ready over her notepad.

'Robert Jameson was photographing Siobhan – what are the dates on those photos?'

Chloe re-opened the files, checked the dates.

'They were taken 3rd March at 10:25 and for the next thirty minutes or so before the following shots were overwritten. Don't know how much longer the session went on for.'

Teàrlach raised his eyebrows as the mention of session.

'It could have been innocent. Just got a bit out of hand?' He didn't even convince himself.

Chloe's wry expression suggested she didn't hold much truck with that explanation either.

'OK, we can't infer anything from these – apart from the fact Robert and Siobhan may have had more going on than a standard publicity photoshoot. Park that for the moment.'

He stroked an imaginary beard as he always did when deep in thought.

'We can't be sure that's Duncan MacNeill's boat that's in the frame on Staffa, but it looks very similar. Is there any chance of zooming in on that shot, see if we can make a positive ID?'

Chloe made the photograph full screen, zoomed in on the boat until it pixelated into incoherence.

'Can't make out the name on the boat. Looks like two people on the back of it, but it's anyone's guess. Might be the boat we saw today, but it wouldn't hold up as evidence.'

'Motive. Everything always boils down to motive.' Teàrlach made a fist with his left hand, raised his thumb and touched it with his right index finger.

'Siobhan may have had regrets over the photographs he'd taken – especially if she was in love with Calum. She wouldn't want to risk any of that getting out. Assume she told her brother, and they asked Robert to delete the shots.'

'That would put her brother in the frame, Duncan.' Chloe wrote in her pad.

Teàrlach raised his left index finger, repeated the process as he named Calum.

'If she told Calum, then he might have been the one talking to Robert.'

Chloe added Calum's name to the list.

'Except Siobhan wouldn't have been keen to let her boyfriend know she was involved with anyone else,' Chloe added.

'That's true. Unless she and Robert had an involvement before Calum turned up on the scene.' Teàrlach realised he'd already accepted Siobhan and Robert Jameson were more than simply friends. After all, she was as good as naked in front of him – although it could have just been a photo session that got out of hand.

'There's also the other guy we saw with Duncan at the boat,' Chloe pointed out. 'We can't rule him out.'

'OK.' His middle finger indicated a third suspect's involvement with Robert Jameson's death. 'Fraser mentioned Calum worked for Siobhan's brothers, maybe this is the other brother? Call him X for the moment.'

An X dutifully joined Duncan MacNeill and Calum Donald on Chloe's pad.

'We need to talk to them – see what they have to say about Robert and where they were on the day he died. But it will have to wait until tomorrow.'

Teàrlach was only too aware they were literally chasing shadows.

FIFTY-SIX

DUNCAN

Duncan MacNeill was alone in his room. It was well after midnight and Morag and Finlay had long since gone to their beds. Siobhan was still out somewhere looking for Calum, driving around the island in the wind and rain. He desperately wanted to sleep but sleep only brought nightmares.

He stared at his diary. Yesterday's page remained blank. It was almost a fortnight since the pink moon, thirteen days since Robert Jameson fell to his death on the rocks in Fingal's cave.

A simple cross adorned the page for Monday, 6th April, inscribed in pencil. A full moon symbol had been helpfully added by the diary printer, warning him to beware. Was he cursed? Duncan had researched the onset of madness with phases of the moon. Modern medicine discounted the theory as antiquated rubbish; a leftover from the ancients' observation that the brain held liquid and was hence susceptible to the same tides as the sea. The same storms as the one raging outside his windows. The word lunacy derived from the same belief.

Siobhan had told him that Robert had come on to her during a photoshoot. She'd pushed him away, reminded him he was married and wouldn't want to hurt Lucy. It was a moment of madness she'd said. Robert had offered to take publicity shots for the band, maybe a cover for the first album. For free, he'd said. She didn't go into detail, but the studio session alone with him had 'got out of hand' – more flesh on show than was necessary. One thing led to another. She'd had the grace to appear embarrassed, even guilty as she swore him to secrecy.

'Why are you even telling me this?' he'd asked.

'Because he won't leave me alone. Robert won't take no for an answer. You have to make him stop or everyone will find out.'

He could picture her black tear-streaked face as mascara stained salt water the colour of sin.

'It's Calum I love – he can never find out.' She was pleading at this point, her soft hands clasping at his.

Duncan had felt angry, tried not to imagine his sister and Robert together.

'What do you want me to do?'

'Just warn him off. Tell him not to see me again. Get him to delete the photos he took of me – he'll know which ones you mean. Please, Duncan.'

He met his eyes in the wall mirror behind his desk. They offered no hope, no promise of redemption. As empty as his future was going to be.

Duncan turned back the diary pages to Friday, viewing the empty page with fear. Perhaps if he just left it blank? The pen moved to the margin, added a cross against the date, then wrote under its own volition. He relived the horror with each revealed word.

FIFTY-SEVEN
TRICKY MICKY

The storm had blown itself out over the course of the night. Teàrlach hadn't been able to sleep even if he'd wanted to, not with everything else going on. A daughter he never knew he had in New Zealand and the promise he'd made to visit, what to do with the cottage and its belongings – and how to break Robert's involvement with Siobhan MacNeill to Lucy. And the second shadow that hinted at Robert's death being anything other than accidental.

He could hear Chloe stirring in her bedroom and put on the kettle in readiness. The sky had that sullen pewter grey cloud that often followed a storm, turning the stretch of sea between Ulva and Mull leaden and ominous. Occasional gusts of wind showed in the movement of grasses, a green seascape complete with moving waves. Only a few white horses reared their heads out at sea, the water taking on an unnatural stillness after a night's frenzy. A curlew flew past unseen, it's warbling cry the only trace of its passage.

'Morning, Teàrlach.' Chloe appeared in the doorway, bleary-eyed and blinking away the sleep from her eyes.

'Do you want coffee?'

'Aye. Let me freshen up.'

She made for the small bathroom clutching a toothbrush.

'Be quick. The ferries will be running again, and we need to find the guy who had Robert's camera before he leaves Mull.'

'I'll be quick.'

He poured two cups, drank his outside whilst he scanned the surrounding hillsides with the uncomfortable feeling that someone had him fixed in their crosshairs.

'OK, I'm good to go.' Chloe was pulling on a winter jacket more suited to the arctic than a Scottish spring.

He smiled. She was getting the hang of island life.

They reached Craignure with time to spare and sat in the car scanning the occupants of vehicles and foot passengers for someone fitting Dee's loose description. The arrival of the Tauth Wildlife Tours minibus caught their attention, pulling up in the dedicated bus parking zone. The driver jumped out, too wiry to be the corpulent photographer Dee had described. He opened a side door, and a small group spilled out onto the pavement; only one of the passengers fitted the description.

'What are we going to do?' Chloe asked. 'Sniff his breath?'

'We'll just talk to him. See if he knows anything about the camera.' Teàrlach opened the driver's door and stepped out. 'Maybe stay upwind of him?'

They were retrieving bags from the back of the minibus when Teàrlach reached them, making straight for the guy carrying a lot more kilograms than was healthy.

'Did you sell a camera to Sam Topping?'

The guy's expression changed from puzzlement at Teàrlach's approach to such obvious guilt that he didn't need to answer. Out of the corner of his eye, Teàrlach saw the same expression flit across the driver's face before he redoubled his efforts to unload his passengers' luggage.

'I may have. What's it got to do with you?' Guilt had turned to bluster.

Teàrlach caught an unmistakable taint of something unpleasant on the man's breath, even outside with a sea breeze scenting the air. He handed over a business card. Podgy fingers turned it over before it was read with suspicion.

'My name's Teàrlach Paterson. I'm a private investigator looking into the death of a wildlife photographer – Robert Jameson. Would you like to tell me where you found the camera you sold to Sam?'

The minibus side door closed with a slam. The driver wished them all a safe onward journey before climbing into the driver's seat and moving away at speed, racing through the gears like a rally driver.

Teàrlach watched the minibus tear off up the road with surprise before returning his attention to the man stood in front of him.

'I got it from Micky. I paid him a thousand for it – he said he didn't want it.'

Teàrlach waited for more. The rest of the group had by now formed an interested semi-circle, waiting to see what this was all about.

'Who's Micky?' Teàrlach persevered.

'Micky's the driver.' A podgy finger pointed in the general direction the minibus had just taken, a thin blue trail of diesel smoke being efficiently erased by the breeze.

'Did he say where he got it?' he asked without any expectation of receiving a meaningful reply – more dutifully going through due process than anything else.

'No. Just said he was going to put it on eBay, but if anyone was interested...'

'So, you bought it from him – Micky?'

'It was a bargain!' he said indignantly.

'Then why did you sell it after only a few days?'

He looked trapped, searching the other members of the group for inspiration.

'Didn't get on with it,' the bluster returned. 'Sam was interested, so I sold it on to him.'

'OK. We'll have a chat with Micky. Thanks for your time.'

Teàrlach leisurely headed back to his car, Chloe by his side.

'Are you not going to take his name and contact details?' she asked.

Teàrlach shook his head. 'No need – they'll be on the passenger manifest, and Tauth Wildlife Tours will keep records. I think our friend realised his purchase was too good to be true and didn't want to be handling stolen goods, that's why he sold it on.'

They started up the road, following the direction the minibus had taken moments before.

'You think Micky from the tour bus knows something about it?'

'Oh yes and judging by the look on his face when I mentioned Robert's camera just now, I think he knows a lot about it.'

He smiled at Chloe. She'd once told him he had a wolverine smile whenever he had a lead to follow.

'Let's have a chat with him, shall we?'

FIFTY-EIGHT
VIDEO GAMES

Inverness was a fading memory in her handlebar mirrors. Dee headed down the A9 south to Glasgow grateful the worst of the storm had passed. All she had to contend with was the odd, squally shower and random gusts of wind. She'd left the hotel just before sunrise and traffic was almost non-existent this early. Speed cameras lined the route, so she couldn't push the bike too fast. Robert Jameson's camera case was strapped into her top box, secured with a couple of bungees. His death was becoming less accidental and more of a murder investigation with each discovery they made – in which case his camera could well become evidence.

That gave her another problem. The police would want to know who recovered the deleted files on the camera's memory card and Dee would prefer to remain very much in the background of any official enquiry. The image of the two shadows outlined on Staffa's rough vegetation flashed through her mind. If only there was some way of making an ID.

Dee arrived back at her riverside flat mid-morning, arms aching from riding the bike non-stop for the last four hours. She stored Robert's camera case in a cupboard, ordered in a pizza and showered away the worst of the road before the food had a chance to be delivered. At least she wasn't covered in dead flies. One advantage to killing the planet, she thought ruefully.

The intercom sounded, and Dee carefully checked the door camera before triggering the lock to take delivery of her pizza. She'd hardly eaten anything since the fish and chips on Tobermory sea front yesterday and her stomach had been complaining all morning. Sat in front of her computer screens, Dee contemplated her unusually serious reflection as she ate. Was it the frustration and worry of attempting to track down her parents that was bringing her down, or was it the knowledge that Teàrlach had a child?

Apart from the one time he'd opened up about the tragic events leading to the death of his mother and only brother, Teàrlach had remained a closed book. A book she'd taken a personal interest in prising open to read. Now she'd caught a glimpse of the contents, was it that good an idea to pry any further?

The discovery he had a child had affected him more than he let on – who was even marked down on the kid's birth certificate as the father?

The thought made her instantly think of her own birth certificate. A fairly unique document with having both mother and father's names absent. Applying for a passport or driving licence – almost any of the documents any normal person required resulted in her having to go through so many checks and interviews that she'd begun to wonder whether she really existed at all. That was certainly the impression petty officialdom gave her. Was that what was behind this sudden decision to try and find her parents?

She shook her head, unable to answer this most basic question of herself. Why should it bother her? It wasn't as if she hadn't managed to get this far without them. And what would she find if she did manage to track either of them down? What-

ever it was, Dee had no doubt it was going to be a disappointment. The sudden decision not to follow that trail caught her by
surprise. Weeks of agonising only to conclude she didn't want to
face the emotional wreckage that lay in wait at the end of her
search. Neither Chloe nor Teàrlach struck her as being fulfilled
by having parents – if anything, quite the opposite.

Three computer screens came to life at her touch, giving her
an update on world news, network traffic and emails. The Oban
police server was top of her agenda, but there had been little
progress since the last time she'd looked. Dee was tempted to
begin the challenging job of finding the real identity behind
Finn MacCool's name – even if it would take hours of
painstaking effort. If only this was a task she'd tried before, then
it would have been an easy exercise with all the firewalls
already compromised.

There was another trick she could try.

Dee set up an alias, calling herself The Merrow Maiden
and selected a suitably fetching mermaid picture for her profile,
gave an address as Fingal's Cave and made damn sure that the
police wouldn't be able to track her if they tried – which they
undoubtedly would as soon as they saw the post she placed on
the dead sound recordist's social media page.

Hey Finn MacCool. I know what you did
I was there, watching you
Both times

She read it through critically, then pressed send. If Finn
MacCool was intrigued enough to respond, then she might just
be able to encourage him to direct message her. Then she'd have
him! Satisfied she'd done as much as she could, Dee grabbed
fresh clothes and repacked her bag. It was time to return to
Mull and help with the investigations.

FIFTY-NINE
SPEEDING

The Isle of Mull has one main stretch of two-lane road in the north, the A484 taking the unwary driver comfortably from the main ferry terminal at Craignure until reaching Salen, when it turns into a single-track with little warning. Sergeant Suzie Crammond picked her favourite spot, partly hidden by trees yet offering a clear line of sight for her LTI 20-20 UltraLyte speed gun to obtain clear evidence of speeding offences. She timed her arrival to coincide with the first ferry boat traffic. After the best part of twenty-four hours without a ferry, people would be trying to make up for lost time and she expected to make a good haul. The ground underfoot was covered with twigs torn off during the storm – at least no major branches had been broken.

She needed to talk to the MacNeills about Calum, something she was putting off for as long as possible. The family still had considerable influence on the island, and this was an apple cart she didn't want to turn over. The only comfort she had taken from yesterday was the absence of any call from Siobhan's mother saying she'd not returned home, and the lack of any major damage reports. There was still the troubling thought that two people had now claimed Calum Donald was missing –

Siobhan and the PI. She'd have to make enquiries, starting with Duncan MacNeill if Calum didn't show up today.

The sound of an approaching vehicle caught her attention, the engine being pushed to its limit. Suzie sighted through the scope with the expertise of an experienced hunter, pressed the trigger and the speed gun growled an acknowledgement. When the laser locked on, she heard two high pitched beeps announcing an over-speed reading had been successfully taken. She peered more closely at the driver through the lens – that was Micky Chambers driving that wildlife tour minibus. She lowered the speed gun, stepped out into the road and flagged him down.

He didn't slow down but continued driving straight at her, so she had no choice but to dive into the verge or be hit. He looked at her in shock as he shot past, his speed increasing at the sight of her uniform. Suzie picked herself up, retrieved her hat which had caught on a branch and dusted herself down. She watched the minibus until hidden from view by a bend in the road, her eyes narrowing like a gunslinger's.

'Now I've got you, Micky. Trying to kill a police officer.'

A car was coming up rapidly behind her and she spun around to catch another speeding vehicle, only to realise her hand was empty and the speed gun still on the verge where she had fallen. She recognised the driver – it was that private detective with some woman passenger. They both looked as surprised as she was as they shot past, following Micky in the tour bus.

'Right! I'll have you as well!'

Suzie ran to the patrol car, checked herself in the mirror and saw dead bracken fronds stuck to her uniform and hair. Her cap was adorned with a twig which had managed to fix itself in her police badge. It took several minutes before she felt able to begin chasing after them. Suzie called for backup on the radio.

There wasn't any great rush. This was an island – there wasn't anywhere for them to run to.

SIXTY

SALEN

'Shouldn't we have stopped?' Chloe cast a glance over her shoulder at the policewoman extricating herself from the overgrown verge.

'Didn't look like a stop signal to me,' Teàrlach accelerated over a bridge where the two lanes separated before rejoining again. 'If anything, it looked like she was trying to speed check us without a radar gun.'

'Was she attempting to camouflage herself?'

Teàrlach grinned. 'I'd guess she jumped into the side of the road when our friend in the minibus kept on driving.'

He slowed as they entered Salen, checking each turn-off for any sign of Micky and his minibus.

'Shit! He could have gone either way.' Teàrlach paused at the first junction, then swung the wheel to the left. 'If I was him, I'd avoid Tobermory. She's most likely radioed ahead for someone to watch out for him.'

He headed past a garage, then a row of newbuilds before the road curved away uphill. In the distance they heard the unmistakable sound of an approaching police siren. Teàrlach checked the rear-view mirror even as the siren faded away.

'She's taken the Tobermory road.'

Ahead of them the road became almost straight for a kilometre or so – there was no sign of the minibus or its driver.

'Think he went the other way?' Chloe asked.

'No telling. If he did, chances are he's going to be caught by the police – especially if he forced her to jump off the road. He may still have gone down here, but he'd have to be going at a fair old rate to have disappeared already.'

Teàrlach pulled into a passing space. 'See where the tour company are based. He may have gone there.'

Chloe held her phone up for him to see the screen. 'No internet,' she explained.

He thought for a few moments.

'We'll go back to Salen. The signal's better along the coast.'

'You not worried about meeting the police again? Looked like she wanted words with you.'

'The police will be chasing Micky, same as us. I don't think we're a priority.' He started a three-point turn, careful not to sink into the soft verges. 'Besides which, we've done nothing wrong.'

SIXTY-ONE

BRACKEN

There were already two police cars at Tauth Wildlife Tours by the time Teàrlach and Chloe arrived. The sergeant spotted them right away and marched purposefully towards them with a no-nonsense expression fixed on her face. He noticed there was still some bracken caught on the back of her uniform.

'I thought I'd made it clear that I didn't want you pushing your nose into anything that didn't concern you?'

Now that her face was leaning in the car window close to his, he was able to focus on the contusions on her cheek.

'You know you're bleeding?' Teàrlach helpfully indicated his own left cheek.

Her fingers explored the area, came back with a touch of blood. She dabbed at her face with a handkerchief, cursing low enough her words couldn't be made out.

'I had to jump out of the way, or I'd have been hit by that!' An incriminating finger indicated Micky's minibus. 'What were you doing chasing after him? I'd have had you for speeding...'

'Except you'd left your speed gun at the side of the verge,' Teàrlach helpfully added.

'Don't get clever with me, PI Paterson.' Suzie took the time to lower her head for a clearer view of Chloe as if committing her face to memory. 'You didn't answer my question.'

Teàrlach thought carefully before answering.

'We recovered Robert Jameson's camera. It was sold to a photographer by the driver of that minibus. I just wanted to ask him how he came by it.'

'And that's your excuse for behaving like you're on a race-track? You know how many accidents there are here because drivers don't know how dangerous it is to speed on single-track roads?'

He shook his head, a response that left the sergeant lost for words.

'Where did you find Robert Jameson's camera?'

A younger policewoman came over, ostensibly to begin checking his car, but he suspected she wanted to hear the exchange for herself.

'One of my team traced the camera to Inverness.'

The notepad made an appearance, the word Inverness neatly written on a fresh page.

'Name,' Suzie demanded.

'Dee Fairlie. She works for me.'

'And who had the camera?'

'Can't say. Dee's on her way back to Mull – I can ask her when she's here?' Teàrlach attempted a trustworthy expression. Judging by the scowl flitting across the sergeant's features, he'd failed to convince her.

'And how did she track down the missing camera?'

This policewoman was being too inquisitive for Teàrlach's liking.

'Don't know. Someone mentioned something I think.' He couldn't have been vaguer.

Both policewomen must have thought the same by the look they exchanged.

'That camera must be handed in to the police. There could

be important evidence and failure to do so could be seen as defeating the ends of justice.'

Teàrlach nodded enthusiastically. 'We'll bring it to the station as soon as Dee comes back with it. Have you seen the minibus driver?'

His attempt at deflection didn't work.

'If I don't see that camera in the station by the end of the day, I'll make your lives hell, and that's a promise.'

She shut her notebook, glared at them for good measure. 'And you leave the minibus driver to us – understood?'

'I understand, officer,' Teàrlach replied meekly.

She hesitated as if she had something else to say, then turned on her heel and walked back to the two police cars with the younger policewoman.

Teàrlach gave a friendly wave, and they turned back onto the road.

'What do we do now?' Chloe quizzed.

'It's an island,' he replied. 'Micky isn't going anywhere. We just have to find him before the police decide to lock him away.'

'Are you going to hand over the camera, like you said?'

He drove in silence for a while, carefully edging out onto the road leading north towards the cottage that was once his home.

'We'll give them the camera after Dee says it's safe to do so. I don't want Lucy Jameson to find out her husband was possibly having an affair – not from someone else.'

'Think it's likely to stay secret?' Chloe asked perceptively.

'I hope so, for Lucy's sake.'

SIXTY-TWO

HOSPITAL VISIT

Siobhan saw no sign of the police on her journey down to Craignure and the island's hospital. Whatever incident had required the use of the siren she'd heard, it hadn't happened on the route she'd taken. The building still gave the impression of newness even after twelve years, surgical white paint contrasting with a single splash of orange. Yellow daffodils lined the access road like protestors, their heads turned away in disdain from the lack of colour coordination.

A receptionist smiled a greeting as Siobhan entered the lobby.

'Good morning, how can I help you?' The woman automatically scanned for markers of illness before meeting her eyes.

'I'm here to visit Fraser Donald.'

'Fraser Donald... Let me see.' A finger traced the monitor screen mounted on her desk. 'Ah, yes.' She paused, allowing time for her to adopt an apologetic expression.

'I'm sorry, but Fraser's not allowed any visitors at the moment. As soon as the doctor says he's well enough, I can let you know?'

Siobhan was taken aback.

'He's not allowed any visitors?'

'I'm sorry, no. I can pass on a message if you like?'

'No, it's OK. Has his son been in to visit, Calum Donald?'

The receptionist's apologetic mask veered towards irritation.

'We don't keep visitor records here.'

'I know. I'm sorry – I just wondered if anyone else had been in to see him? Try to see him?'

'Not as far as I know. The doctor made it clear that he wasn't in a fit enough state to see anyone.'

'So, Calum hasn't been here in the last couple of days?' Siobhan's perseverance was causing the receptionist's irritation to grow.

'Not that I know of. I can take your details and let you know when or if Fraser Donald can receive visitors, other than that there's really nothing more I can do.'

'All right – can I give you my mobile number?'

She left the hospital with the assurance that they'd be in touch as soon as Fraser was well enough to receive visitors. It provided little in the way of comfort. His father's sudden illness was the only rational explanation she had for Calum's disappearance, and his absence from Fraser Donald's side could only mean one thing.

Siobhan searched through her purse for the card Finlay had given her. Teàrlach Paterson, Private Investigator. She called the number.

'Teàrlach Paterson.'

He sounded more like a local than a Glaswegian.

'My name's Siobhan MacNeill. You're looking for my boyfriend – Calum Donald?'

'Just a minute, let me pull in off the road so I can talk.'

The sound of gravel crunching under car tyres was followed by a car engine being switched off.

'Sorry. Hello, Siobhan, thanks for coming back to me. I've

been asked to look for Calum by his father, Fraser Donald. You know Fraser's very ill, he may not have much time left?'

The flat delivery of Fraser's impending death caught her unawares. She'd known he was ill, some sort of brain cancer, but hearing Fraser only had days...

'I'm at the hospital now. I tried to visit, but they're not allowing anyone to see him.' A sob caught in her throat, catching her by surprise. She could feel tears pricking her eyes and wiped them away in irritation. Her emotions had been held in check; this wasn't the time for the dam to break.

'I'll get straight to it, Siobhan. Can you tell me where Calum is, or at the very least can you let him know that his father's ill? I made a promise to his dad that I'd find him before he died. Can you help me find him?'

The dam broke.

'I don't know where he is,' she managed eventually. 'Something's happened to him, I know it.'

Siobhan barely managed to speak, the words strangled in her throat. The events of the last few days came back to haunt her – the last time she'd seen Calum; the argument with her mother and the wild claim that Calum was her brother. It was all too much. She felt as if the universe was conspiring against her. Why couldn't they just be allowed to love one another?'

She broke down, her face buried in her hands and the phone forgotten. Siobhan didn't care that she was on full view in the hospital car park. She didn't care that people had stopped to look at her. She only cared for Calum.

'Siobhan?' The PI's voice issued tinnily from her phone. She wiped her eyes with the back of her hand, held the phone next to her ear and grabbed the last lifeline she had.

'I want you to find him. Please help.' She hated herself for sounding so pathetic, wet sniffs adding emphasis.

The PI waited a respectful time as she pulled herself back together.

'We'll do everything we can, Siobhan. Can we meet somewhere, and you tell me what you know about Calum and where you think he might have gone?'

'I'm sorry.' Siobhan dabbed at her eyes. 'I've been trying to keep calm, but we'd planned to leave together Saturday morning, and he wasn't there.' She swallowed, forcing the cry back down her throat. 'He wouldn't have gone anywhere without me.'

'OK. Look, wait for me there – you don't want to be driving in that state. You're still at the hospital?'

'Yes.' She listened to her own voice sounding weak and hated herself for it.

'We'll be with you in an hour. Think of anywhere he may have gone, any friends he may have stayed with. Does he have his phone with him?'

'I don't know, it wasn't at the holiday cottage. I've tried calling him, but it just goes through to voicemail.'

'Don't worry, I'm sure there's a perfectly rational explanation. We'll see you soon – just stay there.'

Siobhan struggled to see the phone screen through the tears, wiping them away angrily with the back of her hand. She flicked the vanity mirror down and started repairing the damage to her makeup whilst forcing her emotions back under control.

'Where are you, Calum?'

The distraught girl in the mirror had no answer.

SIXTY-THREE

SEXTORTION

'So much for Siobhan MacNeill helping us find Calum.' Chloe viewed the bend ahead with concern. Teàrlach was driving too fast for her comfort – if they met someone coming towards them at the same speed...

'Aye. Now she wants us to find him as well.' He braked as they entered the bend, cautiously craning his head around to check the road ahead was clear and accelerated.

'Are we still looking for this Micky character?'

'He'll turn up eventually – either we find him or the police will. Either way, he's going to have to explain how he ended up with Robert's camera. I don't know how long Fraser Donald has left, and I promised him I'd find his son. Siobhan's the best chance we have of finding him.'

Chloe held back from responding. Siobhan didn't sound like she had any idea where Calum was either.

'She mentioned a holiday cottage. Do you think that's where he has been hiding?'

Teàrlach pulled into a passing place, braking hard enough for her to be thrown forward until held by the seatbelt.

'Sounds like it. We can ask her where he's been staying

when we see her. There may be something he left there that can give us a clue as to his whereabouts.'

'Maybe he got cold feet and decided not to go off with her – or whatever they were planning? That might explain why he's not answering any of her calls.'

'If his phone is switched on, then Dee may be able to track him. We can get his number from Siobhan, that would give us one way of finding him.' He cursed as they met another car head on. 'There's a passing space right behind you!'

They waited as a car pulled awkwardly into a nearby space, the driver glaring at them as if they were somehow to blame for his inability to reverse.

'Tourist!' Teàrlach exclaimed with feeling.

Chloe wondered how long you had to live on an island before you were entitled to call other visitors by that name.

'Do you think this is all connected – Calum's disappearance and Robert Jameson's death? And the drowned guy they found?' She shared his distrust of coincidences.

'Calum was crew on the fishing boat, and that photo Dee sent looks very similar to the boat Siobhan's brother owns.' Teàrlach concentrated on his driving.

She'd made the same connection. In her mind, the Venn diagram circles shifted to encompass the fishing boat, Siobhan, Robert and Calum. She added the brother there as well – Duncan MacNeill. The guy dragged up on the beach still occupied a lonely circle, his link to Robert Jameson ever more tenuous. She visualised him floating away like a soap bubble in the air, his underwater sound recordings left behind as a legacy.

'If that is Duncan's boat, then he or Calum could have taken Robert's camera when they went to Staffa, if Siobhan told them what had happened. Maybe they had a fight, and he fell from the cliff?' Chloe unconsciously echoed Dee's earlier thoughts.

'I've been thinking about that. Put yourself in her shoes,

would you tell your boyfriend about any compromising photographs Robert had taken, or your brother?'

Chloe considered his question carefully. Neither option would have appealed to her.

'Guess a lot depends on what her relationship is like with either of them. When were these photographs. taken?' Chloe started reading back through her notes.

'3rd March this year.'

'Yes, that's right.' Chloe pictured a photoshoot getting out of hand, Siobhan's retrospective concerns. 'You don't think he was threatening sextortion?'

'We can ask her.' He checked the clock. 'We'll be at the hospital in half an hour – if she's still waiting for us.'

'I can't see her telling Calum about it – especially if it went any further than taking photos.'

Teàrlach nodded in agreement. 'That's what I thought too. Again, something to ask Siobhan. If she told her brother to make sure the photos were deleted, it may explain how the camera ended up with this Micky character.'

'And how Robert Jameson ended up dead,' Chloe added.

'Aye. We need to talk to her about more than Calum, and another word with her brother would be useful.'

'Do you think any of this has anything to do with Calum going missing?'

'I really don't know. Not on the face of it. If her brother was involved in a struggle on the clifftop with Robert, then that might explain how he came to fall to his death. There's no reason I can think for Calum to be disposed of, unless he threatened to tell the police?'

'Only her brother can answer that question.'

'Aye,' he said quietly. 'We'll pay him a visit after talking with Siobhan.'

SIXTY-FOUR

HOLIDAY LET

There were only a few cars in the hospital car park. Teàrlach recognised the harpist from Deò straight away. She stared at the two of them as he parked in the next bay, her dark eyes large with worry. They left their cars and stood facing one another like characters in a Mexican standoff. Siobhan's face still retained signs of recent tears, the telltale smudge of mascara leaving shadows on her cheeks.

'Hello, Siobhan, I'm Teàrlach Paterson and this is my assistant, Chloe.'

They shook hands, strangely formal in the setting of a hospital car park.

'Do you want to go somewhere else where we can talk, or is this OK?' He cast a look heavenwards, thick grey clouds making slow progress from west to east. At least it didn't look as if it was going to rain for the next few minutes. A curious gull alighted on a nearby fencepost, bright yellow eyes surveying them for any feeding opportunity.

'Here's fine. Can you help me find him?' Siobhan pleaded.

'Tell me everything you know about Calum's movements,

up to the point he went missing. You said he was staying at a holiday cottage?'

Teàrlach's notebook waited for her to respond. He could see Chloe out of the corner of his eye wandering over to peer through her car windows.

'He wanted to keep his head down, since my mother went completely mad.' He picked up on her mentioning her mother being mad.

'Calum's father mentioned your families having some history?'

She physically flinched at his words.

'It's all a lie!' The words were shouted loud enough to frighten away the gull. It wheeled away into the sky and called a low, piercing keow of displeasure. 'Calum's good friends with my brothers. He said it was best if he stayed out of sight for a while, until we left.'

'Where was he staying? Can we have a look around, see if there's anything that might lead us to him?'

Teàrlach took a note of the address, realised Calum had been staying less than five minutes away from his aunt's cottage.

'When was the last time you saw him?'

'Friday, at the holiday let. I was with him all afternoon.' Siobhan's hands flexed nervously. 'We were planning to get away – the two of us. Somewhere we could just live together without our parents trying to break us up.'

He imagined her long fingers plucking at the strings of a harp as they twitched in front of him.

'I went to the pub with Finlay afterwards,' she continued. 'Wanted to say goodbye to the band and friends – not that anyone knew we were leaving.'

'Are you saying Calum's family didn't want him being with you as well?'

'There's only his dad. His mum died years ago.' She brushed hair away from her eyes, turned to face into the wind.

'Our families have been at each other's throats for generations. It goes way back. There was a big dispute over land, the Donalds won a legal case against our family. David and fucking Goliath.' She laughed mirthlessly. 'There's something else behind it. The animosity between my mother and Calum's father is personal – it's deeper than some historical legal case. I don't know – it's pathetic! Our generation don't want anything to do with it.'

Teàrlach nodded in understanding. The threads of history still ran through Scotland like the warps in a canvas, invisible but holding the wefts of modern society in their place. *'The sins of the father are to be laid upon the children.'* He looked around him at the municipal car park and utilitarian hospital buildings, questioning why his subconscious supplied a line from *The Merchant of Venice* here, of all places.

'Calum's father told me that his son loved you. He didn't mention anything that made me think he was against the two of you being together.' Teàrlach watched her carefully as she formulated a response.

'He may not have said anything to you, but he told Calum he wasn't to marry me or have anything to do with me. Calum blocked his number, so did I. He's just as bad as my mother – that's why we have to get away!' Siobhan spat the words out with real anger.

Chloe stopped writing in her notepad, asked her own question. 'Did anything happen on Friday?'

Siobhan looked at her for the first time, a slight frown appearing as if she had dismissed her as some sort of secretary and hadn't expected her to take an active role.

'My family were all behaving a bit weird when we came back from the pub. Except for Finlay – he was there with me at the pub on Friday night when you lot turned up to play pool. I went straight to bed. We'd planned an early start for the next morning.

I've been looking everywhere for him!' Her hands clenched into fists, pulled in tight against her chest. 'I even stayed at the cottage last night in case he came back – before I thought he might be at the hospital.'

Her tear-filled eyes fixed on Teàrlach as she cried out. 'Where is he?'

He needed more answers from her before the waterworks started up.

'Finlay's your brother, right?' Teàrlach sought confirmation.

'Yes, Finlay and Duncan.' Siobhan managed between loud sniffs.

It was Teàrlach's turn to make a connection, between the two men unloading the fishing boat and the scowling man with Siobhan by the pool table.

'Both your brothers are fishermen? And the *Morning Dew* is their boat?' He couldn't remember the Gaelic.

'So?' Siobhan said angrily. 'What's this got to do with finding Calum?'

'And Calum works as crew?' He persevered with the line of questioning despite her increasing anger.

'Yes. It's Duncan's boat. He can employ whoever he wants.' She nodded as his line of questioning became apparent. 'My brothers don't share this family feud nonsense. They both get on well with Calum.'

Chloe's pen was busy.

'So, when did you discover Calum was missing?' Teàrlach asked.

'Saturday morning. I left home at 7 a.m., went straight to the holiday home. He was meant to be ready. I'd booked the first ferry.' Her voice broke. 'I'm sorry. I don't know what's happened to him. I think he's in trouble.'

Chloe put an arm around her as the tears flowed, shooting Teàrlach an accusatory glance over Siobhan's heaving shoulders.

'Tell me a bit more, Siobhan, and then we can go and have a look around the cottage.' He tried for a consolatory voice and was rewarded with her raising a tear-streaked face towards him.

'What's Calum's mobile number? We may be able to track him that way.'

She shook her head. 'I've tried – he's not picking up and his phone's not showing his location.'

'Even so, we may still be able to find him.'

A look of hope crossed her face as she searched for her own phone, read out a number for Teàrlach and Chloe to jot down.

'Thanks. One other thing.' He hesitated, the thought of hitting her with the next question whilst she was vulnerable giving him some disquiet. 'Do you want to tell me why Robert Jameson had your semi-naked pictures on his camera?'

SIXTY-FIVE
SNAPS

'How could you...?' Siobhan's eyes opened wide in horror. 'How do you know about that?'

Chloe shuffled uncomfortably beside him, giving every impression that she'd prefer to be anywhere else but here.

'We found Robert's camera,' Teàrlach explained. 'Your photos were on the memory card.'

She stared at him blankly, then searched the car park in case anyone was in earshot.

'What have you done with them?'

'It's OK. I just wanted to talk to you about them – we'll do whatever you want with the photos.'

'I want them destroyed. All of them.'

'We'll do that, I promise. Nobody needs to know.'

Siobhan closed her eyes, sighing in relief. She opened them again only to see Teàrlach and Chloe waiting expectantly for more.

'Robert had offered to take some shots for the band,' she began. Her long fingers started playing nervously with her hair, twisting and untwisting auburn strands as she spoke. 'I knew he was a good photographer – he's had pictures published in magazines.'

Teàrlach nodded in encouragement.

'He has a studio – had,' she corrected. Her eyes became unfocussed as she remembered the photography session. 'I wondered why he only wanted me. I asked him about the rest of the band, and he said he preferred working with people individually. It was easier than trying to arrange a group.'

She stopped twirling her hair and her hands fluttered like small birds before clasping together, the thumbs still restlessly circling.

'He was very good, kept telling me how great I looked, how I could be a model. He kept adjusting my position, used his hands to tilt my face towards the light. I wasn't used to being complimented like that.'

She grimaced slightly, then spoke so softly they had trouble hearing her words. 'He made me feel like I was the most beautiful woman in the world.'

A laugh followed, self-deprecating and ironic.

'I should have seen what he was doing, but I got carried away. "Why not try a shot with your shoulder exposed? Look sexy, unbutton your blouse." You know the score.'

The thumbs came to a halt. 'It was just a bit of fun, something that got out of hand. I know Lucy – I wouldn't have done anything to hurt her. Or Calum.'

Her chin rose in defiance. 'I never had sex with him, I'd never have done that to Calum. I told him I wanted those photographs deleted – all of them! He fobbed me off, promised me he'd erase them, but he kept trying to meet me alone. I told him no – said it should never have happened.'

She stopped then, her brows creased with worry.

'What happened after, Siobhan? Did he leave you alone like you asked?' Teàrlach asked.

'He sent one of the photographs to my phone a couple of weeks ago. Said he wanted us to meet.'

'Did you?'

'No! I'd already told him I wanted nothing more to do with him, that it was a mistake. Then he said he'd share the photographs with Calum if I didn't see him again.'

'Sextortion?' Teàrlach put a name to it.

She nodded unhappily. 'I didn't know what to do. Calum and me... We're serious, do you know what I mean? Seeing those photos would have hurt him so much, but I couldn't tell him about it.'

She hid her head in her hands as if to erase the world and her memory.

'I should never have let it go so far – it's all my fault.'

'So, what did you do?' Teàrlach felt he was one step closer to finding the truth about Robert's death.

'This can't go anywhere? I don't want anyone to get into trouble.' She spoke in a rush, the panic evident in her face.

'We're not the police, Siobhan.' He saw her doubting his words. 'The last thing I want is for Lucy to get hurt. She doesn't deserve it, not after losing Robert.'

Siobhan blinked away her tears and doubt.

'I asked Duncan to have words with him. He's big enough to make Robert listen. I said he had some pictures of me that I didn't want anyone to see, and Robert had refused to delete them off his camera. I never said anything about...' She struggled for the word Teàrlach had used.

'Sextortion?' He prompted.

She nodded gratefully. 'About the sextortion. He was just going to make sure Robert knew I was serious about the photos and to make sure they were gone for good.'

Teàrlach joined the dots.

'Did Duncan go to Staffa to "have words" with Robert?'

She nodded again, unable to say the words that condemned her brother.

'And he came back with Robert's camera?'

Siobhan bit her lip. 'No. I don't know. He said he'd sorted it.'

'And what did you think when you'd heard Robert had fallen to his death?'

'I don't know.' She started crying again, her hands hiding her eyes.

'Duncan would never hurt anyone.' The words were broken, muffled by her hands. 'I don't know what happened, but it isn't what you think. What anyone would think. You can't tell anyone – he'd be done for murder.'

Chloe placed an arm around her, opened the car and helped her into the driving seat.

'I'll stay here with you for a bit, until you're feeling better.' She frowned at Teàrlach, as if he'd just done something unforgivable. 'We'll join you at the holiday cottage in a bit.'

'You won't tell anyone, will you?' Siobhan pleaded.

'We'll not tell the police, no. That's not our job,' Chloe reassured her, then locked eyes combatively with Teàrlach.

'We'll not tell the police.' Teàrlach felt like he'd just been expertly manoeuvred into a trap. 'But I'll need to speak to your brother.'

SIXTY-SIX
FERRY

The lunchtime ferry was the same *Loch Frisa* boat that Dee had taken to the Isle of Mull on Friday. It had been touch or go whether she'd be allowed onboard due to the volume of traffic – a backlog from the cancelled sailings the ticketing staff had advised her.

'There's only me and my bike,' she'd explained innocently. 'My family are expecting me.' She'd stopped short at fluttering her eyelids but had still managed to blag a ticket. This time, she avoided the coffee and sat with the aluminium camera case at her feet, tin of coke tilting its fizzy contents down her throat.

The coke finished, she set it down on the Formica table in front of her. A family group had hogged the corner seats, children unable to sit still for the entire length of the crossing had taken to running around the small lounge area. They veered erratically every time the boat encountered a swell, giggling fit to burst. Repeated calls for them to sit down were completely ignored. Dee watched them wistfully, wishing she'd been brought up in a family instead of a succession of orphanages. Maybe then she wouldn't have ended up as a gangster's pet hacker – or using her dubiously illegal skillset working for a private detective agency.

The slight smile she wore slowly erased as she thought of Teàrlach and his daughter. She'd been angry when she'd read the letter. Furious to find he'd abandoned his own child, then conflicted when she understood there was no way he'd have known. Was that what had happened to her – a lone mother unable to manage, taking the only way out of an impossible situation by abandoning her baby? Dee knew she could continue trying to trace her parents, legally or otherwise, but was coming to the opinion of why should she bother? Teàrlach was hardly the poster child for a loving family environment with his dad setting fire to the shelter housing his wife and brother. Her being an abandoned orphan was infinitely better than his being made an orphan through murder. At least she didn't have any reason to mourn anyone.

They were approaching the ferry terminal at Craignure. The family beside her were now together, children and bags being gathered ready for disembarking. She called Teàrlach whilst she still had a signal.

'I'm almost at Mull, where do you want me to take the camera?'

'Take it to the cottage – no, hang on. I'm on my way to a place nearby. I'll send you directions once I'm there. It's a house Calum was staying at before he went missing, a holiday let.'

'You want me to head there instead?' Dee sought clarification.

'Aye. I'll ping you the What3Words once I'm there, be good to have someone else look over the place in case I miss something that may lead us to him.'

'How are you getting on with the other guy, Robert Jameson?'

'We've found out who took his camera from Staffa. I'll fill you in later.'

Teàrlach's voice died along with the sounds of his car. She looked at the phone in disgust – he'd have entered another of the island's communication black holes. Still, at least she had a destination to go to.

The tannoy repeated its multilingual request for drivers to return to their cars. She waited until the majority of people had made their way down to the lower decks before following. Dee was one of the last off the ferry, riding her bike up the concrete ramp and into the quiet little village of Craignure. Teàrlach's cottage was almost an hour away. Dee accelerated through the gears, following the road north.

Her iPhone chimed when she was within reach of Teàrlach's cottage, displaying a location nearby. The holiday cottage was at the end of a gravel road, the bike tyres scrabbling for purchase as the track climbed up the side of a hill. She had to stop to open a cattle gate, then coasted down to park next to Teàrlach's car.

The front door was open, a highly pregnant sheep deciding against exploring any further when Dee approached. It ran awkwardly away from her, belly so full it almost dragged on the ground.

'You here?' she shouted from the doorway, crossing the threshold and into an open kitchen/diner.

'Upstairs.' Teàrlach's voice sounded from a stairway.

She followed the sound and found him rifling through a bathroom cabinet.

'Found anything?'

His head appeared from around the open cupboard door.

'Not a lot. Someone was definitely staying here, the bed's been slept in. Whoever it was hadn't finished packing and left without any signs of a struggle.' He scratched his head, brushed hair away from his forehead.

'Siobhan MacNeill's on her way here with Chloe, she may be able to give us something more to work with.'

'Calum's been hiding away here all the time, then?'

'Looks like it. Siobhan said he was keeping a low profile in case her mum tried to have him locked up by the police or something. They were planning to leave the island on Saturday. She last saw him on Friday afternoon, so something happened to make him change his mind between then and early Saturday.'

'You think he's in trouble?'

Teàrlach shrugged. 'I don't know. What I *do* know is that one of Siobhan's brothers, or Calum, were the last people to see Robert Jameson alive.'

Dee made the connection to the shadow photograph. 'So, it *was* his fishing boat!'

'As far as we can tell.' Teàrlach stroked his chin. 'The only real evidence we have is that shadow, and whoever that belonged to was bigger than Robert.'

'That rules out the younger brother then, Finlay. How about Calum?'

'I've only seen the one photo. He's not as large as Duncan, I'm certain of that.'

Dee now knew who Teàrlach had in mind for Robert's death. She waited until Teàrlach finished the story of Siobhan's publicity shots before commenting.

'I'd have pushed him off the cliff myself.' She felt angry on Siobhan's behalf. Could she actually push a man to his death? Her question remained unanswered. From outside, the sound of car tyres on loose gravel alerted them to another visitor.

SIXTY-SEVEN

FULL TEAM

Chloe sat with Siobhan in companionable silence until the sobbing stopped.

'I'm sorry,' Siobhan managed eventually. 'Everything's gone wrong. I just want Calum.'

'Could he have changed his mind? Taken himself off somewhere to think things over?'

Siobhan's scandalised expression said she thought otherwise. 'He wanted away as well. They wouldn't just leave us alone to live our own lives.' She sniffed loudly, wiped her cheeks dry of tears and regarded herself critically in the mirror. 'We're not children!'

Chloe kept her own counsel. 'We should join the others at the holiday cottage – see if they've found anything?'

Her suggestion was met with a look of hope. 'Do you think so?'

She smiled tightly in response, like a parent would to a child. As Siobhan drove them out of the car park, following Teàrlach and Dee to the other side of the island, Chloe questioned her own judgement about the woman beside her. Was it because Siobhan found no problem in displaying raw emotion in front of them? Chloe tried to remember the last time she'd cried. It must have been when she was a child. God knows she had plenty to cry about since then, but drugs had dulled any feelings to the point where she became nothing more than a zombie. If Teàrlach hadn't found her...

How many times had she played that memory in her head? Dangling on a rope too long to break her neck, too short to reach the floor with anything other than her toes. She'd even managed to screw up her own suicide. Now here she was playing agony aunt to a grown woman who should be able to deal with her own problems.

'What do you think happened on Staffa? Between Duncan and Robert?' Chloe left Siobhan no wriggle room.

'I don't know what happened.' She turned to face Chloe. 'I wasn't there,' she added icily.

'You said Duncan wouldn't hurt anyone.'

'It's true. He's gentle.' She focussed on driving.

'What if there was an accident? They were on top of a cliff. Maybe there was a struggle?'

Siobhan shook her head in denial.

'Nothing happened, Duncan would have told me – or Finlay, or Calum. They wouldn't hide something like that. I know they wouldn't.'

Chloe remained unconvinced. Accidental death was exactly that – an accident. Trying to convince a court someone's death was an accident was another thing entirely. Duncan wouldn't have been exactly keen to be put in the dock with a charge of murder or culpable homicide hanging over him; Finlay and Calum may have discussed being prosecuted as accessories to murder. In either case, once the event had happened, if they all kept it quiet, then they were guilty of perverting the cause of justice at the least. Whatever reason for the omission, it would come back and bite them. If it happened that way, she reminded herself.

'Did you find your brothers or Calum were acting strangely, after Robert's death?' Chloe tried another tack whilst they were alone. She studied Siobhan carefully, saw her swallow the guilt.

'No. There wasn't anything because nothing happened.' She dared Chloe to contradict her.

'OK. Robert must have slipped or something. Just one of those things.' She pretended to have lost interest but knew she'd hit a nerve. Siobhan was hiding something, perhaps from herself. Teàrlach would get to the truth – he invariably did.

Now it was her time to feel guilty. The message she'd hidden from Teàrlach's aunt was burning a hole in her overnight bag. She should have left it concealed in the pages of the book, waiting for the time when he'd discover it himself. Maybe she should replace the letter? Chances were Teàrlach wouldn't check the book for months, years even. She resolved to do so when she returned to the cottage.

They turned off the winding single track, headed up a precipitous hillside. The tyres struggled to find purchase on loose stone, wheels spinning uselessly until forward momentum carried them on to a farm gate.

Chloe wrestled it open, keeping a wary eye on the highland cattle observing her from underneath sharp, curved horns until the car drew to a halt and she was able to close it. She could see the holiday cottage up ahead, and as they swept around the rear of the building Teàrlach's car and Dee's motorbike came into view.

'Full team,' she announced to no one in particular.

SIXTY-EIGHT

FISHY

'Hi, Siobhan, you've met Dee.' Teàrlach indicated her with a tilt of his head. 'We've looked over the cottage and there's no sign of a struggle or any indication that Calum may have come to harm. Do you know anywhere he may have gone? Any places he hangs out? What about back to Tiree – he may have gone back home if he'd heard his dad has taken ill, if he doesn't know about the hospital?'

Siobhan's lower lip curled into her mouth. She looked like she was about to burst into tears again.

'He's not anywhere.' She looked at each of them with desperation. 'I've been all over the island. Nobody's seen him.'

'Does he have a car, we could run a search on the ferry traffic?' Teàrlach's hope was dashed as Siobhan shook her head.

'He can't afford his own car – that's why I was picking him up.'

'Can I have Calum's mobile number?' Dee asked.

'Sorry.' Teàrlach opened his notebook, pointed to a row of numbers. 'Meant to give it to you when you arrived.'

She entered the numbers into her mobile and he caught her sigh of frustration as she saw there wasn't a signal.

'There's Wi-Fi,' he pointed to a bookcase where a single green light glowed weakly. 'Password's in the welcome pack on the table.'

Dee exchanged an ambiguous look with him before reaching for her backpack and laptop.

'We should check with his home address on Tiree.' He wanted to bring this investigation to an end, fulfil his promise to a dying man. If Siobhan wasn't able to find him, the chances were that he didn't want to be found – by her at any rate. But his father had a short time left, and he needed to bring Calum to the hospital one way or another.

'I've checked,' Siobhan countered. 'There's no answer because his dad's on Mull, so I checked with his neighbours. The house on Tiree is empty. No one's been there since last weekend. Calum's still here, on the island.'

The flow of words stopped as she struggled to avoid breaking down again.

Siobhan looked at him in despair. 'I told the police he was missing. I told them Saturday night when I went to the police station in Tobermory, but they were more interested in the storm.'

This resonated with his attempting to tell the sergeant Calum was missing – 'this is the first I've heard of it.' He could hear the policewoman's dismissive tone in his memory. If the police weren't going to take the fisherman's disappearance seriously, at least until they'd spoken to Fraser Donald, then it fell to the three of them to find him.

'What about your brothers? You said they were close to Calum. Have you asked them what they know?'

Siobhan became defensive. 'They don't know anything. They would have told me if they knew where he was.'

Teàrlach couldn't help but question whether that was true.

'I need to speak to Duncan. Where can I reach him?'

'He'll be at home, the weather's too wild for taking the boat out.'

'I don't see there's anything else we can do here.' Teàrlach turned to Dee. 'You want to make use of the Wi-Fi?'

Dee looked up from the laptop screen with a distracted expression. 'There are a few things I can try to do with his phone. I'll see you back at the cottage.'

'OK. Shall we follow you home, Siobhan?'

'I don't think that's a good idea. My mother's not good with visitors.'

'I did get that impression.' Teàrlach thought of the dog. 'Can we meet Duncan somewhere else?'

'The place you're staying at is close, isn't it? The old cottage that used to belong to Rosie?'

He was momentarily taken aback by hearing his aunt's name mentioned so casually, but of course Siobhan's family would have known her. On this part of the coast the houses were spread thinly, a near neighbour could be a kilometre away. Teàrlach questioned how he never knew Siobhan's family that well – he had a vague recollection of 'the big house' yet they'd never been there or met the occupants. Teàrlach would have left the island before Siobhan was born; her brothers weren't that much older.

'The place is in a bit of a state, but yes – we can have a chat there if you like.'

He deliberated what else he should tell her. 'Lucy Jameson came to me, in Glasgow. I said I'd find out what happened to her husband, if I could. Someone tried passing his wildlife photos off as their own and she spotted them in a magazine, which is why we looked for his camera. When you see Duncan, tell him I want the truth. I'm not here to pass judgement on whatever happened on Staffa or inform the police. I may not even give Lucy the whole story – not if it's just going to cause her any more pain. Do you understand?'

Siobhan's big dark eyes understood. She gave a tight nod, pulled her keys out of a pocket.

'I'll talk to him. We'll see you back at Rosie's cottage.'

He watched her leave.

'What do you think?' Chloe asked.

'I think it's an unholy fucking mess. Duncan probably had a fight with Robert on the cliff edge, then the three of them decided to keep quiet about the whole thing. I get that.'

'And the camera?' Chloe added.

'Duncan took that to delete his sister's compromising snaps. Somehow the wildlife tour guy got hold of the camera and decided to make a bit of money selling it on.'

'Are we still going to question the driver, Micky?'

'The local police will get to him before we do. He's not a priority.'

'What should be our focus then?' Chloe quizzed.

'Finding Calum Donald,' he said grimly. 'Something's not right here. His dad's only days to live and Calum's disappeared off the face of the earth. I'm hoping Duncan MacNeill can fill in the blanks for us.'

'What if he doesn't know anything about where Calum's gone?'

'I think he'll know something.' He pictured Duncan stacking creels against the harbour wall, anxious to avoid answering any questions about Calum. Something smelt fishy over and above the natural aromas of a fisherman's pier.

SIXTY-NINE

CELLS

Dee paid Teàrlach and Chloe scant attention when they left, concentrating instead on the data gathered from the island's cell masts. Once Calum's mobile number was entered in her search tool, it was soon apparent that his phone was no longer operational. There could be several reasons for that – his phone was switched off; battery had died; or it was simply out of range. Undeterred, she explored the more difficult to reach data which provided a historical view of where his phone had been. This holiday cottage was in a natural hollow in between two hills, with a limited view westwards towards the sea and outlying islands. Perfectly situated for protection from the elements but a mobile signal black hole. His mobile could still be in the cottage with her and it wouldn't show.

She tried another tack, interrogating the Wi-Fi server for a list of recent devices. The admin password had been left to the factory setting, saving her the job of running a code-cracker algorithm. System log showed as a tab. Dee clicked on it and was rewarded with reams of data. There were mobile phone numbers and laptop names displayed from every guest who'd booked the cottage during the last year. She disregarded them all except for the last two weeks of activity.

Calum's phone had his name attached, as had Siobhan's. The router log had dates and times of every occasion both mobiles were at the cottage. The data validated Siobhan's claim to have last been with him on Friday afternoon. She'd arrived at 1.12 p.m., left at 3:37 p.m. The next time Siobhan's mobile registered was on the Saturday morning at 7:16, staying for only four minutes. That was Siobhan in the clear. Everything tallied with what she'd told them.

Dee studied the router log again, taking note of Calum's mobile. His mobile stayed connected to the router for the rest of the Friday, through to the evening and then it became interesting.

At 7:07 on Friday evening, his phone stopped registering on the server. Dee returned to the historical mast data, painstakingly searched through the traffic to find Calum's number. The geographical data wasn't that accurate – too few masts to provide clear triangulation – but his phone appeared within a one-mile radius of Siobhan's home address for half an hour at which point no further records existed.

Dee leaned back into cushions, her back complaining at being hunched over the laptop for so long. It looked very much to her that Calum had taken himself off to Siobhan's home on Friday evening. That had been the night they'd seen Siobhan playing pool in the Tobermory bar and she'd questioned her in the toilets. The conversation replayed in her mind, Siobhan not initially believing that Calum's dad was critically ill in hospital, then saying she'd let him know. That figured if she was expecting to see him the next morning.

Siobhan had been frightened of something – was fearful someone might catch them talking about Calum. Then her saying it wasn't fair. What wasn't fair? Maybe she'd wanted to make a clean getaway with Calum the next morning and now knew they had to visit his father in hospital.

Dee shrugged. At least she'd managed to discover where Calum went after leaving the holiday cottage. He'd either gone to visit Siobhan at home or somewhere close by. It was a piece of information Teàrlach needed to have before Siobhan and her brother turned up.

Dee packed her laptop into the backpack. She still had the aluminium camera case in the bike top box – Teàrlach could have that as well. Now that she could see an end in sight to all this, Dee began to breathe more easily. They'd more or less discovered what had happened to Robert Jameson, and she'd found the last recorded location for Calum Donald's phone. Another day at most, then they could all return to life as normal back in Glasgow.

A pregnant sheep startled with the closing of the cottage door, running a few steps and looking at her as if to ask why she needed to slam the door so loudly, then bent back to tearing at the rough grass. The bike came to life at the touch of the electric starter, and she moved slowly back down the track, only to stop again in a slew of loose stones. There, at the margin of encroaching grass and loose gravel...

Dee stooped and picked up a smooth white plastic pebble, with no idea how she'd identified it from amongst all the other stones scattered into the rough vegetation. She held it closer, turning the object around in her gloved fingers.

It went into a zipped pocket in her jacket, with the quiet satisfaction that she now had a spare AirPod. Her foot turned over more stones and bent back the grass looking for its pair without any success. Whoever had lost it would have bought a replacement by now – if it even worked after being left out in the storm all night.

She climbed back on the bike, negotiated the farm gate and

steep hill back down to the road without any mishaps and set off to Teàrlach's cottage. Whether the information about Calum's last known movements was going to be of any use or not, at least she had something to give him apart from the missing camera gear.

SEVENTY

CHRYSALIS

His aunt's cottage had shrunk since the time he used to live there. The rooms were all smaller, the ceiling lower. There was something sepulchral about the place with its dust and darkness that the electric lights were unable to dispel. Even having Chloe and Dee there with him couldn't dispel the sensation of emptiness. He was reminded of an abandoned chrysalis after the butterfly emerges – its job done and the empty shell now left to disintegrate. He made his decision. As soon as they'd found Calum Donald and returned Robert's camera to Lucy, he'd sell the cottage to an islander. Not another holiday let – Rosie would have wanted a family to bring life back to these old, stone walls. New life to emerge from this stone chrysalis.

'That's Dee coming back!' Chloe announced the obvious over the sound of Dee's motorbike making cautious progress down the track. 'I'll put the kettle on.'

Teàrlach smiled, watching as Chloe fussed with the taps until the water ran clear. She'd treated the whole thing as an adventure – her first time on the islands. There was something to be said for being determined to enjoy each day.

'Here's the camera gear.' Dee shoved the aluminium case

across the kitchen table. 'I've properly deleted all the pictures of Siobhan so you can give it to Lucy – or the police.'

'Thanks. I'd better give it to the police since I told them the minibus driver had sold it on. They'll be wanting words with him.' He checked his watch. 'I said I'd get the camera to them by the end of the day. Still have a few hours.'

Chloe watched the kettle until the whistle began to warble its intention to shriek at high volume. He wondered if she knew the old proverb about watching kettles.

'Did you manage to find anything else about Calum's whereabouts?' Teàrlach dragged his attention away from Chloe.

'Aye – the house router stores which devices have been accessing the internet. Calum and Siobhan's phones both show up at the times she said she'd been there. Calum's phone stopped registering on Friday evening, so I checked the cellular network data and his phone location was located within a mile radius of Siobhan's home for an hour.'

'Where is he now?' he asked with a sense of relief that they'd finally managed to track Calum down.

'Don't know.'

Teàrlach felt as if he'd been offered a prize only for it to be snatched away at the last minute.

'I can tell you that his phone stopped registering at the holiday home at 6:41 p.m., on Friday, then appeared on the network ten minutes later near Siobhan's home. At 7:07 p.m. his phone stopped registering, and he hadn't moved location.' Dee took the mug Chloe held out with a smile of thanks. 'So, he either turned it off for some reason and hasn't turned it back on again...' She took a sip from her mug.

'Or something happened to him,' Teàrlach added.

Dee nodded happily, her apparent unconcern about the fisherman plain to see.

Teàrlach pictured Siobhan playing pool. She'd been happy,

as far as he could tell. That had been the other brother, Finlay, with her on the night, the scowler. Dee had said she'd seemed afraid of something when they talked together – was she worried for herself or for Calum? If Duncan was at home with his mother, had Calum turned up and how might that have played out? The matriarch's threat had been clear – '*He'd be missing if he showed up here.*' Then Siobhan's mother had threatened to set the dog on him. It wasn't a threat he'd taken lightly – the animal was bred to take down deer. If those jaws reached his throat...

'Here comes Siobhan!' Chloe stretched on tip toe to view Siobhan's car coming down the drive.

They all filed out to watch the car making slow progress down the rough track towards the cottage. Siobhan was on her own.

'Where's your brother?' Teàrlach pointedly looked up towards the road in case another car had followed.

Siobhan was shaking her head. 'He's not at home. Mum said he'd gone out somewhere. May have gone to the boat?' She hadn't stirred from the driver's seat. 'I tried calling his mobile – he didn't pick up.'

Dee stood beside him, viewing Siobhan from over the rim of her mug. He caught sight of her expression. She didn't believe Siobhan and he shared her view.

'Come in, anyway, we've found some more information about Calum. I'd like to run it past you.'

Siobhan wanted nothing more than to drive away, the conflict was clear in her face, but the lure of finding Calum was too much for her. She reluctantly left the car and entered the cottage with evident curiosity.

'Nobody's been here since Rosie died. Is it yours now?' Siobhan's question was aimed at Teàrlach.

'Aye. I've not had much of a chance to do anything with it. Do you want a tea, coffee?'

She shook her head. 'Have you found where Calum is?' Her excitement was palpable.

'Not exactly,' Teàrlach began. 'Dee's managed to track where his phone was on Friday. It looks like he'd gone to your house.'

'No. That's the last place he'd go.' Siobhan started to laugh, expecting this to be some sort of joke. 'I asked mum if she'd seen him the same morning Calum went missing – she said she hadn't. Neither had my brothers.' When she saw they remained serious, her smile turned to worry. 'You're wrong. He'd never go there, not since...'

They waited for her to complete the sentence.

'Since what, Siobhan?' Teàrlach pressed. 'What happened that makes you so sure Calum wouldn't go to your house?'

Siobhan's attention switched between the three of them like a trapped animal.

'It's nothing,' she said weakly. 'I'm just overexaggerating everything at the moment – ever since Calum went missing. I don't know what to think anymore.'

Teàrlach hurriedly asked her another question before the tears started flowing again. 'What happened at the house, last time Calum went?'

For the first time, Teàrlach saw the look of fear cross her face that Dee had described seeing earlier.

'Mum threatened to kill him if he ever showed up at our place again.' Her words came weakly. 'It's because she hates him for who he is! She'll do anything to stop us being together and being happy.' Siobhan shouted the last words with a passion.

She saw their shocked expressions. 'She didn't mean it like that. Not that she'd actually kill him, I mean. It's just this fucking family feud – I'm sick to death of it. I just want Calum back, where is he?' True to form, the tears returned. Siobhan sat with her head held in her hands.

Chloe moved in to hold and comfort her, shooting a disappointed glance towards Teàrlach and Dee who stood impassively by.

'You thinking what I'm thinking?' Dee asked him.

Teàrlach kept his own counsel. He'd met Siobhan's mother. She was unlikely to be able to do much harm to a man in the prime of his life herself, but she had the motive to do Calum harm if she bore that deep a resentment against his father. And with the deerhound she had the means.

SEVENTY-ONE

BASKERVILLES

Chloe remained with Siobhan in the cottage. Siobhan refused to accept that Calum would have gone to her home and didn't want to see her mother, much less talk to her. They had decided descending on Morag all at once would be too much – especially if they wanted to find out what had happened to Calum after he visited the house on Friday evening. The clouds remained grey and omnipresent, leaving the island almost monochrome underneath. There was a tension in the air like the prescience of a thunderstorm approaching, a thin cold breeze ruffled the few leaves that had the temerity to make an early spring entrance. Siobhan's house lay only another mile along the road.

'How do you want to play this?' Dee had invited herself along, sitting in the passenger seat still dressed in her biking leathers.

Teàrlach hadn't formulated any plan, save to avoid the guard dog.

'I'll just ask her straight. As it stands, she's the last person to have been likely to see Calum – her or Duncan. If Calum doesn't turn up soon, then the police will want to start any enquiry with them. I imagine they'd prefer to avoid any real police scrutiny.'

He thought of Robert Jameson falling to his death, and the photograph of the *Morning Dew* approaching Staffa minutes before. She'd not want any of that to be looked at in any detail either.

He reminded Dee about the dog as they turned into the driveway.

'There's a bloody huge deerhound running around the place which she can't control. Watch yourself!'

'I'm good with animals.'

Teàrlach gave her a tired look. 'Just be careful. You may be better staying inside the car.'

She left the car before he did, marching purposely towards the front door.

'OK.' Teàrlach had to sprint to catch up. 'Leave the talking to me.'

He had no need to pull on the doorbell. The dog thundered down the hallway barking loud enough to raise the dead, then threw itself repeatedly against the door. A woman's voice shouted from inside, commanding the animal to be quiet and heel. The door opened a fraction, enough for Teàrlach to recognise Siobhan's mother glaring at them both. A wet nose tried to force the door open, and a familiar struggle ensued between owner and dog, accompanied by angry, short instructions.

'What do you want?' she eventually managed. Judging by her expression as she took in Dee with her red hair and leathers, neither of them were going to be favourably received.

'I wanted to talk to Duncan. Is he in?'

'What for?' The door opened wider, the dog's nose forcing a gap large enough for its teeth to show.

'It's a private matter,' Teàrlach replied as reasonably as he could.

'Well, he's not here so if you don't mind...'

The door would have closed except for the dog's head jamming it open. Its eyes were focussed on them, deciding which one to target first. The fact that a heavy door had just impacted its skull had only encouraged the animal to redouble its efforts.

'Then I'd like a few words with you.'

He saw her refusal coming before she had time to voice it. 'It's about Calum Donald. His visit here on Friday evening.'

Now he had her undivided attention.

'What do you mean? That boy wouldn't dare show his face here. How dare you mention his name!'

'We have proof he was here, Mrs MacNeill, and now he's gone missing. You either talk to us or I'll pass all the information I have to the police.'

She stopped the next tirade before it started, glared at him with calculation.

'Wait here.'

The dog was wrenched back and the door slammed shut violently enough to shed more flakes of paint. They spiralled like miniature sycamore seeds to join others on the concrete step.

'Nice dog,' Dee ventured. 'Like its owner.'

A howl started from somewhere nearby. Teàrlach traced the source to a wrought iron grill along the wall at ground level.

'Hound of the fucking Baskervilles.' Dee was obviously beginning to enjoy herself.

'Come in and wipe your feet.' Mrs MacNeill stood in the open doorway, wearing a face that would curdle milk at a distance.

They were led through a large hall, imposing staircase leading upwards with portraits adorning the walls. A family tree took pride of place, gold lettering depicting family members going back hundreds of years. Teàrlach searched for the ubiquitous stag's antlers and felt hard done by when none were in view. Dee stayed behind him, head down like a penitent returning to church after a long absence.

'Now, what's all this nonsense about?'

They had reached their destination. The family kitchen had been chosen as neutral territory, neither bestowing status on them as equals nor quite treating them as serfs. Teàrlach imagined himself as a tradesman – one with unusual skills.

'I'll get straight to it, Mrs MacNeill. Would you prefer if I call you Morag?'

'No, I would not,' came the icy reply.

'OK. Well, we were able to track Calum's movements until just after 7 p.m. on Friday. He was here, in this house.'

Teàrlach sensed Dee looking at him as he expanded on her report. Luckily, she kept her opinion to herself.

Mrs MacNeill smacked her lips together like someone who'd just bitten unexpectantly into a lemon. He could almost see her attempting to lie her way out of it. Under their feet, the sound of a large animal paced backwards and forwards.

'He came to see Siobhan,' she eventually managed. 'She wasn't in – I told her to go out and enjoy herself rather than moping around the house like a lovesick teenager. Pathetic!'

Some people lie naturally. They exude bonhomie whilst delivering poisonous falsehoods to fool the gullible. Politicians, businessmen, priests – all masters of the art. Mrs MacNeill was as transparent as they come. She had only paused to give herself time to create a narrative.

'I told him she wasn't here, to stop stalking her. He was never good enough for her.' Her chin raised in defiance. 'I sent him off, I can tell you. Told him to never come back.'

Teàrlach listened with apparent equanimity, but he'd picked up on her use of the past tense in describing Calum.

'He was only here for a few minutes, then?' he questioned her carefully.

'Yes, two or three minutes. Long enough to know he wasn't welcome. I don't know where he went after that.'

Teàrlach nodded as if in acceptance of her evidence. 'Trouble is, Mrs MacNeill, we can see that he was here for half an hour. What do you think happened from the time you said goodbye to him?'

'I don't know. I'm not his bloody mother!' Her bluster fooled no one. 'Anyhow, he's not here and I don't know where he is. Nor do I particularly care.'

That at least had the ring of truth.

'OK. Thanks for your time, Mrs MacNeill. If you do happen to hear anything about Calum's whereabouts, I'd be grateful if you could give me a call – before this turns into a police enquiry.'

He had the satisfaction of seeing her face whiten.

'I'll show you both out.'

'Excuse me, Mrs MacNeill,' Dee spoke up in her most innocent voice. 'But I couldn't help but notice there's a lot of blood under your skirting boards in the hallway. Did someone cut themselves?'

SEVENTY-TWO
ELEMENTARY

Teàrlach followed Dee's gaze. The wooden flooring held a number of stains, none of which appeared to be at all recent. The white skirting boards were clean, almost shining. He couldn't see any sign of blood at first, then bent down closer to the floor to focus on the gap between floor and skirting board. There was a thick dark line where some substance had congealed, traces of it were trapped between floorboards. Teàrlach took out his white handkerchief, wet a corner with spit and rubbed at the floor. His handkerchief came back stained red.

'Looks like blood.' He held it up for the harridan to see. 'Do you think I should give this to the police so they can run a DNA test?' He directed this towards Dee.

'No. That won't be necessary,' Mrs MacNeill said quietly. 'Calum wouldn't believe me when I said Siobhan wasn't at home. He became aggressive – pushed his way inside.' She swayed, her skin now as white as the freshly scrubbed skirting boards. 'I need to sit down.'

She returned to the kitchen, sat down with her head in her hands. Her voice came muffled from between her fingers.

'I told him he couldn't just barge his way in, and then Dusk ran in from the back garden.' She raised her head to look at the only other door in the kitchen.

Teàrlach could spot greenery through the window, moved closer to see a walled garden enclosing lawn and vegetable beds. A polytunnel took up a third of the area, the polyethylene yellowing with age.

'He's not an aggressive dog by nature.' She turned her head towards Teàrlach, pleading in her eyes.

He exchanged a quick glance with Dee, saw her mouthing *'aye, right'* from behind Mrs MacNeill.

'What happened?' Teàrlach guessed the outcome – he just needed to know how badly Calum had been hurt.

'I tried to call Dusk off, but he's too strong for me. There was so much blood.'

She tried to pull herself together, taking deep breaths in an effort to calm down.

'I understand,' Teàrlach said quietly. 'How badly was Calum injured?'

'Duncan was in the living room. He didn't hear anything with his pod things in his ears. He could have stopped it all!' The anger returned and with it the chance to blame someone else.

'By the time he heard the commotion, it was too late. It wasn't Dusk's fault – he was just protecting me, you see? He thought Calum was attacking me!'

'What happened to Calum?' Teàrlach asked the question more directly, fixing her in his sights like a sniper.

'Duncan helped him up, took him out to his car. He said he'd look after him.'

'Did he take him to the hospital?'

She looked away, refusing to meet his eyes. 'I don't know where else he'd take him.'

Dee pulled out her mobile. 'I'll call the hospital now, see how he is.'

Mrs MacNeill looked fearful. 'He may not be there. I don't know where Duncan went. I've not seen him much the last few days – I think he's spending time with Calum. Making sure he's recovering.'

Her hopeful expression masked the fear underneath. Whatever she was telling them, it was a truth she wanted to hear.

'Where is Duncan? Where could he have taken Calum?' Teàrlach allowed an edge to enter his voice.

'You'll have to ask him. I don't know.' The hardness returned.

'You either tell us where your sons are, Mrs MacNeill, or I'm going straight to the police. Your call.'

The dog howled from underneath them, followed by the sound of claws scratching frenetically against wood. Teàrlach hoped to hell the dog was secure.

'I've already told you; I don't know where they are. The boys are big enough to look after themselves – unlike their sister. Go to the police if you want. They'll know who to believe.'

She glared at them defiantly.

Teàrlach turned to leave. 'I'll be seeing the police right enough and be telling them that Calum Donald came to harm here. Enjoy the rest of your evening.'

'Siobhan has to be told.' Dee waited until they were alone in the car.

'We'll pick her and Chloe up from the cottage. The police may know how Calum's doing if he's been taken to the hospital.'

Teàrlach exchanged a grim look with Dee. If Calum hadn't been given urgent medical attention, it was a body they'd be looking for.

SEVENTY-THREE
CASE

Suzie Crammond sat in the cold embrace of her Tobermory police station office, her seat pressed as close to the radiator as she could manage. She'd interviewed Micky, issued him with a speeding fine and then had to listen to his denying anything about having forced her to jump out of his way.

'I could have you for attempted murder!'

'I never saw you, honest. I was checking my mirror in case that car that had been chasing me tried to overtake. It's a dangerous bit of road that, what with foreigners forgetting which side they're meant to be driving and everything. That's the only reason I might have been driving a bit fast – you should go after him.'

She had no witnesses, and his smug smile was the proof of it.

'You should wear one of those hi-vis jackets if you want to stand in the middle of the road. It's dangerous.' His advice had taunted her.

The fact was that she hadn't been wearing a fluorescent jacket. Everyone would know the police were speed checking if they caught a glimpse of her standing at the side of the road.

Suzie had clamped her mouth shut before saying something she might regret.

'Let's talk about Robert Jameson's camera equipment, shall we?' She had the pleasure of watching the smile being wiped from his mouth.

'I didn't know it was his. Honest.' His plea of innocence she treated with the same disdain as his declaration of honesty. Micky wouldn't know honest if he was hit over the head with the word carved onto a giant hammer. The illustration had played so happily in her mind that she re-ran the image whilst she remembered their conversation.

'How did you get your hands on it, Micky? Did you steal it?'

He had the gall to appear shocked. 'Me?'

He'd pointed to his chest with an idiot expression, his mouth hanging so far open she could identify which teeth required attention from across the table.

'Where did you find the camera?' Suzie had asked wearily. 'If you don't start telling me the truth, then I'm going to have to arrest you on suspicion of murder.'

That caught his attention, even if she was pushing the circumstantial evidence further than she should.

'I had nothing to do with that, I don't know how he died.'

This at least was true. Micky's only saving grace was that he couldn't lie, not with any conviction that is – despite the practice he'd had over the years.

PC William Aitkin was growing tired of this exchange. His shift had finished twenty minutes ago, and this soap opera had the capacity to run and run.

'Just tell us where the camera came from, lad, or I'll take you into custody myself.'

'I was given it to sell, fifty-fifty like.' Micky had looked at the two officers hopefully, in case he'd said enough.

'Who from?' Suzie had asked, her notebook opening to signify how seriously she was going to take his answer.

· · ·

The sergeant studied the name now, sighing at the implications. Constable Aitkin had left her to it, citing 'previous arrangements' as an excuse not to put in any overtime. He was definitely going to climb up the ranks.

Finlay MacNeill was not unknown to her. The family still held a lot of influence in the places where it mattered – the chief of police, the leader of the council. Despite their apparent poverty, the family still attended those functions where the presence of local aristocracy was as essential as bottles of fine wine. The inescapable fact that this family had aged rather worse than the wine didn't matter, they were still courted by the great and the good to garner influence and further careers.

Finlay had been on the periphery of a few incidents. Nothing more than youthful high spirits: a bit of mindless vandalism, theft, criminal damage. A word in the right ear and he never made the charge sheet, never mind the court. Even if he had, the sheriff attended the same events.

This wasn't going to be an easy one for her to handle, but there wasn't anyone else to do the job. She contemplated passing the information over to Oban, let them get their hands dirty. No, they'd be too astute and risk-adverse – it would only bounce straight back to her and then it would become official and limit her wriggle room.

If Finlay MacNeill had Robert's camera, then he knew more about the photographer's death than anyone else. She could just leave it as accidental death, if Finlay only admitted to finding the camera on Staffa. Another sigh escaped her lips. Here she was, making excuses for Finlay to make any threat of prosecution fade away. Maybe it was for the best.

There was a knock at the door, then a face appeared at her window. It was that bloody private investigator! She was still cross with him for escaping a speeding ticket, then pointing out she still had bracken attached to her uniform. He held up an aluminium case for her to see. Robert Jameson's camera. All her chickens coming home to roost at the same time.

'Have you handled it?' She didn't really need to ask. He'd have been all over it like a particularly nasty rash.

'Checked the contents, looked at a few pictures to check it really was Robert's. I don't have a note of the serial number or anything, but I'd say it was his.'

The case lay on the station counter like an omen.

'Thank you for bringing it in. I'll see that his widow gets it in due course.' *Once forensics have picked their way over the contents*, she thought. Naming Lucy as Robert's widow had brought home his death once more – the head smashed to a pulp amongst the volcanic columns in Fingal's Cave. She found herself shivering, told herself it was the cold.

'One other thing I have to mention.' The PI hadn't moved.

'What is it?' Suzie asked reluctantly. Things were bad enough as they were without these amateurs stirring anything else up.

'I've just come from the MacNeills' house.'

She started at the name, felt as if he'd somehow read her mind. His eyes were serious, face set as if he was about to deliver bad news. Suzie felt her heart beating loudly in her chest.

'What about it?'

'We've been looking for Calum Donald, the missing fisherman.'

She nodded in recognition and felt a coldness in her stomach. She'd only just made his disappearance official since Siobhan's hysterical appearance at the station.

'He was last seen at Fiorlesk House on Friday evening. Mrs MacNeill admitted that her dog attacked him. I can't be sure, but it looks like there was a lot of blood spilt in the hallway – there's traces of dried blood between the floorboards and underneath the skirting. Duncan MacNeill took him off for treatment, but he's not been booked into the hospital – we checked.'

Any thoughts that Finlay MacNeill might be conveniently forgotten about were wiped from her mind.

'And where's Duncan now?'

'That's it. We haven't any idea where he's gone. Him or his brother. I told Mrs MacNeill that I'd be notifying you.'

'Are you planning on staying here on Mull much longer, Mr Paterson?'

'I've made a promise to find Calum. I'll not be leaving until I've found him or in the event that his dad, Fraser Donald, dies.'

'If you want my advice, I'd keep well out of all this. Forget Calum, that's our job now. I think you've done enough.'

He shared an enigmatic look before leaving. It was clear he had no intention of giving up on his search, but she was powerless to stop him.

The phone waited for her to make the call to Oban. Suzie picked up the receiver, hit the quick dial for the Oban detective who'd been investigating Robert's death. Outside the window the sky was turning darker as sunset approached. The wind had picked up in the last few minutes, shaking the glass pane in its frame as if to warn the storm hadn't finished with them yet.

'Oban police?' The voice sounded tinnily in her ear.

'Sergeant Suzie Crammond, Tobermory police. I've got a problem.'

SEVENTY-FOUR

RED KIA

Teàrlach returned to the car. Dee glanced up from the passenger seat as he climbed in.

'Did they have any information?' she asked in a way that predicted his response.

'No, I don't think they've done much about looking for Calum. That's going to change now.'

A voice piped up from the back.

'I told the police he was missing on Saturday night. I knew they didn't take it seriously. Useless fucking bastards.' Siobhan sat there like an unexploded bomb, her fingers clenching and unclenching in her lap.

'Did they have any idea where Duncan or Finlay were?' Chloe asked more out of hope than any expectation.

Teàrlach shook his head.

'The sergeant wasn't in the mood to discuss the case. I think she's got her hands full.' He exchanged a meaningful glance with Dee, reminding her to keep the details of Calum and the dog to themselves. Siobhan was already as highly strung as her harp. There was no point in giving her any more reason to worry in case she snapped.

'I want to go back home,' Siobhan said quietly. 'This is getting us nowhere.'

'I'll take you to the cottage. You can collect your car from there.' Teàrlach started the engine, pulled away from the kerb. 'You can't think of anywhere else your brothers may be staying?' he asked one last time.

'If they're not in the pub or on the boat then no. They're not exactly well-travelled.'

They'd already checked those two locations on the way to the police station without success.

'We'll keep looking out for Duncan's car, in case we pass each other.' He sounded resigned to failure even to his own ears.

'His car's getting fixed – they'll be in Finlay's red Kia,' Siobhan piped up from the back.

Teàrlach nodded in confirmation, with a shrewd idea why Duncan's car may be off the road. If Calum had been badly injured and not given urgent medical treatment, then he might already have bled to death on Duncan's back seat. Why would Duncan not have taken Calum direct to hospital?

'What are your brothers' mobile numbers?' Chloe asked in the back. 'We may be able to get hold of them.'

Teàrlach heard Siobhan recite two strings of numbers for Chloe to jot down. They might come in useful if Dee managed to jump on the internet somewhere. He remembered the holiday cottage Wi-Fi – if all else failed, they could try that.

'They'll be no bloody use anyway,' Siobhan said with feeling. 'All they know about is fishing and football. Although Duncan likes his music,' she added reluctantly.

Teàrlach had something puzzling him. One of those thoughts that originates from deep in the mind and struggles to make it to the surface. He worried at it until the thought crystallised.

'Did you see the news, about the sound recordist the police found drowned?'

'Yeah. What about it?' Siobhan answered distractedly.

'He had a recording of a woman singing underwater. She sounded like you.'

'What do you mean? He had one of our CDs or something?' Siobhan's puzzled face looked into the rear-view mirror.

'No, it was just your voice. Singing in Gaelic. Underwater.'

'How could anyone have that? It's something I was trying out, for a concept album. For when I left the band,' she added. 'It's my voice played back underwater. Those are my songs. How could anyone else have them?'

'Where do you keep the recordings?' Teàrlach asked.

'At home. In my bedroom. There's no way anyone else could get hold of them.'

He changed his line of questioning.

'You said you and Calum were planning to leave Saturday morning?'

'Yes, but he wasn't there.' Siobhan spoke each word slowly, as if talking to an idiot.

'Did Calum have his own transport – could he have driven somewhere by himself?'

Teàrlach watched Siobhan in the rear-view mirror, saw her brows draw down in confusion.

'No, he didn't earn enough to buy a car and I had one anyway. Why?'

'Because whether you believe me or not, he went to your house Friday evening around 7 p.m. We've been able to track his phone and place him there, until his phone was switched off. How do you think he travelled there?'

'He must have walked.' Her words were halting.

'In ten minutes?' Teàrlach quizzed.

'Perhaps he took a taxi?' Dee asked. 'We could check with the local firms?'

'Or someone drove him?' Chloe joined in.

'Why would they lie to me?' Siobhan's face was the colour of chalk.

Teàrlach needed to tell her about Calum's violent encounter with the family pet before she reached home. He watched her in the rear-view mirror whilst trying to work out how to break the news.

'We'll run a check after dropping Siobhan. She needs to get home.'

They drove over the hills as dusk settled, the dark sky tinged with red as they crested the top of the island road and tipped down towards the ocean. The car was buffeted by the wind here on the exposed hilltop, lessening as they entered the protective embrace of gnarled woodland nearer the coast. Here the trees took the full force of the wind with practised ease, bent and shaped by years of exposure, they shrugged off the elements with a scattering of twigs raining down on the metal car roof.

The car lights caught the gate to cottage, and Chloe jumped out to wrench it open.

Teàrlach took the chance to speak with Siobhan. 'We think Calum may have been injured on Friday night.'

'What do you mean?'

He twisted around in his seat to face her, seeing her eyes widen.

'Your mum said the dog went for him, at your house, and Duncan had to take him to hospital.'

'I don't believe you. No one's said anything to me. They wouldn't keep quiet about something like that.' Siobhan's voice broke with emotion. 'Why would you even say such a thing?'

'Because it's the truth, Siobhan. I needed to tell you, before you go home. The police may be there.'

'You're full of shit, do you know that? I don't believe a word of it. You're fucking sick. All of you!'

Teàrlach drove down the track to the cottage where Siobhan

scarcely waited for the car to stop before jumping out and into her own car.

Chloe held the cottage track gate open against the force of the wind, staying put until Siobhan's car reached the road and headed off into the darkness, twin beams tracing an erratic path into the approaching night.

'You could have broken that more gently.' Dee's disapproval was clear.

They stood in the small cottage kitchen, kettle performing its ritual on the gas hob whilst the wind set to shaking the tiles and windows once more.

'Maybe,' Teàrlach replied. 'She had to be told. I didn't know how else to put it.'

Dee was unconvinced. 'Telling her Calum's been attacked by that dog and may even be dead isn't the way to do it!'

'What else was I going to say? Tell her nothing?'

Chloe's struggle with the door against the wind brought their argument to a close.

'I'll phone around the taxi companies then, shall I?' Chloe checked her mobile. 'Seeing as how I have a signal – and 4G.' This was directed towards Dee.

'Aye, all right. I'll see if I can track either of her brothers.' She reached for her laptop, cracked it open and buried her head in the screen, oblivious to the two of them.

Teàrlach stood by the window, looking out at distant, twinkling lights marking a salmon farm way out at sea. Morag had said Duncan took Calum to the house. He had no reason to doubt that on this occasion she may be telling the truth. His hand unconsciously felt the letters in his jacket pocket. Somewhere, on the other side of the world, was his daughter. When all this ended, he'd go and see her.

SEVENTY-FIVE
STUPID BOY

There was a police car on the driveway. Siobhan's heart pounded with panic, fearful that the PI had been telling the truth. She ran into the house as if the devil himself was on her tail. She heard subdued voices coming from the living room and threw open the heavy door to see her mother and a uniformed policewoman deep in conversation.

'Siobhan, this is Sergeant Crammond,' her mother announced with her usual imperious tones. Siobhan hardly paid the sergeant any attention, her eyes drawn to her mother's unnaturally white and gaunt face. She looked as if she'd aged twenty years since their argument the other morning, the lines in her face no longer concealed by makeup, her eyes devoid of mascara, devoid of anything.

'What's she doing here?' Siobhan interrogated her mother, ignoring the policewoman.

'There's been a bit of an accident,' she began hesitantly.

Siobhan clutched at the edge of a Chesterfield, her legs no longer capable of supporting her unaided. This had to be the news about Calum. How badly was he hurt?

'What's happened?' She managed through the tightness in her throat.

Her mother had lost the ability to speak. She sat motionless with her hands clasped primly together in her lap. Siobhan focussed on the hands, skin mottled and wrinkled with age. It looked as if she was praying.

The policewoman gave every impression of wanting to be anywhere other than sat in this formal room with them. She fiddled with her cap, turning it around in her hands so the badge faced forward.

'Someone fucking say something!' Siobhan shouted. Her heart threatened to explode in her chest. Their silence was unbearable.

'It looks as if Calum's been seriously injured,' Suzie Crammond intoned with the solemnity of a judge.

'Looks like?' Siobhan attempted to follow the logic of her pronouncement. 'What the fuck do you mean, looks like?'

She could see her mother wincing at every profanity. Her frustration was boiling over – either they told her what was going on or she'd go completely mad.

'Can someone just tell me what the fuck is going on?'

The policewoman looked over at her mother as if asking permission. Siobhan saw her head dip in acknowledgement, then stay down as if fearful for what was to come.

'Do you want to sit down, dear?'

The policewoman had switched into professional mode, all calm and controlled. Now Siobhan was frightened.

'Just tell me!'

Siobhan had seen a trapped animal once, as a child when her father used to set traps for the rabbits that infested the garden, back when there was someone who actually cared for it. This rabbit was young, still stupid enough to have not learned to distrust men and all their works. Its neck hadn't been broken, but a deep gash oozed blood where the wire snare had dug through fur and skin as the animal had attempted to escape. By the time she'd found the rabbit, it was resigned to its fate – large, dark eyes watching her approach without any fear. Her father had been close behind her, walking so quietly on the soft grass that the first she knew of his presence was when he brought the spade down hard on the rabbit's skull. This policewoman's eyes held the same resignation.

'Your mother has just told me that Calum came here to see you on Friday evening.'

'Came here? Why would he do that? Why didn't you tell me he'd been?' Siobhan directed this to her mother who refused to raise her head and meet her eyes. 'She hates him!' This was directed at the policewoman. 'He'd never come here again, not after the last time.'

The policewoman waited for the outburst to cease before continuing.

'The dog attacked him. I'm afraid it looks as if Calum suffered some severe injuries.'

'What? Dusk attacked him?' Hearing the PI's words repeated by the police had made the unthinkable real. 'What was Dusk doing loose with a stranger in the house?'

Siobhan let go of the chair, went to stand over her mother who still wouldn't raise her head. She grabbed her mother's face, felt the parchment skin crinkle under her fingers like paper and forced her head upwards until their eyes met. Even through her anger she felt her mother's fragility in her hands.

'What did you do to him?' She fought against the impulse to squeeze her hands together, crushing the life out of the woman who hated her man enough to set the dog on him.

'Siobhan, you're hurting me. Please.'

The sergeant pulled at her arms until she had to release her grip. Siobhan stood there with her arms at her sides, shaking with the realisation that she had so wanted to kill her own mother.

'It was an accident.' Her mother's voice had aged with the rest of her, more like a croak than the confident and overbearing tone she was used to hearing. 'I didn't know Calum was coming. Duncan had some idea about making us have a reconciliation – as if he knew anything at all.' Her old voice returned with a vengeance as Duncan's name was mentioned. 'He can't leave anything alone.'

She breathed heavily, preparing for what was to come. 'Dusk heard the door and went out to investigate. It was only Duncan, so he came back into the kitchen with me and started to go back to sleep in his basket.'

Siobhan drew the scene in her mind's eye. Duncan shutting the living room door, putting in his AirPods and turning up the music to give them privacy – and escape the details of whatever it was they needed to talk about. He was a coward in that regard. Not wanting to involve himself in the messy business of personal relationships when being a fisherman was more than enough.

'Calum followed a minute later. He must have been tidying himself up in the car. His hair had been newly brushed.'

This detail brought a lump to her throat. It would have been exactly what he'd do – trying to make as good an impression as he could for the woman whose unaccountable hatred he tried so hard to counter. The realisation for his visit suddenly hit her, and she made for the chair again – collapsing into the cushions with tears in her eyes.

'I didn't know he was in the house. Duncan never warned me or said anything. The stupid, stupid boy!'

The policewoman interrupted. 'Before you say anything else, Mrs MacNeill, you do not have to say anything, but anything you do say will be noted and maybe used in evidence.'

They both ignored her as if beneath contempt.

'He walked into the kitchen, bold as brass,' her mother continued. 'I don't know who was the most shocked – me or the dog. I didn't have a chance to grab his collar, he sprang out from under the counter and went for him. I tried to stop him. I did!' She pleaded now as if her audience disbelieved every word she uttered.

Siobhan couldn't speak or move, her vision tunnelled in towards her mother's distraught face. It resembled a death mask – a premonition of the end.

'Calum made it to the hall before Dusk brought him down. I've never seen him act that way before – it was horrible.' She was reliving the moment, an expression of pure horror in her face. 'He went straight for his throat – there was a tearing sound and blood. So much blood.'

Her mother went silent, her jaw clenching and unclenching in rapid procession. Siobhan realised her mother was silently crying.

'Where's Calum? Where is he?' Siobhan's hands went out, helplessly reaching for her lover.

'Duncan took him. He came out when he heard the screaming. Said he'd look after him. Told me to clean all the blood off the walls and floor.'

'Where did he take him, Mum? What's happened to my Calum?' Siobhan reverted to being a child. Wanting the grown-ups to make everything right. In her heart, she knew nothing would ever be right again.

'I don't know. I thought he'd taken Calum to the hospital. I don't know. I don't know.' She collapsed in on herself, body silently quaking in her chair.

Siobhan watched her mother from a place far away, feeling herself sinking into the chair as if it had turned into the mouth of hell and was digesting her piece by piece.

'Why did he come here? Why?' Her voice sounded distant in her ears, and she struggled to hear her mother's faint reply before darkness enveloped her.

'He came to ask for your hand in marriage.'

SEVENTY-SIX

BALMACH CAVE

'No joy with the taxi companies.' Chloe stood looking at her phone with disappointment.

'That narrows it down, then. I suspect one or other of Siobhan's brothers may have collected him – they were meant to be friends of his, so it's logical enough that they'd help.'

'What do you make of that story about Siobhan's recordings?'

Teàrlach's lips pressed closely together. 'If she kept them in her room, then chances are someone in that house took copies.'

'You think the MacNeills are responsible for murdering the sound recordist?'

'Look at what we do know. John Stevenson was attracting unwelcome attention to the destruction of the seabed around Mull, specifically the use of dredgers and trawlers which leave the area devoid of any life at all.'

'But the MacNeills were creel fishermen. That's not trawling.'

'Aye, but what if they weren't making enough money from that and wanted to trawl? There were boat engine noises in some of the recordings, so someone must have passed close to where he was recording and would have seen him. The fact they knew enough about him to target his social pages means he was already a target.'

'Should we take this to that policewoman, let her deal with it?' Chloe asked.

'Again, we don't have any hard evidence – only conjecture. If the MacNeills have trawl nets stashed on board, then that may be enough for the police to look into it.'

Dee looked up from her computer, her brows drawn down in concentration. 'What's the other brother's name? Duncan and...?'

'Finlay,' Chloe answered. She glanced down at her notepad to check.

'Hmmm. Whoever was threatening the sound recordist was using the handle Finn MacCool on social media.'

'Finlay,' Teàrlach responded. 'I wonder if it's him?'

'I'll know if he ever replies to the message I left him.' Dee returned her attention to her computer as it chimed a notification. 'I've found them!' Dee shouted in her excitement. 'Duncan and Finlay. They're both registering at this point here, along the coast.'

Teàrlach peered over her shoulder to see a map of the island. Dee zoomed in to a patch of coastline where two blue dots lay almost on top of one another.

'What's there?' He asked the question of himself. Neither Dee nor Chloe knew the island as well as he did. The map location was off the road, away from any houses he knew about. Teàrlach wracked his brains, picturing the road down that part of the coast before it climbed up towards steep cliffs.

'Is this live?'

'No.' Dee changed tabs to view a table which to him appeared full of meaningless numbers. 'This was two hours ago.

Their phones will have gone out of range of the mast, but they'll both start moving once they're back in range.'

'They're somewhere in this area, then?' Teàrlach asked.

'Somewhere.' Dee shrugged. 'What's there?' She repeated the question he'd asked himself.

'Nothing that I know of – but I've not been here for years. Could be a newbuild, down a track maybe?' His hand stroked at his chin, wondering at the coincidence of the two brothers moving so soon after he'd spoken to their mother.

'Are we going to have a look?' Chloe ventured. Her head turned towards the window as a particularly strong gust threatened to remove the glass from the frame.

'It's not a great night to be out near the coast.' Teàrlach stated the obvious. It was just after 10 p.m.; clouds thick enough to completely obscure the moon.

The thought of Calum needing help made his decision for him.

'Siobhan's brothers aren't the sharpest tools in the box. They may have left him to recover by himself somewhere to avoid any police involvement.'

'Bit late for that,' Dee commented drily.

'Aye. Bit late indeed.' Teàrlach considered his options, listened to the wind howling around the cottage.

'I'll see if I can reach Siobhan. See if she knows where they might have gone to on this part of the island.'

They listened in silence whilst Teàrlach made the call.

'Siobhan? Teàrlach Paterson here, sorry to call so late.'

'When did you know? About the dog attacking Calum?' Her voice issued tinnily from the iPhone speaker. 'Why didn't you tell me sooner?'

He grimaced. 'I didn't want to worry you.'

There was an unidentifiable sound in response. Teàrlach thought it may have been a derisory snort.

'Look, thing is, we think we know where your brothers are.'

'Where?'

'Bit difficult to describe, they're not at any recognisable location on the map. Do you know anywhere they might have gone to near Balnahard. On the B8035 to Pennyghael?'

Three pairs of ears strained to hear a response.

'Balmach Cave.'

'I'm sorry, didn't quite catch that?' Teàrlach didn't recognise the name and thought he'd misheard.

'Balmach Cave,' Siobhan repeated. 'We used to sail there when we were younger. Not many people know about it. It's dangerous – they wouldn't go there at night. And then the tides...'

'What about the tides?'

'It's easy to be trapped with an incoming tide, the place floods. When our father found out we'd been inside there, he gave the boys a telling-off. Why would they go there?'

Teàrlach had exactly the same question.

'There's no houses there? No huts or barns that Duncan may have taken Calum to recover?'

Siobhan's laughter took them all by surprise. She sounded deranged.

'Recover? My mother has just told the police the dog ripped his fucking throat out so no, I don't think he's recovering anywhere.'

They looked at each other in shock.

'Did your mother say what happened, Siobhan? Are the police looking for him?'

Another derisive snort came from the iPhone speaker.

'He'd come to ask for my hand in marriage and the dog ripped out his throat. That's what happened.'

The phone went quiet before Siobhan's voice came quietly through the speaker.

'I know what they're doing.'

They waited for more. Only silence.

'She's cut me off.' Teàrlach checked his phone for confirmation.

'What do we do?' Dee asked. 'Let the police know?'

He nodded, thinking of the fisherman obeying the ancient rituals of asking for the daughter's hand in marriage only to be brutally killed. There was little hope of Calum surviving an attack from a dog like that – especially if its jaws had reached his throat.

'Chloe, we need someone within dependable reach of a signal. Can you stay here and call the local police, tell them to go to this Balmach Cave and describe where it is from Dee's screen?'

'Dependable signal?' Chloe asked with some justification.

'It's the best we've got,' Teàrlach retorted. 'Dee and I will try and find this cave, or at least find the brothers to talk to.'

'What about Calum?' Dee interrupted. 'Are we looking for a body now?'

Teàrlach thought that was exactly what they were going to find.

'We'll find him, one way or the other. If he's still alive, then we'll get him to hospital.'

The two women didn't want to press him on the other option.

He jumped in the car with Dee, took the rough track fast enough to spray stones into the surrounding bracken. She didn't bother strapping in the seatbelt, ignoring the electronic summons to click in only to clamber out a moment later and hold the gate open for him.

'Do you know where this cave is?' Dee asked once they were back on the road, fastening her seatbelt before she was thrown around every corner.

'I know the general area. There's a car parking space near to where you picked up their phone signal. We'll take it from there.'

Teàrlach concentrated on the road ahead, throwing the car around blind corners in the hope that nobody was stupid enough to be walking along a pitch-black road in a storm.

SEVENTY-SEVEN

BANSHEE

There was only one car in the off-road parking space, and Teàrlach pulled in beside it with the absolute certainty that this must be Duncan's car. With the engine off, they could feel the wind shaking the car like a toy.

'At least it's not raining,' Dee said chirpily. She hadn't had a chance to change out of her black leathers and her red hair stood out like a flame against the darkness.

He gave a wry smile. 'There's a torch in the glove compartment. We'll be needing it.' Teàrlach caught the car door as the wind threatened to rip it out of his grasp, opened the boot and pulled out a cagoul which he put over his top with some difficulty. His face was caught in a strong beam, enough to momentarily blind him.

'Sorry. Found the on switch.' There was the sound of Dee's passenger door closing.

He couldn't see her face to ascertain how sorry she was, just an amorphous negative of his retina hanging purple and red in his vision. He waited for his sight to clear, blinking until he could focus again.

'I'll have the light, thanks.' He held his hand out, took the torch and aimed the beam into the back seat of Duncan's car. There were bandages, a suitcase and overnight bag, and what looked suspiciously like a lot of dried blood.

'Think we've found where Calum's been hiding.' Dee's face screwed up in disgust. 'Looks like an abattoir in there.'

Teàrlach didn't answer. He had enough experience to know Calum's survival must rest on a knife-edge.

'We need to look for him.' He found he was shouting to cover the noise of the wind, which had increased in the last hour to approach a full-on gale. Even standing upright was proving a problem – they both staggered as the more powerful gusts hit them.

Teàrlach swung the beam backwards and forwards, sweeping an arc from the parked car.

'This way,' he shouted.

Dee followed in his footsteps, using the torchlight to pick her way along a sheep track. There were spots of blood adhering to the grass, showing up black against the green of the vegetation.

'They can't have gone far,' he called over his shoulder.

Dee would have been invisible except for the white of her face. He was distracted by her wildness; caught in the spill from his light, she resembled an elemental spirit surrounded by fire. With an effort of will, he forced his attention back to the path ahead, picking out telltale splashes of congealed blood.

He felt the first stirrings of hope that they might find Calum alive. If he was still bleeding, it could only mean he wasn't dead. Teàrlach ignored the small voice telling him this didn't look like fresh blood, more like spillage from a recent corpse.

A light flickered ahead, glinting off the sea. He swiftly turned off his own light, hissed at Dee to keep quiet. They crept off the track, feeling their way in the dark and crouched down in the bracken. At first, all they could hear was the roar of surf impacting the shoreline, then the distant light returned – bobbing and shifting as someone drew nearer.

'Do you think that's Duncan?' Dee's whisper was more of a shout so she could be heard.

'Probably. Maybe his brother too. It would take two of them to carry Calum across this.'

He motioned her to stay low, hoping she could see the whiteness of his hand. Two men approached, voices loud enough for snatches of conversation to be heard above the wind and surf.

'Clean the blood.'

'Find him there.'

'Story straight. We need an alibi.'

'The other guy.'

'We don't know anything about him. What the fuck!'

Teàrlach stood in their path, the bright flashlight shining straight into their eyes, so they had to shield their faces with their hands.

'Duncan and Finlay MacNeill. My name's Teàrlach Paterson, I'm a private investigator.'

'What the fuck are you doing here?' Finlay's bravado was only spoilt by the shake in his high-pitched voice.

'I think you know,' Teàrlach said calmly. 'I'm looking for Calum Donald.'

The two brothers looked at each other with such guilt that Teàrlach actually felt more disappointed than anything else. He was sharp enough to catch Duncan trying to see past the flashlight to work out his odds.

'Don't think of trying anything,' he cautioned. 'I'm not alone and the police will be here any second. It's over, lads. You may as well tell me what you've done with Calum so we can get him the help he needs.'

Teàrlach's heart sank as Finlay laughed in his face.

'You work miracles, mate?' His laughter stopped as

suddenly as it had started. 'He's been dead for days. Starting to smell as well.'

Teàrlach wondered if the younger brother was slightly mad. His attention was caught by headlights sweeping across the sky. The police had made better timing than he'd thought they would.

Finlay took advantage of Teàrlach's distraction, shoving into his shoulder and making towards the car park. He only made a few steps before tripping and flying face first onto the ground. Dee emerged invisible from the bracken, placing a leather boot firmly enough on his back to keep him planted there.

'Don't try and stand. I can kick you in the balls very easily from here – and believe me, I've had practice.'

Duncan's jaw had dropped at the sight of the woman springing up from the ground like an apparition made flesh. The approaching car slewed into the car park, a door slammed and an erratic beam cut a swathe through the air towards them. They were frozen into position, waiting for whoever this was.

'Siobhan!' Duncan recognised her first. 'Why are you here?'

If Dee was an apparition, then Siobhan was more like a banshee looking to exact revenge. Teàrlach backed away when he saw the crowbar in her hand, raised ready to strike. Her eyes caught in the torchlight like a wild animal.

'Put it down, Siobhan,' Teàrlach tried to calm her. 'There's been enough harm done.'

She scarcely paid him or Dee any notice, stepping over Finlay's prostrate body without so much as a glance.

'What have you done with him?' Siobhan directed the question to her elder brother.

Duncan hadn't moved from the spot since Teàrlach had challenged him. He looked lost.

'I've put him in the cave, Siobhan. I've laid him to rest.' His hands went out towards her. 'I tried to help. There was nothing I could do!' His despairing cry was caught by the wind. 'I told

Calum to wait in the car until I was sure the dog was locked up, but Mum wasn't having any of it. She said this was as much the dog's home as hers and she wasn't going to lock Dusk away. Then Calum just walked into the kitchen. I couldn't stop Dusk, he was too quick. By the time I pulled Dusk off him, it was too late. He died before I could reach the hospital. I didn't know what else to do.'

She stared at him with pure hatred, then pushed past him and started running down towards the sea.

'Don't go there, Siobhan. It's not safe...' Duncan tried to make a grab for her, but she'd anticipated his reaction, swinging the metal bar at his outstretched hands. There was the sound of bone breaking, a dry, brittle snap loud enough to be heard over the wind and waves.

'He's all I ever had and you took him from me!' Her anguished cry was swallowed by the wind.

Duncan pulled his hands into his chest, nursed them with a whimper of pain.

'She can't. It's not safe. The tide's coming in. She'll be trapped there with him,' he entreated Teàrlach to stop her.

Teàrlach held still. He couldn't leave Dee alone with the two desperate men. Where were the police?

'Come back to the car. I'll shut you both in there and then go after your sister.'

He motioned the way back to the car park with his flashlight. Duncan turned and ran after Siobhan whilst the light was out of his eyes, calling for her to stop.

'Shit!' Teàrlach cursed. 'Here, take the torch and hit him with it if he tries to move. Hard!'

Dee hesitated. 'How are you going to see where you're going?'

'Just take the bloody thing! I've been on night manoeuvres before – I'll be OK.'

Dee's doubtful expression wasn't what he needed in that

moment. He thrust the torch into her hands, then gave a silent thanks as she swung the beam to illuminate the direction Duncan and Siobhan had taken. The track wasn't at all clear. It would only take one wrong step and he'd fall down to the rocks below.

SEVENTY-EIGHT

LAMENT

It was almost midnight. The night was as black as any he could ever remember, even the sky had lost any faint light from the moon as heavy clouds covered it as effectively as a blackout curtain. The small light from his iPhone barely helped. He felt his way forward, each foot gingerly testing the ground before the next was placed in front. The surf was getting louder, crashing angrily against unseen rocks and threatening him with an unpleasant death if he put one foot wrong.

Then a new sound came from somewhere ahead of him, an unearthly call echoing strangely into the night. The thought of sirens crossed his mind, mythological women attracting sailors to their death. Anything would be possible on a night such as this. Wind howling and threatening to push him off balance, the sea crashing dangerously close by.

A lull in the wind enabled the voice to be heard more clearly. It was Siobhan, crying into the night. It sounded like a lament, every note squeezed from a broken heart and filling the night air with dread. He must be getting close. Teàrlach dropped to all fours, using his fingers to feel the ground ahead of him as the path plunged down closer to the thundering sea.

Siobhan's voice was close, crying now as the lament fragmented into tears of pain and loss.

He jumped when Duncan appeared in front of him.

'Stay there. It's not safe,' he commanded Teàrlach. 'I'll fetch her out. It's all my fault.'

Teàrlach stayed where he was, unsure of the path ahead. There might have been a sheer drop into the sea or a clear path – with the sound of the wind and sea and impenetrable night he was so disoriented it would have been madness to proceed. He was caught in a dilemma – to go after Duncan and Siobhan and risk leaving Dee on her own any longer, or to stay perched at the edge of an unknown drop next to the crashing waves.

Siobhan's wailing abruptly cut off. He strained to hear what was happening just metres away from where he crouched, his vision now all but useless.

Duncan suddenly reappeared, Siobhan's inert body in his arms. He dropped her clumsily at Teàrlach's feet, almost throwing him off the path. His iPhone shone a weak light down to crashing waves and certain death if he'd taken one more step.

'Here,' Duncan cried. 'Take her back to the car.'

Teàrlach shone his iPhone to check Siobhan's inert body.

'What did you do to her?' He shouted to be heard.

'I had to knock her out. She wouldn't leave him. I'm going back for Calum – it's not right leaving him for the sea. I'll join you back at the car, I promise. I'm sorry. Oh God, I'm so sorry.'

Teàrlach heard the unmistakable sound of Duncan's crying fade into the night. He couldn't go after him, not without knowing the lay of the land. Siobhan had to be his responsibility now.

He caught her under her arms and dragged her backwards, awkwardly retracing his steps back to Dee and Finlay. She weighed more than he would have expected, her clothes catching on rocks and stunted bushes as he pulled her along. Dee's flashlight circled the air like a lighthouse beam, and unlike the sailor he used it as a homing beacon until close enough to call out.

'Dee. Shine it over here so I can see where I'm going.'

The light swept erratically in his direction, and he shut his eyes until the beam found them, then lowered to illuminate the path.

'What's wrong with her?' Dee called.

'Unconscious. Duncan must have hit her,' he shouted back.

'Bastard!' Dee said with feeling.

Teàrlach held back judgement on Duncan's apparent violence. He didn't know what had happened in the cave, or what was happening now.

Another car's lights swept across the sky, a familiar blue light strobing behind the headlights.

'Thank fuck!' Dee exclaimed.

That's one of the few times she's ever been pleased to see the police. The thought ran through Teàrlach's mind as he laid Siobhan down. The torch beam swung down to reveal a cut to Siobhan's forehead. She moaned in response to the light, covering her eyes with the back of her hand.

'She's all right, then.' Dee made a swift assessment of the other woman's health. 'Where's Duncan?'

'He went back into the cave to fetch Calum's body. Said he needed a proper place to be laid to rest – not let the sea take him.'

Dee took the opportunity to see to Siobhan, using the torch to check she wasn't too badly hurt. Her eyes opened under the intense light, then immediately closed with a hand going to shield her face.

'Take the torch away, I can't see anything.' Siobhan's voice sounded strong enough to reassure Teàrlach that she wasn't badly injured. 'Where's Calum?'

Dee had to prevent Siobhan from struggling to her feet.

'You can't go back. You can hardly stand after that knock to your head!' Dee had to shout above the wind.

'Give me the torch.' Teàrlach waved it into the night sky, alerting the police to their location. 'I'm going back to help Duncan, the police will be here any minute.' He shouted above the wind and headed back along the precipitous track.

The path was narrow where it twisted down towards the crashing waves. It was a miracle that Duncan had been able to carry Siobhan's unconscious body up such a treacherous slope. Ahead he could make out a cave entrance – how was Duncan able to find his way without a torch? The sea was deafening this close, giant waves smashing into the rocks and throwing freezing spray into his face.

Teàrlach called Duncan's name, but his shouts were caught by the storm.

He inched forward on rocks slick with seaweed, his feet repeatedly slipping and threatening to throw him into the maelstrom of water churning metres underneath. There was nothing to grip, no clear path forward. A huge swell filled the cave entrance, almost taking Teàrlach with it. The incoming tide had blocked any access. There was no way anyone could get in or out of the cave now.

Defeated, Teàrlach climbed carefully back up towards Dee. Duncan's only hope was to stay put and keep above the water.

'Over here, sergeant! I've found them.' A strong Somerset accent bellowed nearby and its owner came into view, closely followed by Suzie Crammond. The look on Sergeant Suzie Crammond's face and that of her male PC suggested Teàrlach and Dee were going to be given a hard time, instead of plaudits for doing the police's work for them.

'I thought I told you to keep your nose out of this?' Teàrlach couldn't see the policewoman's expression with her searchlight planted squarely in his face, but he could imagine it well enough.

SEVENTY-NINE

LUCY

They'd spent hours at the police station in Tobermory. Sergeant Suzie Crammond had taken statements from each of them, cross-examining Teàrlach, Dee and Chloe without giving the impression that she believed a word they said.

The stories tallied, even to the point of unexplained gaps where they were unable to say precisely how they had known where to find the two brothers. She knew they were holding back, and Teàrlach guessed she had a shrewd idea of how they had managed to find them, but she had too much on her plate.

Finlay had given his version of events, saying Duncan had asked him to help move Calum's body and he'd been too frightened to go to the police as he knew he should. He claimed to have no knowledge of how the underwater sound recordist had ended up dead, or any idea that the family dog had killed Calum until last night.

She didn't believe him. Neither did Teàrlach, but without any proof he was going to be charged with perverting the course of justice along with his mother.

They'd had to repeat the whole story in the early hours of the morning when the detective arrived from Oban. Teàrlach had never seen someone actually turn green with sea sickness before, but a trip from Oban to Tobermory in a police RIB after last night's storm couldn't have been a comfortable experience.

Teàrlach had heard that the police dive team had managed to pull Duncan and Calum out of the sea cave, but too late to save Duncan from drowning. The high tide had filled the cave, pushed by the force of gales the water had flooded in faster than Duncan would have allowed for – even with his experience of the local waters. His broken hands wouldn't have been much help to him. Calum's body had been sent for post-mortem, although the ragged tear in his throat was obvious enough cause for death.

Teàrlach knew more than the police, but it wouldn't help anyone to give them the whole story. It certainly wouldn't help Duncan who was in line to be accused posthumously as an accessory to murder. Siobhan had stowed Duncan's diary under Chloe's passenger seat – as if she thought she'd never be coming back. Teàrlach was as certain as he could be that Siobhan had intended to die in the cave with Calum. Chloe had only discovered the diary when they'd parked up near Lucy's house after the police had finally let them leave.

Teàrlach glanced at the pages, scrolled though the year's fish catches, Duncan's concerns about his mental health, his dreams for the future he'd never now have. Recent events had been jotted down in a childlike hand. Duncan had agonised about Calum and his sister, happy for them to be together and unknowing of his mother's concerns. It had been Duncan's idea to drive Calum home so he could attempt a reconciliation with Morag. The outcome of that tragic event was all too clear in his written words. The circumstances surrounding Robert's death was also listed in clumsy longhand. A comedy of errors with deadly results.

Teàrlach handed it back to Chloe.

'I don't want Lucy to see that.'

'Do you want me to come in with you?' Chloe offered.

'It's best if I talk to her alone. Thanks, though.'

'Are you going to tell her everything?' Chloe asked as he opened the driver's door.

'I don't know, Chloe.'

Lucy opened the door before his hand had reached the bell.

'I saw you, outside,' she explained. 'I've been waiting for you.'

Teàrlach stood awkwardly in her living room until she joined him.

'Please, take a seat.' Lucy pointed to the nearest chair.

The words reminded him of when she'd appeared in his office just a week ago. She sat in an adjacent seat, hands linked on her lap and turned to face him.

'I want to know everything, Teàrlach. Please, don't hold anything back. I'd rather hear it all from you than anyone else.'

Teàrlach drew a long breath, saw the quiet acceptance in her eyes. The carefree girl he remembered was no longer there.

'We found Robert's camera.'

'I know. The police have already been in touch.'

What else had they told her? Teàrlach knew then he'd have to tell her everything. It wouldn't be a kindness to hold back.

'Robert had taken publicity shots of Siobhan MacNeill. They were meant to be flirty, provocative, but went too far.' He saw her flinch. Lucy closed her eyes, then nodded to herself.

'Go on.'

'Siobhan had asked Robert to delete the more explicit shots, but Duncan decided to step in when Robert refused. He was threatening to anonymously send them to Calum if Siobhan didn't agree to meet up with him again. I'm sorry, you shouldn't have to hear this.'

'I want to know everything, Teàrlach. I'd prefer to hear it from you than have people gossip behind my back. You'll remember enough about island life to know that's how it goes.'

Teàrlach nodded.

'She asked Duncan to talk to him, make him delete the photographs. There was a struggle – on the cliff – and Robert fell. I'm convinced it was an accident, Lucy. He never meant for Robert to die.'

A solitary tear made slow progression down her cheek. She made no attempt to wipe it away.

'Micky Chambers was given the camera to dispose of, after Duncan had deleted Siobhan's pictures. He didn't know anything about the circumstances – he's not to blame for any of this.'

She made no response apart from another tear joining the first.

'Duncan's dead. He drowned last night.'

'How?' she asked without emotion.

'He saved Siobhan. She would have drowned in the cave where Calum Donald's body lay if he hadn't brought her out. He tried to bring Calum out as well but didn't make it.'

'Calum's dead as well?'

'The MacNeills' dog attacked him when he went to their house. He died on the way to the hospital. Duncan panicked and hid his body.'

'So I'm not the only one left to grieve.' She dabbed at her eyes. 'I want to hate her and now I can't.'

'I'm so sorry, Lucy.' He had no other words to offer.

'Thank you for being honest with me. I know it can't have been easy.' She stood, head bowed so he couldn't see her face. 'I'd like to be left alone now, Teàrlach.'

'Of course. I understand. If there's anything I can do...'

She shut the door on him, muffling the cries of anguish that followed.

'How did that go?' Chloe asked doubtfully once he was back in the car.

'About as well as it could,' Teàrlach replied.

EIGHTY

BLOODY FEUD

The hospital was close to the ferry terminal. Teàrlach pulled into the car park and told Chloe he wouldn't be long. There was one last call he had to make.

He was alone in the hospital waiting room, Duncan's diary open in his hands. The doctor still hadn't come back to say Fraser Donald was well enough to see him. Teàrlach didn't mind waiting. It was better than having to face Calum's father.

He opened the diary to the last few pages, read the account of Calum's death one more time as if to commit it to memory.

"Teàrlach Paterson?' He looked up to see the doctor standing over him in his white coat.

'Aye,' he answered.

'You can see Fraser Donald now.' He smiled as if granting a wish was part of the job.

'Thanks,' Teàrlach replied. He returned Duncan's diary to his jacket pocket, his feet like lead as he followed the white coated doctor into the ward, pulling back a curtain like he was about to put on a theatre show.

'I'll leave you to it,' he said. 'No longer than ten minutes,

OK?' A finger wagged at him as if he was still at school. 'He's on strong medication, don't expect too much of him.'

'Sure,' Teàrlach replied. He sat next to the bed, looked into Fraser's rheumy eyes and saw death waiting.

'The police have already told me Calum's dead.' Fraser gave him that freedom at least – one less burden he didn't have to unload.

'I'm sorry. I'm sorry we didn't find him in time.' Teàrlach spoke quietly. These words were for him alone, not the other patients surrounding them in their own tented beds.

'You tried. I know you tried.' A hand rested on his, cold and wrinkled. A transparent tube attached to a white bandage reaching up to a clear sachet of fluid.

Teàrlach had so much to say, so little time to say it in. Calum was meant to have come to see his father to give his final farewell. How many of us miss that last moment – carrying on as if life goes on forever and we have all the time in the world to see friends, lovers, family one more time. Not for Calum – or for his father.

'He was trying to make peace with Morag,' he started, unsure how far down this road he should travel.

'We once loved each other, Morag and I.' A smile stretched tight skin, the hand patted Teàrlach's. 'When we were young. Imagine that!' Fraser attempted to laugh, and the machines connected to him protested with warning beeps and flashing lights.

'Did Morag tell you Siobhan was our daughter?'

Teàrlach shook his head. 'She never mentioned it. Maybe that explains Morag's attempts to try to stop them seeing each other?'

The laughter died. 'Yes, it would excuse her behaviour, but she knew Siobhan couldn't have been mine.' His fingers mimed a cutting action. 'Had it done after Calum. We couldn't afford any more – and then my wife died. No, Mr Paterson – Morag simply couldn't stand her daughter having the life she wanted. My wife was dying, and Morag never forgave me for refusing to leave her.'

They sat quietly together, the implications for Calum's needless death sitting with them like the ghost at a wake.

'They would have made a fine couple. An end to this bloody feud. I should have given him my blessing.' Fraser's eyes closed for so long that Teàrlach leaned over him to make sure he was still breathing.

Fraser's eyes opened centimetres away from Teàrlach's, making him jump back in surprise.

'I'm not gone yet, lad.' The slight smile returned. 'Do you have children?'

Teàrlach thought of the daughter he never knew he had on the other side of the world.

'One. A girl.' He didn't have the time to explain.

'Good. We need children.' Fraser patted his hand again in benediction. 'It's the only thing that ever makes any fucking sense about this life. Making more life.'

Teàrlach heard the wisdom in the old man's words, so close as he was to death.

'Would it have been quick, my boy's death?' His eyes sought Teàrlach's.

'Aye. Very quick.' Teàrlach imagined the teeth closing on his throat, the jugular spraying blood through torn flesh. Five to ten seconds, his army training informed him.

'That's a blessing. Better than this,' Fraser looked at the medical equipment keeping him alive. 'I'll be seeing him soon enough.' He coughed; a trickle of blood spilled down his chin.

Teàrlach looked for tissues, considered calling for a nurse, but the old man's hand pressed down on his.

'Don't worry about me, son. I'll not see out the day and I'm glad. Thank you again for finding my boy.'

'I'm only sorry I found him too late.'

'No. You found him when he was meant to be found.'

The cubicle curtain drew back, the doctor stood there like an archangel.

'Time's up, Mr Paterson. Fraser needs his rest.'

The hand raised, allowing Teàrlach back his freedom. 'Thank you, Teàrlach. Goodbye, son.'

'Goodbye, Fraser. It's been a privilege knowing you.'

He wiped the tear away as surreptitiously as he could, pulled himself together before returning to Chloe in the car.

The ferry was booked for an hour's time. Dee would already be waiting there in the queue, probably staring at a takeaway coffee in disgust.

'Have you decided what you're doing with the cottage?' Chloe's attempt at making small talk wasn't working as she might have hoped.

'Aye. I'm having the contents cleared: sold or given to charity – I'll let the auctioneers decide. Then I'm selling it to an island family. It's not going to be a holiday cottage; I'm making sure of that.'

He drove the last few hundred metres towards the ferry car park.

'Rosie would have wanted a family to have the place. Somewhere to bring up children and fill the house with their noise.'

He thought of his own upbringing and wondered how much joy he'd brought into his aunt's life. Probably best not to go there.

'There's Dee!' Chloe called out with childlike glee. 'Why's she staring so miserably at her cup?'

. . .

They shared a table in the ferry lounge. Chloe writing in her notepad, Dee reading Duncan's diary. Teàrlach watched as the Isle of Mull slipped past them until Duart Point Lighthouse signalled they had almost left the island behind. His thoughts were on the past, and of his daughter.

'What Duncan's written here doesn't line up with the version his mother gave.' Dee broke the unnatural silence.

'Aye. I know.' He gave a grim smile. 'Morag said Calum had barged in, pushed past her and then the dog attacked.'

Chloe looked up from her notebook in interest. 'What was Duncan's take?'

Dee bent down to the diary. 'He mentions trying to heal the rift between his mum and Calum, picking him up from the holiday cottage and then taking him to the family house. Hang on...'

Her finger traced Duncan's cursive script halfway down the page.

'Here we are.'

She adopted a reading voice as she voiced Duncan's own words.

'Mum wouldn't have Dusk locked away. Then Calum walked in.'

Chloe's eyes opened wide. 'She wanted the dog to attack him?'

Teàrlach shrugged. 'Guess we'll never know. The police were probably given another story altogether.'

'Why carry him all the way to that cave? It makes no sense,' Chloe continued questioning.

'It was their secret. Duncan, Finlay and Siobhan. A child-hood hideaway only they knew about.

Teàrlach saw the isle of Kerrera slide into view. They had almost reached Oban and the road back to Glasgow. 'I don't know if the truth will ever come out about John Stevenson's murder, but my guess is Finlay MacNeill decided to shut him up permanently.'

'Murder someone just because he's trying to protect the same environment they depend upon to continue fishing?' Chloe asked.

'I guess so, Chloe. Some people don't care about the damage they do just as long as they can turn a profit.'

'You think we'll ever find out the truth about Calum's death?' Dee looked up from reading Duncan's diary.

'The only person who can tell us is Finlay or his mother. Calum stopped working for the brothers on the day Robert died and hid himself away in the holiday cottage.'

'Must have had a guilty conscience! Will the police charge Finlay with his death?' Chloe was anxious to see justice done.

Teàrlach visualised the statue of Lady Justice, her scales, sword and blindfold – particularly the blindfold.

'He wasn't around when Calum was attacked, and Finlay's unlikely to incriminate himself any further.'

Dee read through the list of jobs to be done – mending creels; servicing the engine – until she reached the last entry.

'Aye. Duncan wrote it down here.' Dee began quoting.

'The police are going to come and look for Calum. I can't hide him any longer. There's only one place I know. Finlay will have to help. Siobhan must never know.'

'And Siobhan found his diary, knew where Calum was being taken?' Chloe asked.

'That's what I think happened. I'm as certain as I can be that she wanted to die that night, next to Calum.'

Silence followed. Teàrlach looked over at Chloe's notepad. Her Venn diagram intersected so many times it resembled the Olympic games symbol. She noticed his interest.

'Are you handing Duncan's diary over?'

Teàrlach shook his head. 'No point, Chloe. I'll send it back to Siobhan, after enough time has elapsed. It's for her to do with as she thinks best. The police have their version of events. Best let sleeping dogs lie.'

The two women looked at him askance. He could have phrased it more sympathetically.

The tannoy announcement issued words in a language that was as familiar as it was alien to their ears.

'Come on.' Teàrlach stood, swaying slightly with the ferry's motion. 'Time to go home.'

EIGHTY-TWO
OK

A week had passed since the events on the island. Dee still kept an eye on the police reports, providing Teàrlach and Chloe with regular updates into the investigations. Finlay had implicated his brother in the deaths of Robert Jameson and John Stevenson, and the detective leading the enquiry was taking the path of least resistance. Finding a dead man guilty is an easy way of closing down two cases and hitting the solved crime statistics. Finlay was being charged with defeating the ends of justice – facing a fine and the prospect of a couple of years in prison. Morag could be facing up to fourteen years for owning a dangerous dog, but she'd lost more than anyone.

Chloe found herself at a loose end now she'd updated all the paperwork. Dee was buried headfirst in her laptop and Teàrlach had taken to staring out of his window overlooking Glasgow's urban landscape more than he normally did. She sighed as she entered the month's figures into an accounting spreadsheet. More months like this and they'd all be out of work. An invoice lay on her desk, awaiting Teàrlach's approval. She took it through to his office.

'This is Lucy Jameson's invoice.' She placed it down on his desk and waited.

Teàrlach picked it up, held the document at arm's length and frowned.

'I can't charge her for this.' He handed it back. 'She's been through enough. I can't send her a bill on top of everything else.'

Chloe took it out of his hand. 'We made a loss this month. Travel costs, the thousand pounds Dee paid out for the camera. We'll not see anything from Fraser Donald's estate for the best part of a year and we weren't even meant to be working on the John Stevenson case.'

'I know, I know.' Teàrlach looked for inspiration out of his window. 'I still can't ask Lucy to pay anything.'

'Have you decided whether to see your daughter?' Chloe's blunt question caught him unawares.

He nodded. 'I had a video call with them last night. Saw Isla. Her mum's right – she can talk! I scarcely managed a word.'

Chloe could imagine him being tongue-tied, the wee girl talking non-stop and filling any awkward silences.

'I'm flying over next month. I don't know what she'll make of me.' His earnest expression made her laugh.

'God, Teàrlach. She'll love you, of course – and you'll spoil her rotten.'

He smiled and she could see the young boy in him for one, fleeting moment.

'Dunno what we're meant to do whilst you're away.' Chloe covered the surge of emotion with the first words that came into her head.

'Oh, just take it easy for a couple of weeks. If anything big comes in, I'm only on the other end of the phone. Otherwise, you two can do at least as good a job as I can – better if the truth be told.'

'Glad you know it.' Dee made an appearance in the doorway, leaning against the open door. 'I've some news for you.'

'What?' Teàrlach's expression turned from happy to worried in an instant.

'I've had a response from Finn MacCool.'

'Did he take the bait?' Chloe asked.

'Aye. Lucky he's not a fish otherwise he wouldn't last long.' Dee kept them waiting for more.

'Go on then. What have you found?' Teàrlach's impatience was clear.

'Turns out his IP address is the same as Finlay MacNeill's. Quite a coincidence, don't you think?'

'Somehow, I'm not surprised.' Teàrlach linked his fingers together and stared into the cage he'd just made.

Chloe knew he was imagining the creel and trap that had drowned the sound recordist.

'Dee, can you make sure the Oban police make that connection? Without it coming back to us, of course.'

She nodded brightly. 'Or I can send it to your sergeant in Tobermory as you two were getting along so well together?'

'Aye, give it to Suzie Crammond. She deserves some credit out of all this.'

'I guess that wraps it all up, then?' Chloe tore the invoice in half, looking expectantly at Teàrlach.

'Aye. Not that we had much success.' He sighed heavily.

'Oh, I don't know.' Dee sounded more like her chirpy self. 'We found what happened to Lucy's man – which is all she wanted. And you were able to tell Fraser Donald what had happened to his son, before he died.'

'And we've helped the police with John Stevenson's murder – except they'll never know it was us,' Chloe added.

'Aye, I suppose.' Teàrlach didn't sound convinced.

'And you found you had a daughter,' Dee said quietly. 'Which is the best discovery of all.' She turned on her heel and left them. 'I'll send an anonymous message to that sergeant,' she called over her shoulder. 'She can take it from there.'

Chloe had seen the sadness in Dee's eyes and looked at Teàrlach sharply to see if he had noticed, but his focus was back to the cage his fingers had made.

'It will be OK,' she said quietly. 'Isla's going to be a lucky girl. She'll have two dads to wrap around her finger.'

'Thanks, Chloe.' Teàrlach's tight smile wasn't enough to hide the emotion in his eyes. 'You know what, I think we're all going to be OK.'

A LETTER FROM THE AUTHOR

Thanks so much for reading *The Graveyard Bell*. If you want to join other readers in hearing all about my new releases, you can sign up for my newsletter here.

www.stormpublishing.co/andrew-james-greig

Please consider leaving a review. This can help new readers discover a book you've enjoyed and gives us all a big boost!

Scotland's islands have always held a fascination for me. They are unique microcosms of society, each with their own personality and character. Returning to Teàrlach's home gives me the opportunity to share those parts of his early life that he tries to keep secret and I hope helps the reader understand more of what makes him the way he is. I have made this a slower and more considered storytelling, reflecting the pace of island life.

I very much look forward to sharing my next book with you. You can peer under this author's bonnet at:

andrewjgreig.wordpress.com

f facebook.com/andrewjamesgreig

X x.com/AndrewJamesGre3

instagram.com/andrew_james_greig

tiktok.com/@andrewjamesgreig

bsky.app/profile/andrewjgreig.bsky.social

ACKNOWLEDGEMENTS

My thanks to Claire Bord and the team at Storm Publishing for their hard work, expertise and enthusiasm; Dushi and Catherine for their eagle-eyed edits; my family and friends for their support and encouragement, especially Shona. Special thanks to the reviewers, bloggers and everyone who makes the publishing industry work and most important of all to you, the reader.